S0-BOJ-817

3 2386 00078 0184

THE
OTHER
LANDSCAPE

THE
OTHER
LANDSCAPE

Neil Gunn

WALKER AND COMPANY
New York, NY

First published in the United States of America in 1990
by Walker Publishing Company, Inc.

Previously published, in paperback, by Richard Drew Publishing,
Glasgow, Scotland.

Published simultaneously in Canada by Thomas Allen & Son
Canada, Limited, Markham, Ontario.

Library of Congress Cataloging-in-Publication Data

Gunn, Neil Miller, 1891–1973.
The other landscape / Neil Gunn.
Reprint. Originally published: Glasgow, Scotland : R. Drew Pub., 1984.
ISBN 0-8027-1108-1
I. Title.
PR6013.U6408   1990   823'.912—dc20   89-70683
CIP

Printed in the United States of America

2   4   6   8   10   9   7   5   3   1

FOREWORD

★

In 1954 Neil Gunn, one of Scotland's most distinguished 20th century writers, wrote his last novel, "The Other Landscape". Throughout a writing life spanning over 30 years Gunn had used the Highlands of Scotland as the main backdrop for his work but the themes he explored were of a universal nature, themes that were concerned with completeness and wholeness in life. In all his novels there is an element of search for something indefinable, which can possibly be best described by the word delight, a word he used in his autobiographical work, "The Atom of Delight", written two years after "The Other Landscape".

Like many a last novel by a truly imaginative writer "The Other Landscape" differs from its predecessors. Whereas in the preceding books of a distinctly philosophical nature, including "The Silver Bough" already published in the Scottish Collection, Gunn is preoccupied with cultural renewal through the understanding of the rhythms of nature and the observance of the mores of a Celtic civilization that was dying, in "The Other Landscape" he sees cultural renewal more as a positive force in the true spiritual sense. This force represents a creative and beneficent principle, in juxtaposition to its opposite, a destructive and maleficent power. In this book the problem of evil has become undeniably metaphysical. An autobiographical element is clearly present, with the narrator in the novel being the imaginative surrogate. The narrator's philosophising brings to mind Prospero's musings in Shakespeare's "The Tempest", also, interestingly enough, a last work. It is a farewell to the novel and the ultimate acceptance by the author of the unsurpassable difficulties that face any writer in gaining access to the kernel and heart of things.

The story is told by a young anthropologist, Walter Urquhart, who has been asked to find out the provenance of a piece of writing of exceptional quality that has been sent to a London literary magazine. His quest takes him to a remote Highland community and brings him into contact with the residents of a local fishing hotel, its staff and gillies and, of course, the writer of the manuscript. The writer, Douglas Menzies, is a musician, widower and recluse. The opening chapters quickly interweave the three main strands of the story: the tragic history·of the strange manuscript and its author, Urquhart's continual awareness of another landscape and the humour, closely related to tragedy, which bubbles to the surface from the interaction between people of different backgrounds and cultures living in a remote community.

Menzies, the recluse, is on a lonely spiritual struggle to find meaning in a life of tribulations. A beautiful wife dying in childbirth has precipitated a spiritual crisis, which has been approaching for some time; yet for him the "unseen" presence of the dead wife has a healing influence. In the same way, the Gaelic songs of a gillie's daughter have within them the same spirit of reconciliation. As Urquhart so eloquently puts it, "It was a very old Gaelic air; it went back so far that it was timeless or had transfixed time; it had words and those words told a story of human tragedy; yet that tragedy had been so winnowed by the generations that it could be sung, hummed, as a lullaby to a child."

If Menzies represents something wholly positive in terms of a spiritual quest to reconcile the irreconcilable, the negative side of being is portrayed by one of the residents at the hotel, a retired major. The Major, an extremely intelligent and argumentative Englishman, claims to know the local landscape better than the locals do themselves. His arguments with Urquhart and his gillie are saved from becoming too sombre by the influx of humour and it is humour that finally buries the Major.

Through his privileged position of knowing both Menzies and the Major, Urquhart can compare the aspirations of the two, and their stories. A synthesis, he is unable to find. Of Menzies he writes, "I had the feeling that I knew him better than any other person on earth and yet I realised that I would never know him. But this did not offend, hardly disappointed even, for I realised, by a lifting further intuition, that what moves the spirit profoundly can never be fathomed." And of the Major, "The Major was probably more on my level, I thought. A real good-going argument, no hits barred on the road to hell with plenty of knockable things around, and eternity in the offing like a punchball out of reach."

It could be said that Gunn in "The Other Landscape" took unconcealed satisfaction in ridding himself of the unsympathetic stranger — so powerfully portrayed in the shape of the Colonel in a very early book, "The Lost Glen" (also published in The Scottish Collection). That, in my opinion, would be a wrong diagnosis and, worse still, would hint at negative quality that was never in Gunn. I agree with his biographers, Francis Hart and John Pick, when they write in a "Highland Life", "But he did not write 'The Other Landscape' to put the Major in his place. He wrote it to explore the mysteries of death, evil, misfortune and delight. It is beautiful, sombre, alive and positive, wildly ambitious and strangely youthful."

DAIRMID GUNN
Edinburgh, 1988

THE
OTHER
LANDSCAPE

1

It was a small hotel with eight or nine bedrooms and loch and sea fishing, the kind of place that had the same guests season after season. In fact when I arrived Johan, the table-maid, was not at all sure that I could get a bed and turned away with a thoughtful expression on her thin dark features. It was some time before the landlord appeared, a big slow man with a close-cropped ginger moustache and small eyes, greeny-grey, set wide apart in a comfortable face. He looked more doubtful than Johan as he took me all in. Would I be staying long? Only a couple of nights or so, I replied, and as that seemed to make a difference I did not tell him why I had come.

I was placed at a small table in a corner of the dining-room and had to look over my right shoulder to command the main table with its party of nine. That table was like a small outpost of empire where they just stopped short of dressing formally for dinner. Catches of trout were discussed and Highland boatmen or gillies amusingly mimicked, while argumentative cross currents set up a jabble now and then. One of the five men, always addressed as Major, tended to be the focal point of interest or talk, a bulky man with a plethoric face and rather harsh voice. When they rallied him over his not having gone fishing that day he had things to say about his gillie, Lachlan, which were appreciated.

7

Dinner over, the five men and four women, none of them young, left the dining-room and went into the sitting-room, on the other side of the entrance passage, the Major giving me a raking look as he passed. I had hardly begun to wonder if I should follow them when Johan appeared and asked if I would have coffee where I was. It was neatly done in the interest of all and I thanked her. When she was clearing the table I inquired about meal times just to hear her Highland voice. I smoked a couple of cigarettes over my coffee and then went out.

It was a quiet August evening with blue showing everywhere between high white clouds. The landscape had a stillness, a slowness, that rose into a far distance of mountain tops. I kept heading west on a grass-grown track until at one point, when I stopped to look around, I actually saw nothing moving anywhere; but as I listened I heard what I first thought was the faint surge of my own blood but decided, with a touch of excitement, was the lazy wash of the sea against cliffs. However, the track finished at the tumbled ruins of two cottages in a shallow hollow. The trunk of an old tree, with one stunted branch outthrust like a withered arm, had at one time been used as a post for fencing wire. I recognised it as the rowan or mountain ash, grown to keep evil spirits away. This brought back so much of my own boyhood that I stood looking and listening until my mouth went dry.

As I went up the far side of the hollow I glanced back over my shoulder at that still place, for I was used to dealing with vanished civilisations. My thoughts accompanied me over level ground until I reached the cliffs at the end or head of what was, I could now see, a wide promontory.

Two to three hundred feet below, gulls floated languidly, looking no larger than their own wing feathers.

Other white birds in a string swept low and fast over the wrinkled water: gannets. Then a bird rose quite close to me, banked and went down, on outstretched wings that never flapped. The fulmar, I thought, and started back.

As I took my bearings, I could see the inlet on the north side of the promontory going miles inland to a village at its head. To the south, the cliffs fell slowly away from the Head on which I stood, and I decided to follow them, keeping well back to make the going easy. Presently the cliff wall curved round and went directly inland; opposite the bend and quite close was a long narrow rock stack with sheer sides. I could see the noisy birds on their ledges. Beyond it, across two hundred yards of seaway, was the northern end of an island, guarding a wide bay, before the cliffs to the south went seaward again.

Suddenly I saw the white house, down to my left. Something familiar about it was a little too startling to be real. I sat down slowly and then lay flat.

Green turf rolled slowly down to the house before flattening out towards the cliff perhaps a hundred yards from it. There was a small low-walled garden in front and, behind, a long steading with the roof fallen in. No one moved about the place. I watched and listened but heard only the shrill crying of seabirds as if they were being disturbed. Holding my breath, I caught quite distinctly the cavernous or rock-wall echoes in their cries. My eyes roved far beyond the house to a hinterland heather-dark and desolate.

It would have been a sheepfarmer's house, I decided, its green site chosen by the incomers in those days of last century when the crofters were forcibly evicted from their simple homes to make room for sheep. Ridges in the ground showed where the land had been

9

cultivated, but here there were no ruins, for the stones of the vanished dwellings would have gone to the building of the new house and steading.

All the time my eyes never really left the house for I had the feeling that presently the man whom I had come to meet would appear at a gable-end and stare up in my direction. Why I didn't go down I hardly know, for even if this wasn't his house there would be no harm in calling and inquiring. But then I hadn't even asked the innkeeper where Douglas Menzies stayed. I wasn't ready, I felt; and because it becomes a habit to attempt to rationalise any feeling, I searched about until I found a satisfactory reason, namely, that when I did meet him I must have his script with me and talk in a simple business-like way. It was something in the writing that made me hesitate, with a sense of fear going deep, like the cliff-face. The fulmar in its apparently blind weaving had startled me more than a bit.

But let me tell at once how the typescript came into my possession. I am not a literary man though I have done a fair amount of writing, mostly about primitive societies or the primitive in societies. The subject has interested me ever since as a boy in the Highlands I hunted and fished as naturally as any primitive man or otter. I confess it is one of my ambitions to write something on the mind of the primitive hunter, with special reference to the interactions between that mind and the hunting background, particularly at the most vivid moments when a certain kind of communion or integration takes place. Then to trace that primitive aspect into our present-day island society, with the Highlands as its sporting preserve for the leaders, the headmen (aristocratic or plutocratic), of that society, might add something to our understanding of what politicians call the Highland problem. For when all aspects of

10

living are narrowed to the economic, the complexity that makes the whole pattern of living, the culture pattern as we call it, is vitiated if not quite lost.

Anyway, that's the kind of argument I used to have with David Townbee, who edited *Serpent*, and it was enough for me to find some of his "new" writing but a vivid piercing through of the "primitive" to start the kind of endless discussion that had the effect of foreign gin.

I was back in town and having a drink with him before going on to a show when suddenly he slapped the bar counter and mentioned Douglas Menzies' piece of writing. "My God, it's terrific!" He laughed and stubbed his cigarette out. He could never get his tie straight and his gestures were awkward, upsetting things about him as if waving them away from the tremendous fun of what he had discovered. By the time we remembered the show we were too late for it and I went back with him to his rooms.

First, one or two odd facts. The script was very neatly typed, almost professionally, but did not carry the writer's address. The heading to the initial page was: CLIFFS *by* Douglas Menzies. Then followed twenty-six quarto pages of double-spaced typing. But from a tiny fleck of paper which David discovered under the fastener he had deduced that a front page had been torn away. No covering letter had accompanied the script. The postmark on the envelope, however, was quite clear and David looked it up in a postal guide and then in a gazetteer. It was obviously a small place in the north-west Highlands and a letter to Douglas Menzies should either have reached him there or been returned. David sent two letters but got no reply, nor were the letters returned by the postal authorities.

"What did you say to him?"

11

"I said I was very interested in his work and should be glad if he would communicate with me as no covering note or address had been enclosed and I was chancing my arm by sending this to the postmark on his envelope. I admit I also said that as his contribution seemed in the nature of an overture which he might care to say more about—and so on. You see, in a way—had I been given the right to publish? Who sent it to me? Did he?—or did someone else tear off the front page, stick it in an envelope and bung it off? When you add to that the nature of the stuff! . . ."

I took it away with me and read it and didn't sleep much. I saw what David meant by overture. In fact I got haunted by a sort of mad music. Cliffs and storms and the almighty Wrecker. It was, as David had said, terrific, for it also had an extraordinary intimacy between a man and a woman that was more than disturbing, almost unbearable, because it was carried beyond the personal. But I need not say more about that now; it will be dealt with later. The background excited me, too, stirred up such a lot of atavistic stuff that I lay awake wondering whether I shouldn't take the opportunity of ten free days to go north and meet the man.

The following night David laughed. "I knew it would be bung into your barrel. And I'm glad you're going to investigate on the spot. You can now test out some of your theories about those who go hunting natives anywhere but at home. Make a record of your total experience and we may even serialise it! But, remember, the *Serpent* must have its sting." And he thrust two pronged fingers at me.

That was only two nights ago and now here I was with the overture coming into play before anything had happened!

How long I lay there watching the house I don't know—perhaps half an hour—but in the end I got sensitive about being seen. I found myself looking over my shoulder. No one appeared. I slipped back the way I had come until I reached the ruins of the two croft-houses. In the half-light there was not a breath of wind, just stillness, a doorstep, weeds smothering a hearthstone, the tragic thrust of the rowan tree's withered arm against the sky.

But there was something more than the tragic. Many are susceptible to the peculiar power of the twilight, particularly in lonely places. For me it can evoke figures I knew as a boy; tranced hunting moments at the back of woods, in a glade, eyes staring at a cleft rock, ears hearkening for the inaudible. Two orders of being, the visible and the invisible, pause on the doorstep of this grey hour, and which is going to advance upon you you hardly know. Tension gets drawn out until it is time that is drawn out, so thin, so fine, that its range becomes enormous.

When at last I came in sight of the hotel the lights were on and I stood for a while uncertain, reluctant to enter the place and lose what I had found again. Then I went down through the soft night and quietly into the dining-room.

I listened for voices in the sitting-room but heard none and wondered whether it was too late to ring for a drink—I could have done with some tea—when I heard footsteps and the Major came in. His head turned on his short neck and I acknowledged his muttered "Good evening." Then he paused on his way to the sideboard to ask, "And what are you doing here?"

"Not much," I answered.

"A tourist?"

"No. An anthropologist."

13

His eye gleamed as if recognising a satiric intention to choke him off.

"Your profession?"

"More or less."

"Come to study the native on the spot or just writing for the press?"

"Not necessarily the native only."

He gave a gusty snort. "A Highlander, aren't you?"

"I'm glad my accent is so obvious."

"Not so much your accent as your evasiveness." His heavy features puckered in a combative grin. He could be brutal, but he was intelligent and his intelligence wasn't getting enough exercise.

"Sometimes one is forced to take evasive action."

"Out of politeness, uh? But you're afraid to say it."

This was too much and I looked at him deliberately, when his head lifted, listening. "Wait a minute and you'll see the real Highland evasiveness in action." His eyes glinted with satiric intention and he went out.

I could hardly believe that all this had happened so quickly. The Major must have been about sixty, was plainly southern English in origin, spoke French well and had lived abroad. At twenty-nine I was a mere youngster he could order around. I remembered the way he had drawn out a chair for a woman in her early fifties, thin-faced with greying hair, whom I took to be a widow—correctly, as it proved—while he murmured a French phrase and inclined his head with some grace. It was a momentary bit of acting with just enough of the genuine in it to bring a smile to the other women's eyes.

Now he was coming back. He entered followed by a local man, perhaps in his middle fifties, but straight as a

14

bulrush and lively on his feet as a dancer. This time the Major went all the way to the sideboard and produced his whisky bottle.

"You turned up this morning, Lachlan, didn't you?" The Major poured a gush of whisky into a tumbler.

"I did turn up, sir."

"You what?"

"You told me to——"

"Do you think I don't know what I told you?"

"You'll know best yourself, sir, what you told me. I'm not denying that." As Lachlan shifted on his feet his politeness flew about his thick unruly hair.

"If you're not denying it, what the hell are you trying to say? Here!"

Lachlan took the glass. "Here's my very best health to you!"

The Major made gruff acknowledgment and Lachlan swallowed the dram in one swoop.

Then back to the charge came the Major with his maddening air of being contemptuously abrupt.

"All I'm saying, sir," responded Lachlan, with the glancing, sensitive smile that suggested this was an old game, "is that I understood what you said to me was that I was to be at Loch Dubh at ten o'clock——"

"What *you* understood?"

"Yes, sir," replied Lachlan. "What I understood. Ten o'clock was what you said to me, the usual time, and if it had been any other time I would have noticed it, and by my watch——"

"*Your* watch? That turnip!"

Thus the Major introduced the time theme, stirring Lachlan to an involved wordiness, showing him off, showing in particular that though Lachlan would not give in neither had he the courage to accuse the Major of being in the wrong. Lachlan had pride but

15

apparently not pride enough. He would give in if only it would also appear that he wasn't giving in. As an exhibition of evasiveness it could not for the Major's purpose have been better staged.

My discomfort was turning to anger and this should have astonished me because any anthropologist could hardly have hoped for a nimbler display of two cultures in conflict; but it didn't. And when the Major, who was devilishly adroit for all his appearance of abruptness, introduced the motive of servility by trying to draw out of Lachlan how long he would have waited by his turnip watch supposing his employer had not turned up, I began to feel hot.

For by this time it was perfectly clear, of course, that the Major had not turned up at the loch at all, though he had made the appointment the night before with Lachlan, his boatman or gillie, for ten o'clock that morning. Lachlan knew he had not turned up. But this cardinal point was now becoming unimportant, for Lachlan was playing his part only too well, too tiresomely well, for the Major. He could throw his head back and smile, a curious strained smile, but still a smile, not a grimace, as though he could be depended upon to keep the argumentative game on its needlepoint, let the Major say what he liked, and even find time to throw me, the stranger, a glance to indicate that it was a game, that the Major just wasn't getting off with everything, no fear, until even my anger began to curl in on itself with a sort of anguish.

But by this time the Major's own face was getting congested. He had set going what he couldn't control, and was growing more and more impatient. Lachlan might now have been playing *him* on the end of the line, trussing him up. I saw the Major was going to explode. Then he exploded: "Oh, shut up!"

"I can shut up if I like," replied Lachlan, "but all the same if you're trying to accuse me——"

"You're a damned fool," said the Major. "Get out!"

For a moment Lachlan's eyes glittered and across my mind flashed a vision of the black-handled knife which the kilted Highlander of an older time was in the habit of carrying in his stocking to settle such an argument at just such a point. Then—Lachlan was going but not going, almost telling the Major what he thought of him but not quite, until the door was slammed on his heels.

The Major plunged about the sideboard like a heavy animal in undergrowth, rooted out a couple of tumblers and thumped into a chair by the table. "Blurry ass!" he muttered. "A jumping jack!"

"He outlasted you," I said.

His mouth came adrift. "What's that?"

"You're getting out of form; deteriorating." Never before had the thought of sticking a knife in a man passed so vividly into my hands.

"What are *you* trying to say?"

"I have said it. You staged the performance but could not last the pace. Your superiority got the better of you. You went brutal and commonplace like the bloodiest tyrant of your race."

"And you—smile." If his face could not register awe it did its best.

I smiled.

"Good God," he muttered and pushed upright. A real snake in real undergrowth could hardly apparently have astonished him more. I gathered myself. But the Major merely reached for the bottle. "Have a drink." He poured two whacking drams. I was so taken aback I could neither refuse nor accept, though I intended not to touch his stuff. I wasn't letting him off with anything from now on, and age could look after itself.

17

So we got going and presently I heard myself meeting his challenge with a description of the culture out of which Lachlan had come. I used the word "culture" with the detachment of an anthropologist at work in a given field. Lachlan's culture, his Gaelic culture, I explained with cold simplicity, was based on personal relations. Not on empire, not on bloody conquest, but on a way of life among human beings that in terms of the accepted canons of our European civilisation brought out the best. This could be tested in the sector of art by consideration of his folk music and traditional poetry. In short, Lachlan's background did not readily permit him to be directly brutal in a personal approach. Thus if he appeared in certain circumstances evasive it was only to those whose intelligence was so crude that it required to be told that a spade was a blurry spade.

The Major did not charge the red light. He sat back to look at it properly with an expression of infernal anticipation.

"Culture," he said. "Civilisation. Here!"

"Not exclusively here," I said. "In the higher spheres of other civilisations the same evasiveness appears. For example, in the diplomatic service. At least it *was* found there before it became the fashion to call your opposite number a bug-scattering cannibal."

"What do you know about the diplomatic service?"

"For that matter," I inquired, "what do you?"

"I was in the diplomatic service for thirty years."

To slip against an upper cut when you feel your footwork has been fairly good is more than surprising. Worse than that: I had been talking too much, just like Lachlan.

"Hurt, are you? Peeved, uh?" probed the Major.

"Not at all," I said.

"Equating the verbal inconsequence of a Highland

18

gillie with the verbal usages of a diplomatic service that normally was run by the cream of the English aristocracy."

"Precisely."

"Damned interesting." His body gave a roll in its chair; his enjoyment was not only ironic, it was gargantuan. I was obviously going to be an even better subject for the Major's probes than Lachlan. As he lifted his tumbler, he nodded to mine and waited with a certain assessing and at the same time compelling light in his eye. All right, I thought, accepting the challenge. So I pulled a chair out from the table and sat down opposite him.

He looked pleased at having compelled me to do this but not smugly, rather as a hidden test of a fellow's manners. "Huh!" he grunted, lifting his glass. We drank and started on the second round.

Whereas he had probed Lachlan with, as it were, his fleshy purple thumb, he used words on me, language, with lights from many cultures that shone and vanished round sudden chunks of downrightness from a cluttered throat-box. Occasionally there was even a gesture that recalled the way he had moved the widow's chair. My effort at analysis had provided a whole counter of toys or memories for the Major. He could pick one up, expose its works and negligently throw it away—into my face. I let him see that he had thrown it into my face by taking it, breaking it in two, and letting him have the pieces back by way of a right and left. We landed in literature and Persia, and presently were quoting Omar Khayyám.

But if I thought I knew the *Rubáiyát*—and I could repeat swatches of it—the Major soon undeceived me. Not that his scholarship was obtrusive; it merely emitted illuminating glints that a podgy fist dismissed like a jinnee's hand. But at the same time his eyes, dark blue and watchful in shots, let me understand that I didn't know an awful lot, not nearly so much as I fancied; I might have acquired some knowledge, some human facts here and there, but that was a long way from understanding, from the experience that had gone beneath the surface and endured what was encountered there.

True enough—but, equally below the surface by this time, I had my own understanding of the way he had treated Lachlan, and if he thought he could manoeuvre me into a position where I could forget it, because it was too trivial to remember now, he was mistaken. There had been poets in more places than Persia.

From diplomacy, or politics, or even oil, I could make a show at countering a sudden thrust. But a time came when the Major leaned heavily on the table, pushed his head forward and held me with his intent eyes.

"Have *you* ever heard," he asked me, *"the beating of a distant drum?"*

It was a splendid punch. It knocked me into deserts. The world rolled back to its far confines. I had heard drums, but never that one, the one which the Major had heard, and which for a moment had reverberated in his voice. Even tom-toms were hardly enough now. I put out my hand for my glass and found it empty.

The Major charged both. "Have you?"

The blue in his eyes was dark and emphasised the pin-points of light. His cheeks were full but not pendulous, a weathered red with a suggestion of purple. But up above where the brow passed into the hair was a sort of washed smoothness as if a sponge had swept the hair back before a couple of brushes had completed the job. Dark grey and still thick enough to show nothing of the scalp. The effect was neat, clean, and youthfully intellectual. Down below the face carried an almost brutal charge.

I admitted that I hadn't heard his drum. I was still under the effect of the desert, aware of an Eastern illumination—when an extraordinary thing began to happen. The satire in his face was growing dim; his head and shoulders were losing their solid outlines; he was fading away as if some jinnee were in fact withdrawing or dissolving him in an Eastern magic.

"Come," he said and solidly got to his feet.

I blinked once or twice before I realised that the light in the white globe was actually going down.

I followed him into the passage that led to the back premises, then followed the sound of his footsteps, for here it was quite dark. I was so careful not to bump him that he got ahead of me, and I kicked something that clanged. I heard his growl and made towards it, hands out. A warmth met me, a feminine warmth, a red eye of fire diffused a faint glow; we were in the kitchen. I could see him now passing through a door on the right and I got on his heels. The darkness became complete again until a match flared and abruptly went out. "Hell's drums!" said the Major flipping his burnt fingers. The next match broke. His vocabulary expanded. I struck a match and the Major found the candle. After some reluctance the flame rose slowly.

We were in an outhouse and the Major manœuvred into position beside an iron wheel like that on an old-fashioned clothes mangle. As he turned the handle, interlocking teeth growled softly and weights began perceptibly to rise.

"Light," said the Major. "Got to wind the thing."

In this remote spot they would have to manufacture their own gas. I made some thoughtful comment and between his puffs the Major said, "You think light is laid on."

The remark suddenly shook me but I tried to keep my laughter noiseless, while the Major's solid torso dipped and rose and dipped. As a gust of wind came from him I offered to relieve him on the wheel and after a few more turns he let me.

It was still the cold war, but personal relations were being established. The Major even explained the mechanism. He looked about him and handled things. I could see he was not annoyed at having to do all this, however disgruntled he might appear. His restless intelligence liked to poke around and into things. He emitted critical snorts, and then suddenly he swore, for having stumbled against a wall he had brought a heavy coil of rope about his neck. What he said I didn't quite catch for his toe had kicked into some metal sheet that reverberated like thunder; but his malevolence passed quickly into a thick humour as he apostrophised the rope and those behind the rope, in an intimate way.

"Enough!" he said presently after a glance at the weights. As we stumbled back to the dining-room I felt certain that every soul in the hotel must now be awake.

The Major tossed off his drink exactly as Lachlan had done. I followed suit, not to be outdone.

What the time was it didn't even occur to me to wonder, for the Major had gone back to Lachlan and we started over the same ground again, but this time more explicitly. Deliberately he recalled the words of abuse which I had directed at him. As rationally as I could I did my best to justify them. This went on for a long time. It seemed an endless wrangle.

"I am deteriorating, you think?"

"Well, if I was rude, so were you."

"Rude to you?"

"To Lachlan."

It got raw and might have been nasty but for some weird element of speculation. I find it difficult to explain this, to suggest that there was some other place where we did meet, much as there had seemed to be another world behind the ruins.

"So you think I have come here to deteriorate?" the Major persisted.

"I never said that."

"No? What did you say?"

"I don't want to be personal."

"Shouldn't you have thought of that before you were?"

I wasn't going to answer. Some day Lachlan would bash that face in. "As you like," I said. But I was disturbed. The fellow wanted to worm about the roots.

"Evasive, uh?"

"Not at all. There is merely a limit. And, anyway, if you want to know," I could not help adding, "I got the impression that here you were, a man of high intelligence, if I may say so, not being able to last the pace in—in that sort of—of miserable game you started with Lachlan."

"You're beginning to stutter," he said; "you're losing your precise anthropological tone."

His sarcasm was solid as his jowls, dominating, yet subtle as hell where the roots are. He had worked things round until he was on top again.

"You're deteriorating," he added and pulled his face back.

The hidden gleam of satisfaction hardly showed in his eyes. Knocking me out was almost too simple a game for this tried dyed-in-the-wool diplomatist.

"It happens," he continued. "This is the place for it. Your local culture pattern, if that's what you called it

23

—or Gaelic culture, was it?—is in process of deterioration and so draws within it those elements that are, for one reason or another, attracted by it."

"Are you giving a picture of what has happened to yourself?"

"First you stutter; now you become crude and rude. You cannot last the pace."

He lifted my verbal pieces one by one from the board. "But perhaps you haven't had time," he allowed, "since you arrived here this evening, to get the full picture of the local—uh—culture pattern—or did you call it Gaelic culture?—anyway, that culture—very good word—which retains within itself, if I remember you aright, the finest—the best, I think you said—elements of our Western or European culture or civilisation, as exemplified particularly, I gathered, by the behaviour of Lachlan."

I swallowed my anger in a desperate effort to get a grip of myself. I begged him to proceed.

His eyes narrowed on me slightly, his fleshy lips pursed. "You command me? I was merely going to make the suggestion, permissible perhaps out of my superior years if not superior experience, that although, being a Highlander, you may consider yourself an expert analyst of Lachlan's evasiveness, still, as an anthropologist, you should for that very reason have exhibited a more objective approach."

"You are quite right," I agreed; "it is part of the training. At the same time an innate knowledge of, an interest in, any given quality is supposed to help both in its understanding and in its elucidation as part of the whole pattern. Or would you say not?"

A faint assessing smile, an imperceptible nod, acknowledged that I was getting control again. It was maddening.

"You mentioned also the traditional poetry, the folk music. We haven't a mad poet here, so far as I know, but we have a mad musician."

"Really."

"You should investigate him." He was watching me. "He would be—he is—the complete study in deterioration. He has come wholly under those local influences that—uh—produce the best."

The cold crawled about my spine. Menzies, the writing! It was like falling over cliffs.

I became aware of the silence and asked as calmly as I could, "What's his name?"

"So you *have* come to see him?"

I could not mention Douglas Menzies' name.

"High time," nodded the Major, but when he inverted the bottle only a few dribbles came.

I had had enough in every sense and pushed my chair back. "I'm afraid it's been all your drink," I said getting up.

"Uhm." He rose and put the empty bottle inside the sideboard. He shambled round the table and turned off the light after he had got his matchbox in his hand. On the small table by the foot of the stairs were two candlesticks.

As he stumped solidly in front up the stairs I did not know whether he hated me or not and I did not care. I would be rid of him in a moment and in my own room.

My surprise was bewildering when he paused before his door, turned to me and asked, "Like to see my room?"

But I must have indicated that this would be agreeable. In fact, at all points there had been a certain underlying politeness between us. The Major had not only made me aware of my comparative youth but also had drawn out of me some deference for his superior years. That, with a certain amount of drink, one could still coldly retain something of the gentleman was the kind of thing he had an eye for.

After setting down his candlestick on the commode by the bed he took out his box of matches and then followed a performance, or a ritual, so utterly unexpected that I must have gaped. He lit a second candle. He moved on a step or two and lit a third. He wasn't going to light a fourth? But he was. A fourth—and a fifth—and a sixth. They were stuck on or in all kinds of receptacles, including so far the neck of one empty whisky bottle, and so far he wasn't half round the room. A seventh was stuck on a round tin lid at a low level. Then he rose to the height of the mantelshelf and added two more, aspiring ones in slim old-fashioned brass candlesticks. Beauties. In the corner to the right stood a small round three-legged stool, a perfect stance, with a flowered china saucer for holder. When he reached the wardrobe I held my breath, for he turned to a bedroom chair. Not on top of the wardrobe, under the roof? No, because the chair itself held its brass ashtray with candle.* I wouldn't swear to a total of eleven, but it was in that region. And it wasn't a large bedroom. In fact it was a small, an ordinary, cheap-looking bedroom, that very badly needed doing up. When at last he turned to me I murmured that he had a lot of candles. No remark could have been more apt, apparently, for he invited me to inspect an American trunk that stood under a dark window curtain. He slung back the rounded lid and exposed large bundles of candles neatly swathed in brown paper, a whole nest of them with a huge packet of matches as the cuckoo's egg. He was, like any schoolboy, showing me his treasures, but not with eagerness, quite practically,

26

puffing a bit. I was touched. Strange boys, up for their first term, coming together by that odd chance . . .

I don't know yet if there was anything of peculiar or special significance which he had invited me in to see, but I doubt it. Anyway, there I was outside again, with my host in his doorway, and all those candles flickering behind him like memories of chandeliers. I was just about to nod farewell when his hand came out a short distance but quick and straight. I grasped it without a fumble and if the clasp was strong and warm it was not overdone. I bowed my acknowledgments of his hospitality and withdrew.

I had the extraordinary impression of entering my own room on tiptoe, of floating to the window, borne, as it were, by the candle in my hand. The pale cream blind had not been pulled down. Across the backyard, over the zinc roof of the garage, up the slow slope my sight travelled to a far ridge beyond which the dawn was coming in a reflection of opals and silver.

As I pulled the clothes round my neck I had the notion that the whole place might go up in flames from the embassy candles, and I thought that if it did, taking everything into account, from the beating Eastern drum to this silent silver clarion of our northern dawn, it would be remarkably funny.

2

I heard the knock but must then have dozed off, for next there was a trampling of feet; voices called; it was not going to rain. Breakfast was over and guests were getting ready for the day's sport.

Outside my door was a can of hot water but I found my shoes in my room; I hadn't put them out. A couple of men were talking by the garage door and one of them called "Ian!" Ian appeared with a trout net and a fishing rod in its brown cover. There was a mild joke and then the same voice called, "Hi, Lachlan!" Their faces were expectant but Lachlan must have been intercepted.

It had an old familiar air, easy going, not over-concerned with time. It suited a head that could be cooled at the back of beyond where healing airs sifted the heather. I certainly didn't want to meet the Major.

As I came out of my door someone moved along the corridor, and glancing over my shoulder, I stopped. It was the chamber-maid, a girl of twenty or so, with a bundle of white linen in her arms. She was waiting for me to go on. She smiled spontaneously, brightly rather than shyly, yet shyly too, before looking down at the bundle and so giving me time to move off. Fresh and warm and quite lovely, with fair hair and light everywhere from the linen to her eyes.

This was Catherine, and to me at that moment, with my head as it was, she was the grace of life.

In the dining-room, which I had to myself, I apologised to Johan for being late. She was around thirty, very dark, with noticeable cheek bones. Her manners and voice were quiet and responsible and she gave the impression of having thoughts and worries of her own. She had, as I found out, an ailing mother whom she loved in her over-concerned way and supported.

But the chamber-maid got into the butter. And it was real butter, with a buttercup gleam. I could not get over that sudden vision of her.

Outside I ran into the landlord who saluted with a slow smile.

"I hope we didn't disturb you last night," I said, though I hadn't meant to refer to the midnight bangings.

"Not much," he replied with a reticent humour which I liked. A mild man, an easy masculine man, with girth and a bull's strength in his shoulders. His small eyes were unobtrusively taking me all in.

"Major—uh—what's his surname?"

"Thornybank. Major Thornybank."

"Very interesting man. The lights went down."

"Ay, sometimes the lights are a worry."

I glanced at him and he smiled.

"Does he come here every year?"

"Last year he didn't go back," said the landlord.

"You mean he stayed on all winter?"

"Yes. The winter nights are long."

"A real worry?" I was thinking of the candles.

"They are that." He had read my thought.

If Lachlan said nothing with many words, this man said a lot with few.

That the Major could do without his London club in the winter seemed extraordinary, I suggested.

29

"He was retired," said the landlord.

The tense of the verb—did he mean dismissed? But neither of us knew the other well enough to put the matter bluntly.

"He had to retire, you mean?"

"What with nabobs and women and oil, they will be saying strange things can happen out East. But mostly yarns, you may be sure."

"Women?"

He couldn't resist replying, "They say the Foreign Office was more concerned with the oil."

I laughed, but he had his purpose in all this.

"It was you mentioning the lights. The one thing that might worry us is not turning the tap at the lamp right off before going out to wind up."

As I was working this out he went on, "You see, if you didn't shut off the pipe below the lamp and it went out, as it would, then when more gas was made it would come pouring through and flood the room and every place, particularly if you didn't think of lighting the lamp again at once."

And I had been concerned only with the candles! I could not help laughing and the landlord looked as pleased as though he had made another joke.

"You'll be wanting sandwiches?"

"Well—I hadn't thought—is that the usual custom?"

"It is. But if you come back for lunch we could manage something, I'm sure."

I thanked him and said I should like the sandwiches.

"It's such a good day. You'll not be wanting to fish?"

"As a matter of fact I have brought no tackle with me."

"Och, we could always fit you out with a rod. But maybe you are just wanting to—take it easy?"

He was making it as simple as possible for me to

tell him why I had come. In fact he was curious. But somehow I couldn't mention Douglas Menzies. As a taboo it was absurd, for this man was no gossip; he could be helpful, beneath the surface, too.

"To tell the truth," I said, "what I want today is your fresh air. I have come up from London for a short holiday. I'll have a look at your seabirds. You won't have a boat for sea-fishing?"

"Well, we have an arrangement with Dan Maclellan, south there. You'll see his small croft once you go over the rise. But Mr. Lockworth—he's a barrister in London—the tall straight gentleman—he's fixed it up with Dan—he always does, for it's the sea-fishing he's keen on, and especially the lobsters. Dan has two boats, one with a small motor in her. He supplies us with our fish. But he has a smaller row-boat . . ."

By the time I left the landlord I had the odd feeling that he was wondering if I had come to see Douglas Menzies. It brought back the real reason for my visit in the old disturbing way. I began to see the Major's face when he had mentioned the mad musician. Even now I concentrated on the Major, for when a vague premonition becomes too disturbing the mind will dodge it at all costs, dodge it yet be drawn by it; as I was drawn to have a look at Dan's croft.

The "rise" was farther away than it had seemed and all the farther because I did not wish to go along the cliffs and so approached it from the landward side. I struck a burn and following it came on the croft, pleasantly situated in a scoop of ground where the southward run of cliff dipped to a tiny shore before rising again on a westward sweep. A dun-coloured cow was tethered not far from a patch of corn and a smaller patch of potatoes. The visible ruins of at least two houses suggested that this had once been a small

31

community of crofter-fishermen. Dan's house had a sky-light in a slate roof and very blue smoke ascended from the near chimney. There were hens about the door and a white one on top of a rick of hay.

I crossed the burn to avoid passing too close to the house, but a dog barked and an elderly woman stood framed by the doorway, looking over at me. I pretended not to see her and went on down to the beach.

A small boat of about twelve feet was drawn up above high water mark. From her stern a shingly slip slid down by a low spit of dark rock. Some wooden rollers, old lobster pots, a broken rudder and other junk lay around.

It would have been an exposed shore but for the southern end of the long island. Only a dead westerly blow would come straight in.

Big ports make one forget the clarity, the purity, of water that swells up on the shingle and chokes tiny crevices in the rock. A little way out and it is green, a bottle green. The marvel of translucency washes over the skin.

I sat on the beach for a while. Here a bit of old iron stuck out of the shingle, there a rib from a buried keel. The sea water brimmed with a soft hiss. One listens as naturally as the sea brims, listens *back*. I realised I hadn't done this for a long time.

One can see mute things with an extraordinary clarity. Then a touch, just a touch, of clairvoyance seems to come out of the listening and the mind grows abnormally sensitive. The slow movement of the water, its mounting rhythm, the crash, the recession . . . all in miniature, like the memory of a full theme . . . I broke the hypnotic effect by getting up. But the shingle now roared under my feet. I had taken only a few steps on the quiet turf when I jumped and the heart went across me. The dog had sniffed my legs, a black collie bitch with a white star on her chest.

The woman was spreading dish cloths on the low stone wall in front of the house. The wall surrounded a small sloping garden containing cabbages, leeks, very large rhubarb leaves, some berry bushes. I got a scent from the past. It was southernwood.

I greeted her and asked if this was Mr. Maclellan's croft.

She had the kind of light-brown hair that doesn't get grey, clear bone in her spare face, and eyes, a grey blue, that sent an engaging friendliness over her face as she smiled.

I introduced myself, and said I was stopping at the hotel. The landlord had told me about the boats here and I wondered if, sometime, I might hire the row-boat for a look around the rocks. I was interested in sea-birds.

"Surely," she said. "You can have a talk with himself. He's at the sea just now with Mr. Lockworth, but he'll be taking the fish back to the hotel in the evening and maybe you could see him then."

I thanked her, explained that I had only arrived last night and was enjoying a lazy day having a look at the country. I had liked her expression "at the sea" and wanted to keep her talking. After London, I said, it was wonderful country.

"They all say it's very nice."

So we got talking and I asked about the past.

"When I was a little girl there were four crofts. Before my time there were more. You can see where they took in the hillside."

"Where the heather comes down. Is that a cairn above the bracken?"

"No, it's a ruin."

33

"The old race seems to be going."

"Ah well, the young go away. There's not much for them here."

"I wonder what they get that's better anywhere else?"

"They get a living," she said.

We both smiled. It was not good manners to be mournful with a stranger. Where the living meet, the absent and the dead understand this.

"Tell me," I asked; "in the old days were the crofters cleared off the land here, evicted from their holdings? The Clearances."

"Yes," she said, "there was a lot of that. In fact this place here, it was a corner that they were driven to—some of them that weren't shipped away to America. It was the shore, the sea. They were left to live on what they could get from the sea. I have heard my grandfather on that, and he would be very bitter often." Her smile excused her grandfather at the moment.

"They wouldn't have much in the way of boats either?"

"They hadn't," she said. "It was very hard on them for a long time and many died."

"I am a Highlander myself."

We had been introduced at last and she gave me a gracious nod.

So I had to tell her a little more about myself before asking about the land, for if her people had been driven to the shore, how did they manage to get and cultivate the land, their crofts?

"Little by little, they broke in the land and cleared away the stones and rocks. And when they began to do that there was trouble, for the shepherds would drive their sheep down and they had dogs."

"So the people were driven from most of this district

34

and the land given to a sheepfarmer from the south?"

I did not look at her for I was getting round to the white house.

"Yes," she said.

"I suppose," I said, "the landlord, the laird, would make more money out of the sheepfarmers than out of what he called his own people? It was a miserable business."

"It was," she said.

"And who's the laird now?"

"The whole estate was broken up and sold many years ago. There's none of the old laird's family left."

"So they were 'cleared' too! And the sheepfarmer—what happened to him?"

"Well, after a long time the sheep didn't pay. And then it was the deer. When the estate was broken up, many changes took place. There hasn't been a sheep-farmer in the white house for many's the year."

"Who lives there now?"

"Mr. Menzies," she said quietly.

I glanced at her and looked away, excitement stopping my breath.

"What does he do?"

She hesitated. "He makes music," she said, "but I knew his wife better."

Tragedy was in the very tone of the woman's soft voice. But there was also a reticence, a reluctance, that would normally have shut me up.

"I heard about him in London. In fact, I thought of calling on him."

"I wish you would."

I glanced at her and met her eyes. Their grey-blue had a light, a pleading, that almost made me uncomfortable. I looked away to the bracken, the ruin.

"Tell me why—that might help."

35

"You did not hear about—what happened?"

"No. Please tell me about it, Mrs. Maclellan."

"I never hear a storm in the night but it comes over me."

I waited.

"Terrible it was. They were a fine couple—good neighbours. He had a joke about being a Scot from the Borders, where the sheepmen came from who took the land in the Highlands. Some of his people, he said, did actually come north, if not to this part. So he had something to repay, he said. But that was just his joke. For his wife explained it to me, about him composing music. She was lovely."

She talked as though they were both dead.

"I'm standing here and have never asked you in!" she said.

"It's far too early in the morning to trouble any woman's house."

"Perhaps you would take a glass of milk?"

She was about to usher me into the parlour on the left when I said, "If it was the kitchen it would be a cup of tea."

She paused for a moment as though she had heard a ghost's voice. Then she took me into the kitchen, smiling and quick on her feet now.

The hearth was swept; the dark peat about the central glow sent up the blue smoke I had seen outside. When she had me seated in her husband's chair she attended to the kettle, the cups, got the lid off a tea caddy that held biscuits, livened up the very air into swirls. This eagerness of hospitality I had also forgotten.

Over the tea she told her story.

Three years ago last spring Douglas and Annabel Menzies had come to the white house. Annabel was then just on thirty and her husband a year or two older.

36

The white house had been advertised for sale for a long time but no one would buy it. They had got to hear about it as a house to rent when they were doing a tour of the Highlands, came and saw it, fell in love with it, could not buy it and actually got it to rent. It seemed it was just the very place for the work he wanted to do.

"I remember so well the first time she came. It was a bright April day with the wind blowing off the land. Dan was away somewhere and the dog with him. I heard the knock on the door. I knew it must be a stranger for no one called out if I was in. When I went to the door, there she was and she smiled. She had the loveliest smile ever I saw in a woman's face. She was not in a hurry, she was looking at me and telling me they had come to the white house and I was welcoming her and we were shaking hands. There are some people you just know. And with it all, she was so natural and sensible. She was wondering about eggs and things she needed. I told her that was easy and I told her she had brought the spring with her. Indeed it was only then I remembered my manners and asked her in. I was going to take her into the parlour when she said something about the kitchen—so I took her in here. You'll have another cup of tea?"

I thanked her. When old as the hills this woman would tell a story warm as the blood, because she was born to love certain things, like Annabel's smile.

"What was she like?" I asked.

"She was lovely in herself."

"I mean in appearance."

"It's not that she was tall, though she was tall, too, it's the way she moved and held herself. When she laughed she swayed. Nothing hard and lady-like about her; she was the lady born. But she was gay. Ach, she was lovely."

She smiled, the light in her grey-blue eyes. She was moved but not by what she had told me so much as by what she had to tell me.

"Was she dark or fair?" I asked.

My interest made her feel she wasn't talking too much. She lifted her face with confidence and some tinge of colour brought up a picture of her freckled youth.

"She was dark, but not black. I remember—it was some weeks after that first time—I remember coming out of the byre and seeing her down there by the burn humming an old air as she picked some primroses. The sun was shining on her hair and strands of it glistened with brown. It surprised me because I thought somehow she was quite dark. Her eyes were brown, too, brown as the bottom of a hazel nut. It's funny how you don't notice most people's eyes. But her eyes looked at you. It was always such a pleasure to have her coming about the house. I went down to see the primroses. I said she had found them first, the first of the year. She lifted the little posy to her nose and her mouth couldn't laugh."

Mrs. Maclellan glanced about her tea things to make sure I was being properly attended to. She was putting off what she had to tell me, but the more she put it off the worse it was going to be for her. I may have been trained well enough in my job to know that emotion has its own truth and that you sometimes have to go an uncomfortable distance to find it.

"Where did she come from?" I asked.

"Ach, that was it!" she said. "She came from Sutherland and she had the Gaelic. Her English voice was that beautiful you would never guess. An M.A. she was of Glasgow University. But when she spoke first in the Gaelic—it was an old rhyme about running water—I was that surprised it was like seeing her for the first time in a strange way and I couldn't believe it. She laughed then."

"Ah," I said. "That explains a lot. Clannish."

"Perhaps," she said. "Perhaps so."

"But you think it would explain more if I heard the sound of the running water in Gaelic?"

She looked at me then and I think I understood what she meant about the way Annabel had looked at her. Still looking at me she let her voice run away in the water rhyme in Gaelic. Still looking at me she saw I did not understand, and at that moment there was a distance and a veil; or at least there was a place where we could not meet, an experience I could not share. How vivid, almost calamitous, such a moment is, with its implication of failure, of emptiness.

"Ach well," she said, "it's just the Gaelic," putting the language in its subordinate place and letting me off.

"You would always talk the Gaelic after that."

"No, no," she answered. "We only spoke the Gaelic at times. It was—it was——"

"Saved up for something special."

"Yes," she said and I was in the circle again. "You're Highland, too, and if you haven't the Gaelic——"

"They took more than the language from us up here in the Highlands," I said.

She smiled, too, into the distance where her thought was. If she indulged her emotion too much, she might break down, become incoherent, then ashamed. So I asked her a few questions about Annabel's early life; then quietly: "Tell me what happened."

"Oh, I—I can't." Her lips trembled. Her eyes suddenly swam. "It was last winter, a January night, terrible night of storm. An awful sea was running. You

39

could hear it in the cliffs, the awful shock and the boom. At high water on the edge of the dark Dan and me had been hauling the big boat round the spit. It came on suddenly though the sea had been muttering all day. I remember us in our bed thinking we would hear more of this and I prayed for them at sea. It was after two in the morning when someone came knocking at the door. Dan got up and took Ian in, Ian MacLennan, he works at the hotel. He was in his long black oilskin and he told us that a ship was in distress off the Head. She had been burning flares. They had been in touch with the Coastguard away north at Kylessen. But on this coast there is no lifeboat and what could the Coastguard do? Ian was talking like that while Dan was putting his clothes on. He was standing there like a black figure come out of the sea itself and no hope in him. It's a terrible thing to hear men talking quietly, knowing they can do nothing, though they would do everything. The old men when I was a girl were like that. Quiet. And you listening to them and to the night."

I waited for her.

"She was lost with all hands," she said on a fatal tone. "There was nothing anyone could do. She broke up and went down."

I could not even ask how the vessel came to be there, what had gone wrong. She was a tragic figure, with her still hands, and I saw that the final tragedy is the woman's, the creator's tragedy.

And I knew that I was using even that involuntary insight to put off what had to be told.

"That awful black night," she said. "I still think I heard on the wind the cries of the drowning men." She had half turned and was looking into the fire. "Her time wasn't until February and she was awful happy about it. Someone had gone to their door, too. All the

40

local men were needed, for if the ship came inshore, maybe with ropes and lights they might save some of the crew. They had to do what they could. Good men will always do that. But she broke up on the low rock out from the Head, the Cormorants Rock. . . . It was their second child. She had lost the first before coming north. That's why they came. She had a great longing to come, she told me. Many a thing she told me, and many a thing she asked me without asking me, for she had a lovely way with her. I had two sons myself, one was killed in the war and the other, after the war, went back to New Zealand. Dan has a brother out there. So we spoke together, as women speak of their own affairs, for though she was happy she was frightened of what might happen again. Not that she was frightened either but there was a fear deep down in her. Natural enough. I told her she mustn't worry. For nothing kills like worry. But I think, maybe, she had other worries, or imagined them, for at times a woman can make an awful lot of very little. I shouldn't be saying it, but I had the feeling that maybe he wasn't getting on as well as he had expected. It was something she let drop about a musician needing to be in touch with people like himself in a city."

I could hardly listen to her and the urge to get up and go away almost overpowered me. For what he had written in that extraordinary piece called "Cliffs" was coming up through, like a first terrible exposure, up through my reluctance to look at it, to think of it. The Wrecker's motif, which David and I had thought symbolical . . . appalling. Good God, the fellow had been writing about——

"So he set off for the Head with the man who had come for him, as Ian had come for Dan, and left Mrs. Menzies all alone. Half way to the Head he took a

41

thought and turned back for the big torch. When he reached where she lay the pains were on her."

But I won't make any effort to recall her words after that. I can still see him going through the night, rushing for the doctor. He met someone who told him that the telephone to the hotel had gone dead and he thought he would save time by taking the short cut over the hills to Balrunie. Somewhere near Loch Dubh he fell and burst the bulb in his electric torch. After that the night, that dark night, takes on the appearance of phantasmagoria in my mind. The doctor wasn't in. Someone had called for him. But the nurse might be in. Would he go for the nurse, or would he make for the Head, where the doctor might be? He decided to go for the nurse. If he got the nurse directed to his house, he could then hunt the doctor. The nurse lived alone in a small croft house which had been reconstructed for her. He went to the wrong house twice because there was no light in the nurse's house. She was out. The doctor had actually called for her and left her at a case before he himself had gone on to Badlister, the first small creek inside the Head on Loch Runie. But Menzies did not know that and would not have found his way anyhow. He had spoken only to two old mournful women in the houses he had called at. They had been in bed and he had shouted to them through the window. God knows what they thought or what answers he thought he got. There were queer enough stories about it. On his way back along the road he saw a light in the hotel and desperate now for help of any kind he went there. But the landlord was out, Johan had gone home, in fact there was no one in the hotel but the Major, who was in his dressing-gown trying to bring life back to the sitting-room fire. What passed between these two Mrs. Maclellan did not know, though what

42

could the Major do anyway? In mid winter the hotel staff was small, a barman and a girl to help Johan. That was about all.

He must have been in a desperate condition now. It was a long time since he had left Annabel. Would he still hunt or would he go home? He took his burden on himself and headed for home.

Like Mrs. Maclellan, I want to get it over. He found his wife in labour. He did what he could to help. She died of haemorrhage. The child was dead.

Before the day broke Dan, who had heard the news on the cliffs, came back for his wife. With a storm lantern they hurried to the white house. The doctor was there and the nurse. Mrs. Maclellan saw Annabel laid out on her bed. The bare naked simplicity of her words could hardly be borne.

Menzies' hands were bloody and there were blood smears on his face. He was unhumanly composed. "All of him wasn't there," was how Mrs. Maclellan put it. One sentence he did speak, the most terrible words she said she ever heard in a man's mouth. He was looking at the doctor, who was trying to reassure him, to bring him back from that place where he was. "I did not know enough," he said.

3

I ate my lunch on top of the north-eastern wall of the Head and could see the flat rock on which the vessel had foundered. What I could see of it wasn't much bigger than the floor of an ordinary room and at times it gave the effect of motion, of being alive, as the sea curled and uncurled languidly about it. A cormorant was fishing not far from it. Or were there two cormorants? There were two. Beyond the rock, a dozen razorbills, flying fast in formation, swept north. In no time they were specks on that vast extending floor. Off to some new fishing ground, sib to the tides. I lost them and found the remote horizon and over all, everywhere, the sun shone. The land lay quietly under it, flattening itself in repose, and the sea's movement was a movement in an affectionate dream. A shadow came on a hill and I looked at the sky and saw a cloud like a galleon. There were smaller clouds coming up out of the east after it, puff-cheeked like the angels of an old master. The blue was high and serene and its dream began in the stillness that lies beyond the last thought. Down below one of the cormorants left the water. How black it was, its outthrust head like the tip of an arrow. Then under the water I saw an incredible movement of blue-green silver, thick as the body of a man and about a man's length. Swiftly it thrust through the sea, this way and then that. Before my surprise could realise itself it vanished, and on the surface of the water was a small dark ball—the head of a seal.

I watched that seal hunting for a long time. I had never heard or read of this under-water phenomenon before and it held an enchantment which I wished to prolong. Gaelic legend is full of the seal. A beautiful woman sits on a rock combing her hair and a fisherman captures her before she can get into her seal's skin and escape into the deep. He hides the skin and she rears his children—her earth children—and she listens, at times she listens, to the sea. She listens back, and because what she hears cannot be spoken it is sung. Muted and haunted but rising with the storm, coming through, until the allurement that cannot be heard is strongest of all.

Land under the Wave. Such song titles came back to me. The old Paradise, the land of perpetual wonder, was under the sea. I had never quite understood how it could be under the sea. That it could be an island or islands in the West where the sun sets, throwing its silver path back to those wandering or waiting on the shore they had to leave, I could understand: The Isles of the Blest. *Tir nan Og*—the land of youth, of the ever young. But *under* the sea: that required an extra effort in understanding.

/ The waves that curled about the rock were rising higher. A small crevice was filled for the first time. As the water choked the inmost fissure it creamed, hesitated, then fell away in a tiny rush. At high tide the rock would be covered. The vessel would have been piled up on the rock by a huge sea, then as the water fell away she would have fallen back and over, filled and gone under even as she was being hurled against the rock again. The end would have been fierce and fast.

After leaving the Maclellans' home I had made a wide detour, as I did not wish to be seen anywhere near the white house. It might look like prying. Mrs. Maclellan had moved me in a manner I had not believed possible. In a way I laid myself open for it; yet to do so was natural enough to a man in my profession, who has to make sure that traditional modes of behaviour or response are not confused with so-called fundamental truths about human nature. A job has to be tackled objectively and the facts recorded as clearly and inclusively as possible so that others, working outside the field, may make assessments or reach conclusions, like psychologists or even psychiatrists.

When I find myself using this kind of stock argument on myself I generally look into it for it may be a blind. On this occasion it went on and on until I suddenly swore as a darkness rose from a muscle spasm and passed away leaving me sitting there on the cliff top in the sunlight of this quiet day.

Now one thing had troubled me already and that was the way I had turned on the Major and told him he was deteriorating, behaving like a bloody tyrant. It had been as surprising to me as to the Major.

I got up there and then without looking into anything and began following a sheep path that ran inland along the cliffs on the south side of the sea inlet. Sheep were dotted about and the thin turf was yellow in spots with tormentil and crowsfoot. Diminutive violets also, and eyebright, and, in a small hollow, lovely yellow-faced mountain pansies. When I squatted and looked at their faces they did the heart good. They were here always. This was their place.

As I followed the path, the air of remoteness grew. At one spot, where the cliffs disappeared in green braes, I saw three cottages down below with black skerries sheltering the smooth sandy shore. Human feet had made natural steps in the steep green brae. Everything would be carried up on a man's back or a woman's . . . or taken by boat when sea and tide permitted.

Where the steps ended and the path up the slow slope began I was tempted to follow it but didn't, driven on, as I now admitted to myself, to get some picture of the country through which Douglas Menzies had passed on that wild dark night.

But distances were deceptive and when at last I did get up onto the main road I was still a mile or more from the village at the head of the loch. It was a gravel road, narrow, full of pot-holes, with an occasional rough bulge or "passing place". Hardly an inviting road for curious tourists. The bus driver had told me that his garage "on the east side" made more money out of hauling tourists' cars from ditches than from the normal transport business. And there were spots where it needn't be ditches but twenty-foot drops and a long bounding roll after that.

When I saw a footpath leave the road my instinct for country was good enough to suggest that this was a short-cut over the hill back to Dalaskir. Besides, there was a sort of gluttony in me now for off-the-road places.

Well up, I paused to look back, saw scattered houses out from the village and wondered which of them was the nurse's, then I passed into hill country and in time came round a slope and saw a fishing loch below me. The gillie was tying up the boat, a man and woman were stamping their feet and moving off. I looked at my watch. It was twenty minutes to six.

After resting for a while I followed the track until I saw the sweep of land below me, the hotel looking small but comfortably settled, before that slow sweep

47

began to rise beyond it and level out towards the Head. Southward, in an instant, I saw the white house like a lonely beacon pushed back by the cliffs.

Dan's cottage in its hollow I could not see, but a boat was heading towards it from the direction of the island. I watched it until it passed under the land. The barrister would have had another good day. On this side of the hotel the thin brown road ran south. I lost it long before it entered the glen or pass between the mountains. I had probably saved myself over a mile by taking this short cut, but it was not the kind of path I would have taken in the dark, as Douglas Menzies had done.

I sat down again for there would be arrivals at the hotel, and drinks and talks of catches, while there must be some kind of bathroom arrangement, some system of priorities for so congested an attack on dressing. I couldn't imagine the Major being hurried or bounced out of his bath.

Had he been fishing today? I doubted it, but then I wondered, for his nocturnal habits must have achieved a norm of some sort. And what about Lachlan? Ah, so there would be that in it: the question of Lachlan's employment and pay as a gillie. When I was a small boy the charge for a gillie was ten shillings a day. Now it would have to be a pound at least. If it was still a daily engagement—and clearly it would have to be in the ordinary way—then in last night's dispute between the Major and Lachlan the money motive had been darkly concealed. I had never thought of that. Lachlan would have been fighting for his pound and the Major, knowing this, had been playing on his fear. There had been that over and above! The cash nexus!

When I got to the hotel there was no one in the hall. Trays exposed a meagre catch of trout, though one spotted beauty was well over a pound, perhaps a pound and a half. It was so long since I had been in this sporting world that the red spots, the dark gold, and here and there the slimy peat black of a poor specimen with a large head, affected me oddly. But then it seemed I could hardly stir about this place without having obscure atavistic feelings aroused. As I went upstairs, the day went with me, its expansiveness, that airy sense of insecurity on the Head, the underwater green silver of the hunting seal, the remote mountains against the blue, the lonely cottages by the sea. I heard splashings and a woman's voice so high that it sounded querulous behind a bedroom door. I went into my own room and sat on the bed.

Never had I felt so utterly aimless. When I had washed I looked through my belongings and decided all I could do was put on a new collar and tie. But my eye had been caught by the thick envelope into which I had stuck Menzies' script.

I couldn't look at it now, I just couldn't read it. Besides, it seemed extraordinary that he could have written it at all. And that aimless thought, coming from heaven knew where, arrested me. Like a dog, it shepherded my woolly wits from where they had been straying. I sat down on the bed again. It *was* extraordinary.

How could the fellow, after going through that experience, sit down and write about it? He couldn't, hang it he couldn't, not if it had been as intense, as shattering, as Mrs. Maclellan had made me feel it was. It's all very well saying great writers used their experiences in their work. Well, of course. But before they could do it they must have got over or digested the experience; the experience was now secondary to the work.

I became excited because I saw where my thought led. If Menzies had been able to sit down and write about what had happened, he wasn't now in such a bad way as they made out. If he had cut himself off from everyone, if it appeared he was going fast to the devil and death, well, naturally, for in digesting such an experience things happened to a man's system. He sweated blood. The demoniacal could glower in his eyes. Sweating blood becomes a cliché only in the mouths of those who in their creative efforts cannot sweat even ordinary sweat.

My excitement carried me into sweeping statements of that kind. They were heartening; and humbling, too, because I glimpsed the terrific effort involved, the appalling fight. But when they wondered how he lived, where he got the food and drink—for, of course, he *must* drink, though no one had ever seen him drunk— they could not realise that anything at all in the way of nourishment, even the same old stuff and very little of it, was enough. The pitcher of milk that Mrs. Maclellan left by the corner of some stone dyke mightn't always be emptied, but it was now and then. And that same woman would occasionally leave more solid stuff than milk, if I knew her.

I became charged with a drunken hope in my realisation of what happened—and was no doubt still happening, for writing wasn't his true field, and he would have switched to music. And once he had switched to music, for the writing he wouldn't have given a damn. In his marrow he would know that any writing of his could only be amateurish, a fumbling. David's letters to him would have been worse than meaningless; a sort of literary chatter, particularly—and now the thought came to me with horrible significance—if his real creation, his music, had been—was being—ignored. I saw Mrs. Maclellan's face as she told me what Annabel had said, or hinted, about his being "out of touch". I was hardly able to bear it then, for I realised what it meant; in music, of all the arts. There were editors and journals and publishers waiting for the written word of every kind. But music . . .

I had moved among coteries. To criticise or feel superior to them is silly. In any society there's a way of getting things done. Society evolves the way. It's a matter of the behaviour pattern and I'm not thrusting my anthropology down anyone's throat. You cannot sit on a rock and write major music about seals and wreckers or annihilating tragedy and expect a full orchestral production in a capital city next season. There's a limit to what even one's belly laughs at. Beethoven and Mozart were "in the swim" from the child prodigy stage.

But such argumentation can itself grow intolerably inflated, and to cut it short I suddenly fished the manuscript from my bag, opened it in the middle and began to read.

I got a slight shock. This wasn't quite my memory of it. It's not that it seemed smoother, less obscure. Its strength, its force, was being manipulated by another kind of power than the demonic; there were imaginative eyes behind it with a certain serenity, even when the demonic was being dealt with.

Besides, the detail wasn't right. It didn't belong to the actual experience, the tragedy. "And the horizon is set upon the sea," I read. "I hadn't noticed the sea, not particularly. I observe it now with an obliterating sense of shock. My eye travels down it. The grassy bank on which I lie is the cliff-head. The cliff-head! Down beneath me—the jagged rocks, whereon his body lies impaled. *She does not know.* Terror dwells in me without death."

Then it came back to me: this had to do with a dream. I felt completely lost. At that moment the gong went. I stood looking out of the window and saw Lachlan jerk his head away from Ian, who was smiling at him, before walking out of sight. Ian continued to clean his hands with a piece of waste, the humour lingering on his eyelids.

They were all at table by the time I entered the dining-room. The Major looked up so I said, "Good evening." "Evening," replied the Major before turning his head to the widow. I listened to the talk. After a few moments some point in the conversation, or aspect of character in the voice that made the point, would set my mind off on its own. Perhaps a man cannot get past his job, but the contrast between this group, with their southern voices, and this land and its people seemed quite dramatic. The dining table and those around it made an oasis almost to a point which transcends criticism and evokes wonder, and this somehow is pleasant.

The barrister did not say much, but he was a strong self-contained man in his forties, with a straight back, a round head, neatly brushed hair and rather hairy hands. When the Major asked him how he had got on, he started talking as if he had only a sentence or two to say. But more sentences followed, precise, short, and I realised that he was telling a story about Dan and a cave and shags. The story hadn't any particular point, it was simply descriptive, evoking Dan and the cave and the birds in a matter-of-fact manner that yet was somehow amusing in the driest fashion. They all laughed.

The man who had caught the big trout had a face like a butler's and he didn't tell his story very well. Sneddon was his name and the Major poked fun at him. Mrs. Sneddon had her thrust at the Major by asking ever so innocently how Lachlan had behaved.

"Lachlan is a very good gillie, ma'm."

"When he's employed," she said.

"Naughty, naughty," said the widow.

But they all knew how far they could go, and the Major didn't appear in the least disconcerted.

"And what a stroke as an oarsman!" he added. "It was getting very dull, sitting in a flat calm. Then wind darkened the other end of the loch and I told Lachlan to get going. I asked him why he lifted his oars so high. 'Because if it was blowing and I didn't lift them,' he said, 'I would wet you.' 'But it's not blowing just now,' I said as he heaved higher and harder. 'No, sir, but sometimes it is.' "

The barrister appreciated that one.

"When we did get to the other end," pursued the Major, "the wind had gone. Another flat calm. Lachlan looked back at the end we had left and the wind was there now. I saw the satire on his face. 'You could have told me that?' I said. 'I could have told you that easily enough,' said Lachlan."

As they were laughing, the door opened and Johan came in with her tray.

After that the talk got into a bit of a tangle, for Sneddon had caught his wonderful trout on a dry fly; he had stalked the rise. The Major didn't fish dry fly, was apparently more interested in puncturing Sneddon's triumph than in any kind of flies. Others joined in. The barrister was silent. But the women could always ask an absurd question.

As they got up and left the room I sat on. I had heard that Highland hotels had a poor reputation for coffee, but here it was quite good and I told Johan so. Her rather tense expression relaxed.

"I'm glad you like it," she said. Her words were a change from the "Thank you, sir" of the city waiter. But I couldn't think of anything else to say.

I smoked a cigarette and finally decided I would go out for a stroll and get to bed early. I certainly didn't want to make another night of it with the Major, even if he felt that way, and he hadn't shown any sign of it. But that was nothing to go by. And I could bet, too, that his argument with Lachlan over the wind on the loch hadn't stopped at the slight joke!

When I was sure the way was clear, I went out and upstairs quietly. I paused as I heard a girl's voice humming in that mindless or unconscious way that is, in a moment, so intimate. And it was one of the old sea melodies or seal songs, it seemed to me, that had affected me that morning. Actually it wasn't, as I later found out, but for the moment I was swept into that region. Though "swept" is quite the wrong verb: I simply was there, still as a tree in a landscape. This kind of "translation", if I may use the word, gives me at least more insight into the meaning of "magic", in my professional sense, than any amount of effort at intellectual apprehension. It was a very old Gaelic air; it went back so far that it was timeless or had transfixed time; it had words and these words told a story of human tragedy; yet that tragedy had been so winnowed by the generations that it could be sung, hummed, as a lullaby to a child. I know of no essentialising process more profound than this.

I knew now it was the chamber-maid who was humming the air; and when I heard water being poured into a pail I realised she was in my room. As I stood in the doorway she deftly turned over a corner of the bed-clothes and looked up.

"Don't let me interrupt."

"It's all right, I'm finished." She moved lightly and quickly to the washstand and picked up her bucket. But I couldn't get out of her way.

"What was—what was that you were singing?" An absurd boyish gulp in my throat made me stutter.

Her eyes flashed on my face. I knew what her look meant. "Something you were humming."

"Don't know."

"Sorry." I got out of her way, and her clothes brushed mine as she passed.

Really this was going too far! Cornering the chambermaid! I listened to her footsteps in the next room. She was preparing the bedrooms for the night. And she certainly didn't hum anything now.

How could I tell her that I meant nothing? And, anyway . . . what had I meant?

She might tell the others in the kitchen. In no time I was worked up to a ludicrous pitch. I hadn't been in such a knot since I was a boy. I remembered the girl then and the half-choked calf love she had run away from.

Only when I heard her footsteps going downstairs did this surprising gaucherie begin to drain away.

Too much had been happening too quickly; not enough sleep last night and less travelling up the night before.

I sat staring at my window, through the window, beyond the top of the garage, at the light in the evening sky.

What, in fact, had been happening? A few drinks with a Major, a story from a croft wife whose naivety at times had surely been too much, a seal, a girl humming a tune. One could hardly call them happenings. I must put the branks on such irresponsible emotionalism.

For take the tune. When the girl had murmured something like "Don't know" she really hadn't known.

She wouldn't have known that she had been humming . . .

Then I suddenly thought: *What thematic stuff for Douglas Menzies!*

The thought mushroomed up until it was the dome of the sky.

I got onto my feet and looked about the room wondering vaguely what I had come up for. I couldn't remember. In this state of mind I went downstairs and outside, meeting no one.

Everything seemed to work round to Menzies! It was like an obsession, I thought, rather enjoying the bitter tang now that I was in the broad world. Colours were intensified after the glare of the day. A tall grass hung its head in a brownish glow. Grasses were separate and shapely, graceful. The girl had grace; that was her glow from within. She had that quality. Usually one thought of it as slow in movement. That girl would run like a hind.

In time I found myself back where I had eaten my lunch. There was a little more of the Cormorants Rock exposed. So the tide had come full in and was ebbing. The approaching night was draining the vivid quality from the blue and the green, but the white on a frothing tongue of water in a fissure was whiter than ever, spectral. The birds had gone home to their roosts, their high ledges. A desire crept over me to crawl to the edge and look down. The grassy slope was not very steep and at the end of it the rock ledge stuck out a foot or two over the sheer drop. That ledge should stop me even if I slid. A yard short of the ledge my heels and fingers dug into the turf and I held back against an intangible but sickening pull. At that moment a fulmar rose in front of me, wheeled and went down.

My muscles were trembling by the time I returned to my starting point and, deeply relieved, I lay there for some time on my back.

The serenity in the sky had a beauty that was utterly unhuman and I lost myself in its detachment. My very skin got washed by its high air. . . . To demand nothing, to lose the self, was exquisite and rare. But fleeting, and, in a moment, gone; but not for ever, I thought, though a wry smile was already on the move.

This small event had a curious strengthening effect and none the less because I thought I could assess it for what it was worth. This losing of the self: it was an old concept, a bird that was usually shot at sight. Then I thought of coteries as rookeries and my stomach gave a heave or two on its own.

Very necessary those coterie critics, I thought; preservers of the pattern. But this airy argument was being used to keep me from realising where my feet were going. Yet the mind is so devious that I was aware even of that. Only when I stood beside the ruins of the two cottages did argument fade out.

I went on, then looked back over my shoulder and saw what were once the little cultivated fields, could hear what cries I wished to hear, young running feet, the woman singing in the byre's deep dusk as she milked the cow . . . and I saw the dismembered rowan tree, the tragic gesture of its solitary arm against the sky.

When I came in sight of the white house I sat down. I didn't know what to do. And I hadn't the script with me. This had to be a business interview, at the very furthest remove from the personal; to suggest that I knew what had happened would be intolerable.

There was no life about the place, no smoke from a

chimney. The walls of the house must have been lime-washed, perhaps when they moved in. In the thickening dusk these walls were more spectral than the sea froth. Get up and go down!

All right, I agreed, I'll get it over. So I got up and walked down.

4

Not a sound could I hear as I approached the house. The steading was over on my left, its roof fallen in completely at one end, but towards the other end were gaunt ribs or couplings, with bits hanging like rags. The near gable of the house was white but soiled in whorls. I had to leap over a choked ditch for the flagstone that spanned it had slipped sideways. Clumps of rushes were here and there and broad-leaved docks. Then I was in front of the house, passing the near window. The stone doorstep was chipped round the edges and muddy. The low wall ran round a patch of garden completely neglected, wildly overgrown, but with some flowering stocks holding their own by growing tall. These bright flowers momentarily astonished and affected me, like the flicker of a woman's summer dress.

The dark green of the door was blotched and I was just about to knock when a deep throaty growl came from inside, from the room beyond the door. It took me a moment to realise it could only be the growl of a dog. I hadn't heard of a dog and I didn't like the sound. I knocked. The dog growled again and a human voice growled at the dog. But no one came to the door. I all but stole off, so next time I knocked loudly.

I heard him coming. The door scraped as it was pulled inward and there he was with his ashen face and eyes black in the gloom. An extraordinary sort of burning force came out with the look at what was on his doorstep.

"Mr. Menzies?"

"What do you want?"

"I have come up from London. The editor of *Serpent* asked me to call on you about a manuscript which you sent to him. My name is Urquhart, Walter Urquhart. The editor asked me to act for him."

He wasn't suspicious, he didn't glower, he just kept on looking at me, but never before had I met so repelling a force. Whether my words had conveyed any meaning to him I didn't know.

"I would like to discuss it with you," I said. "It is called *Cliffs*."

In the silence I knew somehow that the title had registered.

"What do you want about it?"

"One or two things we weren't sure of." I had had to control a certain nervousness in my voice, but now it was so obvious he didn't want to have any truck with me that the nervousness cleared.

"What?"

"In the first place, we weren't quite sure if *you* had sent it. There wasn't any letter with it. Not even your address. An editor has to be sure of his rights."

"Rights!"

"Yes, rights. Someone else might have sent it for all he knew."

"Who could have sent it?"

"I don't know," I said quite definitely. A certain dull anger was stirring in me and I had meant to be diplomatic, persuasive over an indefinite time.

"Is that all?"

"No," I answered. "There are a few points I should

like to discuss. In the first place, has the editor your permission to publish?"

"He can do what he likes."

"Right. I'll tell him."

"Why do you think I sent it to him?"

"Right," I said. "That's fine."

"Rights!" The satire may have been blasting but the artist in him savoured the word, and this affected me with an inexplicable familiarity, as though I might be tipped over into his stark region any time. Besides, I fancied I got the smell of rum.

"An editor has got to be very careful about his rights," I said. "He thinks it a first-class bit of work. Was quite excited about it."

He didn't explode, but for a long moment things hung in the balance.

"And what do *you* think?"

"Genius," I said.

A harsh sound from his throat hit me like a flung sod.

"Wait a bit," I said, though if the door had shut easily that would have been the end of it. "Just hold on. Hang it, you know it's great work. Why not—complete it?"

My challenge took the wind from him. That I could have used the word genius so glibly might have sickened anyone, but this was in the dumb blasting region. However, something was now taking place beyond our words. His curiosity might be of the infernal kind, if curiosity it could be called, but if a man talks at all he can be kept talking. What this man would hate and repel would be the social touch, the human hand, the intolerable warmth of human sympathy.

"Come in," he said.

"Thanks," I said coolly and groped in after him. It was dim in the room, with white paper scattered about.

61

I saw the dog's eyes, heard the thump of his hind
quarters against a table leg. There was no fire and
the air was infested with the thick warmth of lamp
black, paraffin and a conjunction of smells including
the pervasive pungency of rum from his breath.
I stood still, lest I trod on or knocked things over,
while he busied himself with a lamp. I let him
grope and search for matches before I offered him
mine.

The lamp was a tall affair with a double wick. The
slim funnel hadn't been cleaned for some time; it was
yellow and cracked near the top. As his hand screwed
up the wicks the fingers straightened out from the
knuckles in fine bone. These fingers would take a relentless grip. An old greeny-blue tweed, dark-blue shirt
with collar attached, no tie, a chin rather pointed, as if
the underlying bone in the man would not be denied,
and then the face long, with a straight nose, a steep
forehead and vertical puckers as the eyebrows gathered
before the growing light. The skin was not ashen at all,
it was drained of colour as if it had been washed incredibly clean, shaved and washed after a few days'
growth. He was about my own height, five feet ten,
spare, but, again, with bone that showed at the shoulder
ends; not the cerebral or cerebrotonic type; slim and
smooth, but bony and strong or, rather, enduring,
like the old hunting men.

I glanced about the room. The disorder was of long
standing. Books and music sheets were piled up, strewn
around. One solid table, a flimsy card table, an upright piano in the inner corner, a disrupted wooden
packing case, a writing desk, a portable typewriter, a
violin case. When he dumped its load from a chair,
the uprush of dust caught my throat. I thanked him
and sat down. He stood over by the fireplace, as if he

still had something to find, looking back at me. If his intention was to make a fire he forgot it.

"From London, are you?"

"Yes."

"Specially?"

"Yes."

And suddenly I realised the enormity of my mission: I could come all that way about a piece of writing that did not matter, wasn't worth putting his name to, could be burned for all he cared; not for his music, not for his real creative work but for a single chance piece of perishable writing. It even wasn't true that I had come solely for that, and now I couldn't tell him as much.

"The editor wondered—because it's difficult stuff even for his readers—he wondered if there was more to follow. It seemed to him in the nature of an overture."

"Overture!"

His ironic utterance of that one word was so charged with implication that it made me feel futile and commonplace. Whatever I would say would be on the wrong level. Commonplaces for him had got burned up. We couldn't meet.

My eyes wandered over the scrawled lined sheets. "You write music," I said. Terrible!

He didn't even answer. He stood watching me, the measuring satire quite undisguised. The lips were slightly parted but straight, drawn thin. There was a movement at the corner of the left eye, a flickering. If I got up and went off now I would be conscious of having behaved in a way so indescribably trivial that I should never be able to recall it without a knot in the flesh.

"If you compose music," I said, hanging on, "if that's your real creative business, then writing is secondary?"

"Thirdly," he said. "Third-thousandthly." The penultimate syllable was a lingual test which he surmounted to his satisfaction.

"Why did you write, then?"

"Is that what you have come to find out?"

"No," I said at once, avoiding him. "It's no business of mine. But there's this about it: if you can write like that without caring, then what you could do, if you gave your mind to it, would be tremendous."

But he was searching me out. I had come "to find out". It was a hellish moment. And look how I would, lean back, I knew that he had searched me out.

But he apparently hedged and that gave me a first feeling of assurance.

" 'Write like that'," he repeated. "Like what?"

"I can't go into its merits. I can only tell the effect it had. It had a terrific effect on me. I was born and brought up in the Highlands. Apart from anything else, this background came alive, I mean it became part of life, outside and in. It brought things to life I didn't know or had forgotten. But it also excited the editor and he's English. So it wasn't local or personal; that had been lifted up——"

"Sub specie aeternitatis," he said as I fumbled.

"Exactly," I said; "it needs a cliché." I didn't even bother to look at him.

"Let's have some more of your clichés," he said, glancing about the dark corner of the floor behind him. For a moment he was quite still, then he turned and sat down. "This is interesting." I realised that this man would use talk like a weapon.

"Parts of the writing are obscure, but whether that's your deliberate intention or a failure on the reader's part, I don't know," I said. "I may rate lucidity too

64

high. If I mention it it's only to bring it to your notice, to leave it to you. That's what we felt. With this extra, —and that's perhaps where the word overture came in—this extra, that we got the impression that you start a theme which you might in further work expand. That's the kind of thing I wanted to discuss. However, that's up to you, and—let me say it—the last thing on earth I want to do is intrude." Aware I should not have introduced that personal touch, yet relieved I had done it, I went on at once, "For us, it's all right as it stands."

"But it could do with more lucidity?"

I reacted with the flick of dumb anger that clears the brain. "It might," I said, "be worth considering. The Wrecker's motif, for example. I found myself lost somewhere between symbolism and actuality. That may be your intention. The reader feels that the writer has experienced with an intense clarity of vision what he, the reader, can see only as—as——"

"As in a glass darkly."

I looked straight at him. "Yes," I said. I held his eyes and added, "The degree of darkness being in inverse ratio to the intuitive insight."

That did something to him. Anyway, it cleared his face. Possibly I knew then what my words meant. I was dead solemn, too, and very pointed. The humour of it got him in a way that made of his smile almost a silent laugh as he swung off the chair and from that obscure corner, which he had considered twice already, picked up a small tin milk-pail by its wire handle. The bright tin winked in the direct light; it would hold two to three pints of milk. Twice the fellow had denied his instinct to be hospitable. Now he was going to give me a glass of Mrs. Maclellan's milk. Take it canny, I cautioned myself, you'll get him yet.

He found a couple of cups. One apparently was clean, the other he blew into and then set down on his side. The dog stirred but the brute was under the table and I couldn't see him. He emerged and looked at his master, a tawny collie with the shoulders, the head, of a development beyond the wolf. At least so he appeared in that light. The hair seemed to stand up on his shoulders. He was lean but powerful. He would hunt for his food; reverting to the wild. I would no more have thought of patting him than of putting my hand in a trap.

I watched the brute as he padded slowly and flopped between the card table and the piano. When I looked back at Menzies he was pouring two drinks not from the milk pail but from a black bottle. As he handed me a cup I thanked him and got the smell. It was rum.

We drank.

As my throat burned I choked but made a stupendous effort to get the cup back on the table without spilling the whole content. The skin on my wet hand went cold, anaesthetised. Then I tried to cough up my suffocation, and kept coughing, tears smearing my cheeks, until I got some breath down my windpipe. Gradually I came panting round.

"You like water in it?"

It was hardly the moment for his infernal humour, I thought, but I didn't say so. "It's rather strong," I croaked.

He must have drunk his off like so much water, for he put his empty cup on the table and arose. Beyond the table, from under the window, he picked up a zinc bucket, peered into it, gave it a slight swill.

There was only an inch or two of water in that bucket, yet he contrived to pour the right quantity into my cup without spilling onto the table more than a spoonful or so. But that wasn't all. Setting down the bucket he mopped what was spilt with a blue silk handkerchief. Out of consideration for his guest.

Had he been consistently ruthless, let the papers swim in the water, one could have understood him, known exactly what one was up against. He made a detached job of the mopping then pushed his handkerchief back into one of his pockets. About the whole little act there had been the exactitude, the precision, of a musician, or of a surgeon.

And all the time I knew that that rum was over proof in strength, the kind that cannot be bought in any hotel or other licensed premises. So I couldn't refer to it. All I could do to equal his consideration and possibly cool my burning throat was pick up the cup and try its contents a little more carefully. This I did and after that I automatically fished out my cigarette case. Would he have one? No. And then he took one.

I suppose I had an abnormal awareness of what was happening because of the unthinkable that might happen beyond.

The talk went on and he sucked in words like "symbolism", "actuality", with the smoke which he obviously hadn't tasted for a long time. We cut the old patterns on ice thin in parts and rough in others. It's a preliminary game in which you learn about the other fellow. On the thin ice you drive yourself to an extra intricacy, and on the rough the steel checks and growls with a dismissive intolerance.

He was extraordinarily expert in the use of the image. I do not know how I am going to indicate this. But I sensed it at once. The obvious was no longer of any interest to him.

Perhaps the simplest way for me would be to illustrate it from my own experience. For example, when

I looked back over my shoulder at the little landscape of the two ruins and saw finally the dismembered rowan tree with its one arm thrust against the sky, I had a feeling of turning away from a landscape behind the physical one I looked at. Analysis here can go on for ever and ad nauseam, but "the other landscape" remains as at least a useful label. To put it naively for the moment, it stands for something.

Again, consider normal talk or conversation. I meet a man for the first time and have a few polite words about the weather, the crops, the stock exchange, football coupons, or whatever it may be, and leave him, thinking: that's a decent fellow. I have the same conversation with another man and leave him, thinking: I wouldn't trust him as far as I could throw him. So behind the words another silent conversation must have been going on, "the other conversation", that for each is the important one.

But Douglas Menzies was the metaphysical Scot who had got bored even by metaphysics, wearied of the words that endlessly analyse one another, and had passed over into "the other landscape" where labels or symbols do the work. And if it were contended that labels or symbols could here, again, perform only a metaphysical exercise, the answer would agree but indicate "the other metaphysics".

I know that sounds worse than "neat" and leaves behind it an excessive looming pretentiousness, a trick to give the pretentiousness body and immanence. So I'll have to stop it. For apart from elementary logic, nothing for the human mind is ever as neat as that. The landscapes interpenetrate.

In the beginning I tried to hang on to something, even if it was no more tangible than a rational point of view.

For presently, without my quite noticing how we got there, I was at sea. Perhaps it was his of the word "bollard". The sound, the very shape, of the word stuffed the throat with a sardonic fulness. Yet a darkling waste of ocean did begin to roll away into the gloom. I could see it. And when he said, "There's no bollard for your head-rope," it was beginning to be only too true.

So I countered by remarking that security had its points.

Irony did not visibly touch his features, there was merely a searching humoured light in his eyes. "When the old landmarks fade out, you panic." He could keep his feet and steer where he wanted.

But I wasn't going to be swept away too quickly, so I sensibly agreed that out in the void there were no bollards.

"Except the spectral ones, and you can hardly hitch up to a spectral bollard." He knew perfectly well that I was uncomfortable.

"Hardly," I agreed, without looking at him.

"You cannot contemplate the void indefinitely, surrounded by spectres."

But this was getting too near the bone.

"That," I explained, putting my own helm over, "is why I want to stick to the rational viewpoint even in the matter of writing."

"For after all I did write it, didn't I? And you attribute certain motives to the act. Let a man dissemble as he likes, but he doesn't indulge the creative act without getting a considerable kick. Your editor will know a thing or two about that."

My editor did. As a matter of fact David had used some such words as a spur on me. I admitted the fact at once—as a challenge. For, after all, why had he written it?

For two or three seconds he looked at me, silent, weighing me up, with that glimmer in his eye. Then he did not answer my question. He went a step beyond it and began talking of our need to rationalise the irrational for our own comfort.

But the irony was just a bit fine for me so I let myself go, and I have the foible that urges me at such a pass to pin a man down.

There is always, however, the implication behind such talk and it can be more elusive than a serpent. This man could at any moment pick it up by the tail.

So we took the next step beyond the irrational to the non-rational, where rationalising, strictly speaking, was no longer possible. What now?

The non-rational evoked God, and God evoked Mammon, and for a while some queer spectres inhabited the void. Then he said something which had an instant and extraordinary effect upon me. It was as though our talk in its loops and twists had been a mysterious build-up for his final sentence.

"God's ways are non-rational," he said, "either non-rational or there is no God. Were it otherwise, did God exist and were he rational, then his doings would be susceptible of a logical exposition. His horrors wouldn't call for faith. So if there is a God—*he must have a different system.*"

It had the shock of an insight for me at that moment and words vanished.

Perhaps I was unduly susceptible because of the notions that had been obsessing me about the other landscape, the other conversation. For God—*the other system*. And then I knew, in a moment, that for Menzies the penetration of the other system was now all that mattered.

70

I drew back. There are places which some ultimate instinct of life warns one to avoid.

"His ways are not our ways," I said with solid worth, and added as lightly as I could, "it's an old notion."

"Become a glib one."

"Glib or not, hang it, beyond rationality there can only be insanity, God's or not. The void and the—the spectral bollards: that way madness lies, death."

He was watching me. "So you see the spectral bollards?"

"I can see them all right." They were shaped like real bollards, squat affairs with a small mushroom head but without a quay wall. Imaginative images, easily induced. But wander there long enough and you are in a waste where images will howl like dogs.

"They're difficult to look at," he suggested, "out there in the void." As he went on to describe the waste I cooled down, got my bearings again. I could see that the bollards were spectral memories: that or nothing. And both meaning and memory can elude the mind, as a real bollard a thrown rope noose when the water is heaving around and the light bad. "This way and that . . . there is no way . . . and even one's precious viewpoints, carried over from the past, they grow pretty spectral, too." But there was more than viewpoints. For a man can't hitch up to a viewpoint. In this particular void it doesn't hold any kind of rope. A rope is rational. He went on in this inexorable way, never wildly, but with an abnormal penetration. And then I realised that he was hunting *me* out as well. He knew what was going on inside my mind. He had become an expert hunter of the inner region. He knew my impatience, my discomfort, my awkwardness, my urge to hitch up to something. And then at last he mentioned it: the urge to hitch up to *"the* spectral bollard".

Don't ask me why at these three words Annabel his wife came before me as if all this conversation had been about her. She stood in the doorway of my mind looking at me and I switched my eyes.

"That way madness lies, you think?" He waited.

"I was too glib. I withdraw it."

"Too personal?"

So he knew!

"No," I said. "When a vision is too profound one blacks out—for comfort's sake." I felt exhausted and unthinkingly glanced at my cup.

He got up at once and poured a couple of drinks neatly, spilling not a drop. But the mouth of the zinc bucket was too wide for my cup and again he mopped up the overflow, pushed the same sodden handkerchief back into his pocket and sat down.

I had been in some wild, some mad enough company in my time, but this wasn't mounting in that way. The more you got inside the abnormal the more normal it became. Douglas Menzies was becoming, as we say, more human. Not altogether, not quite, and his bone was hard and ruthless, but his movements—they were easy, apt. That an innate politeness can be more deadly than any bluster of the ego I know only too well, but I prefer it that way.

We drank the rum. Mine, with the water, was probably about the strength one buys in a pub. It was not at all harsh, easy on the palate, good rum.

Where had he got this powerful stuff? I remembered, too, a phantasy which David and I had evolved from what we called "the Wrecker's motif". We had placed the scene in Cornwall because we knew some old wreckers' haunts there.

But I was troubled by the personal note, by my remarks about blacking-out, so I said, "That's the kind of stuff—what we have been talking about—that comes through in your writing." Because I didn't know what to do I drank some more rum. "So I hope you can believe it excited us." I took out my cigarette case but this time he didn't have one. I lit up. "Did you write it lately? I mean is it recent enough for one to hope that, perhaps, it might be added to? I don't want to appear persistent but this is a materialistic age, complete with appropriate ideologies, and unless someone or something breaks through—and it looks as if art is all that's left to do the business—well, I don't know."

"I don't write."

"You made a damn good shot at it."

But there was no humour in this. It was the wrong approach. Commonplace and arid. Materialism, ideologies, philosophy, the new physics—they were different in kind. Irrelevant and, after a certain point, very tiresome.

My eyes wandered over some music sheets on the table. Had this fable talk anything to do with musical composition? I knew enough to know that normally it hadn't, at least not in the literary sense.

"My wife got me to write it."

His words, uttered so casually, stunned me. I actually experienced the sensation of being walloped on the back of the head. I tried to remain quite still, without showing much. He could not mean—he could not mean that his wife had appeared to him after her death and told him to write it?

But he had apparently explained enough and that was that.

There was nothing more I could do but get up and go. I had thought we had been drawing near some sort of human level of understanding, and because I had

73

begun to like the fellow the sense of my own insufficiency came down on me in a dark cloud.

At that point say what you have to say out of the remnant of manhood that cannot be less. "I heard about—what happened," I said.

"You would." His cool voice had hardly a trace of satire.

I glanced at my cup again. I finished the rum. "I suppose that's as far as we can go. I'll tell the editor." I got up.

He got up also.

"I only heard about what happened," I said, looking for my cap, "since I came up here."

"You wouldn't come specially on that account."

I wondered if the fellow hated me; if all the time he could have seen me far enough, and was now saying as much in his own bitter devilish way. The only expression on his face was a smile.

"No. I had the feeling I shouldn't have come. Now I know." But I wasn't bitter against him, only against myself. I couldn't find that accursed cap. I looked about the floor and saw the dog's eyes. As I straightened up I staggered. "It's the rum," I muttered, giving him his smile back.

"Like some more?"

Why I hesitated I don't know; perhaps the vanity that just couldn't be beaten like this, stronger even than the hatred of being where I wasn't wanted.

He poured out two more drinks.

At that moment the man was an absolute enigma to me. If his behaviour meant polite forbearance it was frightening. Not that I was afraid. I just didn't care what happened.

"If we wondered when you wrote it, it was because —but I told you that." My mind was slipping.

74

"I wrote it last winter."

"You mean you wrote it *before*——" I stared at him.

I saw the shadow come into his face as he stared back. "You didn't think I wrote it *after* it happened?"

I gripped the back of my chair, cold sober. Then I sat down.

5

I realise that it would save time and make the story more intelligible to the reader if at this point I just set down quite simply what I subsequently learned about Annabel and Douglas Menzies before they came to the white house. I gathered the facts from many sources, as will be seen.

Annabel's father had had a small sheep farm in the county of Sutherland. From a secondary school she had carried a bursary to the university of Glasgow, with the intention of taking an ordinary M.A. degree and going in for teaching: an almost hackneyed proceeding for a Highland home where the mother can contrive to save a few pounds and hold on to them in a snowstorm. She took her degree and found she did not want to go in for teaching. Her student life was rich on the personal side, for no girl as attractive as Annabel could have avoided the usual ardent *affaires*. So common sense becomes a simple matter of self-protection. That she was balanced in this way to a remarkable degree becomes quite clear.

Balanced to the point of being cunning, for where she would have liked to have gone was to the Art School. That was the world, the new world, that really fascinated her. Shapes or forms, yes, but colour in particular. Heaven knows if there is anything of heritage here, of what produced the vivid colours of the tartan, say, and then set them arithmetically in their squares. The arithmetic of the abstract. Style.

More than that, for colour here may be vivid but also it is deep. In her native tongue the colour adjectives suggest this depth, and translating them into English literally translates them from a deep to a surface manifestation. Something of this must have affected me when I saw the sea water below the Maclellans' cottage. The near green, the bottle green went down through the water. It made, as it were, the crystal clear water visible down to the sand or pebbles. As the eye travelled slowly out to sea the green deepened, and presently was blue, where the deeper depth is.

Even more than that, for the colours for the tartan were got from flowers, from lichens, and some of the most vivid from flower roots. From things that grew, right down to their roots. The "vegetable dyes". And one had only got to compare two pieces of tartan, one with the old vegetable dyes and the other with modern synthetic dyes, to perceive the difference between the soft, the deep and the hard, the superficial.

Yet never with anything merely vague in the soft and deep. The old weaver counts his coloured strands of yarn for his sett, so many for the green, so many for the blue, the red, the yellow. The result may be gorgeous but it is arithmetically, practically, contained.

Annabel had this basic practical sense. She would never have dreamed of writing home and saying she would like to go in for Art, even had the cash, at a pinch, been available. The thought was too shocking even to be laughable. Though knowing this she probably laughed too. The money spent on her over these years at the University to be thrown away! She knew her background too well right down to the startling colour that could be squeezed out of its last pale root.

She did her year at Training College, got her teaching certificate and a job in a Glasgow elementary school. She now had money in her pocket, was on her own feet. And there were night classes for all kinds of subjects, from leather work to commercial design, weaving to drawings from the nude.

She was "very nearly married" to a wealthy business man in the whisky trade when Douglas Menzies came into her life. This business man was himself Highland, and, like many of his kind, an unostentatious supporter of those social gatherings or ceilidhs where the traditional songs are sung, like the one I heard the chamber-maid humming. The hard-headed business man who can go soft over a song would go a long way for Annabel who sang them. When I think of her singing to him— singing could be as natural as talking in that milieu— I am moved to compassion. That scar he will die with.

She fought for her comfort against Douglas Menzies. She hated, too, hurting the whisky man. But at first Menzies and his music and ideas were very exciting; she was interested before she was disturbed. When the disturbance started she lost her real footing for the first time. The easy pictures, the comfortable designs, got a jolt. What lay beneath the night school game came up stark. But she counted her strands. She held on to her pattern, her sett. Even the whisky director's money; the picture of herself as a woman sending home cash to the old folks. Not a romantic business at all; a rending affair, with her awareness, at last, of how she was going to hurt the man who had offered his wealth and his all. Then the plunge, and the coming up naked and shivering cool in the pool, and looking around at the newness of things in the world.

At that time Menzies had been "a music teacher", though just what that meant exactly in the way of

78

employment I don't know. Nor does it matter. What matters is that he disliked teaching, that already he was not only composing but getting certain things accepted for public performance, arrangements or background music for short B.B.C. pieces or stuff of that kind. Getting his oar in, making contacts, taking the steps away from static teaching that would lead ultimately to the world of "free" musical expression. The parallel in writing is that of the freelance who hopes one day to write the books that he believes are inside him. But every artist knows this struggle, only more difficult in certain media than in others.

The contrast between him and Annabel here must have been quite marked. She found teaching not so uncongenial as she had expected. At times, particularly when things were rich in her personal world, she had swift insights into the minds of the children, understood them and led them, let the tiniest tots whisper in her ear. This beautiful woman with the luring voice and the smile that Mrs. Maclellan had tried to describe would have had her response from them, sometimes no doubt to the point of embarrassment. She had, too, glimpses of the greatness of true teaching, the personal giving, the selflessness. That is quite certain.

Then all of a sudden it was the cinema world. They got married in a whirl and set off for London. Douglas Menzies had written the incidental music for a film "short" which achieved more than a *succès d'estime*. A larger contract was arranged with the same studio. All studios were in London. The world was there. And, over all, the categorical imperative: one has to be in touch.

At any time, and anywhere, Menzies' personality would have been felt. The most commercially minded film producer would believe in him—and hope that the fellow would have sense and not go high-flying. As it happened his luck was in, for he had to deal in the big film with a hurricane and the wreck of a ship. The breadth and sweep, the elemental power, of the sea, and, through all, the restraint that intensified the power. I can even understand how his restraint could be more terrifying than the forces it controlled. Anyhow, an audience can go a long way with the elemental in a feature film of the sea let loose.

All this took time, of course. In the film world things which are going to happen in a hurry next week, and indeed do begin to happen feverishly in a preliminary way next week, may then be dropped or shelved, as suddenly picked up, dusted and revived, pushed out of sight again, and actually to everyone's surprise get off the mark next year with a haste that outstrips its own fever.

But meantime Douglas Menzies was finding his feet in the reaches of that sea which washed about the names that mattered, the salons that were ports en route, the skerries of jealousy, the simplicities of a refinement stark as a wreck, the beacon, the baton, the first nights and the last bitter drinks.

When things get too involved a man turns in on himself and asks the old questions about the eternal verities, with mockery or without. The pattern never varies; only the answers. But I doubt if even in this vague way I am getting anywhere near conveying the position he had reached when, after almost three years in London, Annabel began to have her child.

In the practical matter of making contacts she had been wonderfully successful. There was even some normal bother with a film company director who so fell for her in his sentimental way that he decided she could be groomed for stardom. Annabel, who said she couldn't act, so acted him off his feet that he withdrew to a respectful distance, impressed by his own integrity.

But even in the more cultured realm of sophisticated women with assessing eyes, Annabel enjoyed herself. She did not drink much. She smoked less. But she quickly picked up the jargon, because she knew what it was about, and all the more surely after her husband indulged at some later hour than usual in remarks that suggested they were up to the knees in humbug if not plain mud. She would look at him then. She was a fast learner and adept by this time at what went on behind his words.

Her child was born dead after a street accident for which she blamed herself at first to an obsessive extent. But she had been anxious about the first performance of a quartet which her husband had composed. The conductor, the hall, the programme were "important" and everything seemed to have been settled when a woman rang up and, as Douglas was out, told Annabel of a "hitch". As it turned out there was no hitch at all, and indeed the woman, whom Annabel knew quite well, said that she had "just heard of it" and that there might be nothing in it. Only perhaps at that moment did Annabel realise how much her whole heart, her whole being, was utterly given to her husband and the need for his success. In her condition, this feeling, this emotion, became heightened to an unbearable extent, particularly after she had rung up three places and not found him. But he had been in the third place a few minutes before and she correctly guessed that he had gone out with a friend for a cup of coffee. She knew where the unpretentious café was, she even thought she knew its name until her fingers began to drum on the telephone book. She wasn't going into hospital until the following week. She was feeling perfectly all right, and less than three hundred yards away they could almost always get a taxi. That café's name she could not remember, if she had ever really known it. So she slipped into her big coat and set off for the stance.

She was troubled about doing this, perhaps because of the expense—for some time she had been in a saving mood—but more particularly because if Douglas wasn't coming home for lunch in an hour or so he would phone. She was only too well aware that she shouldn't be getting worked up in this way, not because she thought it was bad for her but because he did. It even made him impatient, but with the sort of anxious impatience that she didn't really mind. In a perverse way she liked it, just as she smiled when his male reason worked out "ordinary common sense", as if she were a child who had forgotten what one and one made. But she knew they made three.

And as for the performance of his piece, that made a number beyond all calculation. Besides there was that particular woman who had phoned up. But what really made her hesitate near the corner where they usually crossed over was the sudden thought that she could have asked the name of the café at the third place which she had rung up. No sooner did this enter her mind than she impulsively started to cross the street, for what she really wanted to see was his face. He had one terrible weakness: at a certain point in personal or business relations he just didn't give a damn for anybody. He never flew off the handle; he looked at the face before him and analysed its underhand intention with a ruthlessness that left nothing unargued.

There were two horses in a dray beginning to move towards her on her side of the street. She had plenty of time to pass in front and cross the rest of the vacant way to the pavement opposite. But she hesitated when she saw a taxi coming up to overtake the dray, which had screened it when she started out. She glanced to her left, which was clear, then back at the taxi, thought she had time to cross over in front of it, took a step, hesitated, decided to turn back. The driver of the dray saw she was going to make a fool of herself and hauled on his reins. The horses reared. That frightened her. In a moment there were other vehicles and the taxi driver at his miraculous best did no more than hit her a glancing blow with his mudguard.

They helped her into the taxi which took her back to her own door. She had assured everyone she was all right. She held on to herself with extreme cunning, got up the flight of stairs to their first-floor flat, put through an urgent call to her doctor and reached her bed doubled up.

After losing her child, her convalescence was a slow affair. The plunging horses against the walls of the houses troubled her dreams. Something archaic here drove her back to remote regions in herself. And somehow it wasn't just the horses that frightened her; there was also the awful static menace of the imprisoning street walls with their high jagged roofs against the sky. Those great brutes of horses might have been "explained" in some psychoanalytic fashion. There was something at a deeper level than that, as if the horses, too, were imprisoned. Then one day, as she was waiting for some milk to boil on the electric ring and had fallen into a mindless state, she heard herself singing softly under her breath, one ·of the old airs. Tears began to roll down her face and in no time she was weeping as if her flesh as well as her mind were dissolving and running away.

Douglas was full of an understanding she had not believed possible in any man. This gave her a rare almost detached feeling of intimacy that quite overcame her at odd moments when she was alone. The only incident in the whole affair, which had brought the ruthless look on his face, draining the skin on the bone, was the initial phone call which had started it off. "Hell, that woman!" he had said.

And she knew, as indeed she had suspected, that the woman had been trying to make her particular kind of contact with Douglas. Not that she was the only one. And not that it had mattered. His three words slew her. It was part of the game. And she had "influence".

Outside this inner life was the reasonably bright conduct of a girl who had been through a difficult time and wasn't bothering her friends too much with it. It was the same Annabel who answered enquiries, who met her friends, who would be quite all right, quite her old self, given time.

Then one day he said abruptly, "Let's get away. You need a holiday."

She couldn't find words for a moment.

"You look alarmed!" he said.

"I don't know," she murmured. "We needn't." She was bewildered.

"Look, Anna. You try your best, but you can't. You know that."

She began to weep. "I'm so sorry," she stuttered. "But—but——"

"There you go! Can't you understand how it breaks my heart?" He smiled. "A change of air, my girl. That's what you need."

"No. Just give me time. Please."

"If it's the money you're thinking about, don't worry. We have enough, for long enough. A plunge is indicated, another wild plunge."

84

"Not now. In another year when you—when you have——"

He looked at her narrowly and saw deep down the practical sense that had been guiding his destiny. Another year and *they* would be coming to *him*. A shrewd estimate, that momentarily embittered him.

"If I don't get out now," he said, "I'll hit someone."

A shrewd hit that brought them into the same boat.

"But—where?" she said, groping for time as she wiped her eyes.

"Your native air."

She looked at him with an almost anguished doubt.

"Not Glasgow. No," he said. "The Highlands. Say two months of the bens and glens, roaming in the heather."

He saw the wondering look, then he saw the smile coming, he saw it brim and break.

"Oh yes," she breathed.

As he held her in his arms he knew one more rare and lovely moment to add to the slender string, the immortal tally. Extraordinary the life-giving effect of it, the renewed essence. In a few moments they were chattering.

"Stale, that's what I'm getting," he said, "just damn stale. Up yonder we'll have breadth to see miles. Think of a nor'-wester breaking on Cape Wrath. The swing and the surge, the tumult, of it."

"Yes," she said.

"Drown them in it," he said. "And high time."

"A symphony," she said. "A masterpiece. Oh, I know! And you have sea themes already——"

"You wouldn't waste anything, would you?"

"Don't mock me," she said. "But do you really mean you would—work?"

"A slave driver, that's what you are."

He saw some of the old assurance dawning. "I thought you said a holiday?" She mocked him.

"That's better." He nodded. "Think of a sudden inspiration and me trying it out on you, on a cliff top."

"I could push you over." Her hand came up to her heart as she heard what she had said.

He laughed.

"Tell me," she pleaded. "You're not just saying all this—for me?"

"Tell me," he replied. "Do you think I need it *almost* as much as you?"

She did not answer, her eyes on his face.

"Tell me," he pressed her.

"Yes," she answered with courage.

"Tell me this," he said. "Supposing I was attacked by some big idea and had to settle for a couple of months in a quiet spot—would you mind?"

The light went deep in her eyes then. "That," she said, "would be divine."

Presently as she turned hurriedly away he stopped her. What was she going to do? Get supper, she answered. But he had other ideas. They dined out and drank wine and even in the small hours she had a surprise left in the name of a couple to whom they could sublet the flat.

And so in time they came to the white house.

Douglas Menzies composed many works in this house, including at least one symphony, which I may call the Cliff Symphony. I have often speculated on that body of work. I have even found myself inventing ways by which I could have borrowed the symphony from him under the pretence that I knew a little about music and then have hung on to it or done something about it. But that is in the light of what happened. And how could I have foreseen that, any more than I could have foreseen his writing of a tragedy before it happened?

Two factors, I suspect, helped to defeat Menzies in the practical matter of getting his work acknowledged. Even in the ordinary social way he would grow on people. He could not have been ignored—*until he wasn't there*. The other factor was this, for there are decent helpful men everywhere behind the rivalries and the rest: his work may have become too profound in an idiosyncratic way.

However, it is certainly clear, from what Annabel said to Mrs. Maclellan, that there was a lack of contacts. Even the crofter's wife divined that he wasn't getting on very well. The failure on the practical side may be all there.

And he would not have helped himself much, for he now had enough experience, knew enough of ways and means, to let himself go, in the first year or so anyhow, on the real stuff, to let himself go hopefully. The plunge —and to blazes with hack jobs until he had produced a body of real work. That year must have been a wonderful one for him and so for Annabel. For when he returned from the wildest flight, or even before he started on it, while the conception of it was still "impossible", Annabel was there.

There must have been a third factor, though I hesitate to mention it. But once he had taken off in this kind of country, he was bound in some measure to have got used to the nature of the flight and the scenery. Even in London he did not anticipate using old sea themes (his successful cinema ones) in the new context. He was not going to be so poverty stricken as all that! For, of course, he knew then of the traditional airs of this particular land, the songs that Annabel hummed or sang, particularly when she did so almost unconsciously, to herself, using the rhythm to carry her mood. Here the sea rhythm became the sea's own rhythm. Tradition had put all the rhythms through a winnowing process. Tradition eliminated the temporary, as the crofter's winnower eliminated the chåff. What was left was cleansed of the personal in the sense that all great art is impersonal and thereby achieves the ultimate expression of the personal. At this point only paradox is left; paradox and the urge to give it form or shape in myth or image or symbol. That Douglas Menzies had reached some such condition even in talk, I have already tried to hint. Nothing short of it brought him alive.

But meanwhile, in this wonderful burst of creation, he would have got used to his musical country. In some measure it would have become normal to him. He could not have uttered a tag like "sub specie aeternitatis", hardly bothering even to be ironic about it, unless all the implications which the term "provincial" has for the urban critic had long ago been exhausted and dismissed. The sea, after all, is hardly provincial, and urban critics can be left with their urbanities. Heaven knows what urbanities may have accompanied the return of his symphony from London. But they must have struck Douglas Menzies with an intense dismay. Incredible that what he was trying to do could not at least be perceived. It was so familiar to his marrow now that surely, surely it could be seen.

Annabel began to perceive the need for returning to London. She knew how things had to be "worked", a footing here and then a footing there. Even in a Highland burn stepping-stones are in the order of things, and often slippery and unstable ones enough. Than a really new kind of work that takes in new and strange territory, nothing is more actively disliked, especially in the realm where it belongs. All that is normal too.

But just here she came up against the element in his character which had set her off on that disastrous journey to see his face once she had told him about the "hitch". Where he met the underhand, the wangle, he had no sense of temporising. He went straight for it, whatever the consequences. It had, of course, to be important or personal enough to set him going. He could tolerate a whole lot. But once on the war path he went to the end of it.

In this instance it would be a case of: to hell with London. London wasn't going to put him off. He would do more of the same, and tougher work at that. He was thrawn in the Scots sense that is hardly translatable. He could hang on and live on dry bread and find the bread enough. I have never met a man who was so utterly without self-pity.

And Annabel backed him up. When she saw how things were, she dropped all mention of London. Everything came in the fullness of time. So would London. He had a lot to work out of his system first! This might be his great creative period. Indeed she was quite certain of it because he told her what he was doing. They had evenings when they lived in it. Because she was happy where they were, happy in his work, these little talks gave her spells of intense happiness, the primroses against her laughing mouth. And dancing behind all that was the practical certainty of his acceptance in due time, his fame. Even more practical than that: what he was doing now was putting money in the bank. A beautiful sort of wild flower, wind-blown joke.

When the time came at last for mentioning London, there occurred what put London further from her intention than his. Not even the wild horses of her dream could have hauled her back now. She would have her child in this land.

So she did not tell him right away; she began to scheme for something more than his dry bread, for real money in a household purse. And she became as cunning and pleased and anxious about it as any blackbird over her nest in the spring. Their diminishing resources were entirely under her control and she could always convey to him when necessary that perhaps in another year or so they would have to begin to economise or see how they stood. Actually she had long pared down living costs to a simple minimum.

But she was fighting against London now herself, so she turned to London.

She couldn't have been with Douglas Menzies long before knowing that she herself would never be an artist in the true sense. So, being Annabel, it wouldn't distress her. She would merely be delighted at understanding what being an artist meant because of the interest, the companionship, it gave her and the companionship she could give.

Among her friends in London had been an English woman of about forty, who edited a woman's magazine. Annabel had done some illustrations for this magazine, dress affairs, with some letterpress on, for example, how, when and where to wear Scotch tweeds, with emphasis on the right accessories, stockings, shoes and all that. But it hadn't amounted altogether to much more than the price of a portable typewriter, with which she wrote one or two general articles, then tried her hand at a short story and failed. That was about the sum total.

But now her need was much more urgent than it had been then and she resumed a personal correspondence with the editor, who was happy to renew the old friendship, and who actually asked her straight away if she had a "new line" on tartans, then the vogue of the moment in Paris. Annabel knew exactly what was wanted and made a "story" of it in the American fashion, producing soft wonderful colouring from common plants or weeds, glancing at an old woman gathering lichen off a rock, at a Highland chief's kilt to show that the older the tartan the better it looked, giving the "right" knowledge, the authentic, the inside view, and finishing up with the specialist's exclusive practical hints. She took great care to give the article the intimate touch that let her reader share the appropriate sense of "style" over seven hundred words.

"Excellent," replied the editor, "and what about another seven guineas for Food Hints from the Highlands—and increase the personal touch?" Then it was a Highland garden. "Keep up the personal, the intimate, the surprising incident and you'll become our Scotch Feature."

Seven guineas a month! It was stupendous. It solved Annabel's whole feeding problem and a bit over. This may seem surprising until one looks into it—and remembers Mrs. Maclellan. For when Annabel told that lady her private news, all kinds of services came into action from those of a medical advice bureau to the supply department of a canteen for fresh food, but so unobtrusively and irregularly that Annabel was never really embarrassed. When the fish, straight from the sea, cleaned and wrapped in paper, was handed over with the milk, before Annabel could begin to ask the price she was forestalled with an "Ach be quiet!" Between neighbours, what was an occasional bit of fish? The hens came "on the lay" in so remarkable a way that they couldn't count. Did himself like crabs?

Because the crabs that were found in the lobster pots were just thrown away. As for potatoes it's not that they were worth giving, but they were "that dry for earlies they're real tasty. Dan says it's the light soil in that bittie of land across there". Rabbits were a plague in the turnips, and it was easy for Dan to skin two as one when he was at it. Annabel continued to pay sixpence for the "drop of milk" that filled the tin pail and something weekly for the eggs. When Annabel did a water colour of the cottage, with a small female figure at the garden wall before the front door and a male figure with a creel of fish on his back coming towards her, two white hens on top of a screw of hay, a dog on the run between a cow and the green corn, and presented it to Mrs. Maclellan in an old frame, that kind woman was so overcome with pleasure that she had to wipe the weather off her eyes before she could see it properly. Of the featureless male figure she said, "If that isn't his dead spit!"

I have seen a simplified line drawing of that picture in the magazine to which Annabel contributed her articles. It came about in an odd enough way, for I was back in London and had been taken to a cocktail party by David. I hadn't wanted to go and wouldn't have been in town at all if I could have avoided it, for my mind was still strangely saturated or obsessed. The Highlands were mentioned. I had been there? But I had just managed to get off the subject as our little group was broken up and had turned away when a woman intercepted me. "I heard you say you've been in the Highlands?"

"Yes." I did not know her.

"I don't suppose you could possibly have met a very charming young woman who contributed to a magazine I happen to edit?"

It's the absurd kind of question—for she meant it really as a question: expectation was in her eyes—you can encounter in southern regions, as though the Highlands were a small place where everyone knew everyone else.

"I'm afraid I didn't meet anyone who contributed to a magazine."

"Ah. Foiled again. Pity."

"It's rather a large stretch of country."

"I know," she said and tilted her glass straight. "I never could get a reply." She looked the capable business woman, but there was something in her eyes, a regret, that was secretively genuine. "Even the last cheque remains uncashed." Her lips twisted slightly with the humour appropriate to so unusual a situation and she glanced at her drink and drank. Then she smiled. "I just thought you might know her. She was so charming. Used to be in London with her husband, a composer."

"Afraid not," I repeated, feeling my mouth go dry and wanting desperately to escape. I knew it was Annabel.

David came to my rescue. "We can slide now," he said as we steered our way to the door.

Once outside I asked, "Who was that woman?"

"Thought you were looking a bit strained. But she's really a decent sort. Edits one of these magazines in the what-d'ye-call-it group." Then he remembered the group and her name, Alice Kent.

"I just wondered if I should know her," I said and passed it off, for I couldn't begin on the subject of Annabel again even with David.

The following afternoon, I rang up Miss Kent's headquarters, got in touch with her and introduced myself by recalling the conversation which David had interrupted. She remembered it.

"I have been rather troubled by your question about that nice girl in the Highlands who wrote for you. Could you tell me her name?"

"Annabel Menzies."

"You see, I didn't know she wrote."

"So you know her!"

"She's dead."

I heard the breath in her throat. Quite a few seconds passed before she said in her business voice, "That explains it."

"I was wondering whether it might be possible to see the magazines with her contributions. I have a particular, personal reason."

"Should be possible, I think, yes."

"Would it be an awful nuisance if I came round some time?"

"No. But—let me see——"

"Would you mind," I suddenly asked, "having dinner with me tonight?"

We had dinner the following night and when we got to her flat there were the five magazines and Annabel's correspondence file.

I liked Miss Kent. She was rather short but compact; her shoulders were squared off and her face suggested that lack of feeling which must at a difficult moment have been forbidding to a junior. Her office desk would be tidy as the room we sat in. But that room showed a definite, quiet taste. Where sentiment was what I didn't want, the efficient Miss Kent was the very person. She had savoir faire too, not to mention extra years in the matter of age that found out a lot about me quite naturally. It was when we were talking of David that she said, "I recognised I had rather rushed in when he came to your rescue. Will you help yourself?" She had produced drinks from a cabinet.

"Thank you. Did I hang out signals?"

She smiled back. "You did, you know. And I was annoyed with myself. In fact when you rang up I was feeling rather cool towards you."

"Quite right," I said. "But then you hung out your signal also."

"Really?"

"A tiny one, I admit. No more than a small light of *genuine* regret that you were to hear nothing about Annabel, a momentary desolate light," I went on wondering how she would take it, "at the back of your rather attractive grey eyes."

She took it very well and, civilised usages having been established, it became easy to become natural.

She told me about Annabel at length, described her in little incidents and conversations, tried to define the "freshness" which had obviously had such an appeal for the used and sophisticated because this freshness "was motivated by a charm which the sophisticated never quite achieve, however much they may strive to achieve the same", explained Miss Kent, who could be verbally elaborate in need. "It was God-given," she concluded, with a bitter little slant on God.

But Miss Kent used elaboration sparingly when it came to Annabel's bewildered time after the accident. Describing an occasion when she had rung up Annabel and then gone round to see her and Annabel had broken down and they had talked, she was very simple indeed. If I may have wondered now and then just what Miss Kent's real attitude to Annabel was, I was left in little doubt. There was nothing much perverse in Miss Kent, and I suspect a tragic element in her past which could harden the surface but not the depth. Annabel had drawn the woman out of the shell, in some measure, despite herself. I say "suspect" because I find I really know

95

nothing of Miss Kent's life although she contrived, doubtless by way of precautionary assessment, to uncover quite a bit of my practical doings.

At a rather late hour she decided to make some coffee "to sober us down" as she put it, and when I wondered over anyone's not liking to be "lit up" she took the wonder for exactly what it was worth and smiled at me with just a suggestion of warmth in her pale skin as she left the room.

There could be tenderness in that same woman all right, I thought, glancing around. The magazines and the correspondence file. Heaven knows, I thought, why this reluctance dogs me. I hadn't looked at the stuff, and Miss Kent had simply left it lying. Perhaps we were both bothered in the same way. I got up and looked at the room's appointments and down at the magazines on the small mahogany table and then at the file. I swung the file open and there in ink under the typewriting was the signature, Annabel Menzies.

It had its effect; more than a ghostly impact; at last I lifted the file and began reading.

When I was taking my leave with the magazines under my arm, she thanked me for a nice dinner.

I did not know how to thank her and was about to suggest another meeting sometime when she smiled, "Good night", and quietly shut the door.

So I am driven back, having at least possibly made clear much of what I did not know then myself, to the room in the white house, with Douglas Menzies standing there, looking at me, after uttering the words, "You didn't think I wrote it *after* it happened."

6

I was quite witless and sat like a burdened lump.

"I just didn't know," I said and looked at my cup full of the brown rum. I took a drink. I was drinking too much. "How could I?"

"You merely thought I did. You thought I had discovered a good subject."

"No need to say that."

"No?" He sat down. "Could you suggest, then, a better or bigger subject?" He drank the neat rum.

He had the air, the reasonable appearance, of one dealing with facts. The tragedy was quite a big subject for a writer, and if one thought so one should admit it and be done with it. Why not?

"There's nothing wrong with the subject," I said. O God, was I getting fuddled?

"It's big enough to stretch the best mind, you feel?"

It was too much for me. I could not carry on the argument at that extra remove, where the facts are merely used to point their implications. For moments, yes, but not all the time. I could not breathe in that atmosphere. And then it seemed to me that I understood. The fellow had distilled and redistilled his bitterness until it was overproof, like the rum. But it was bitterness.

Then I found that it wasn't bitterness. Bitterness was the fact or stuff that had been distilled. The sugar of the sugar cane had been distilled—into that spirit in his cup.

He stripped me bare.

Only after that was I able to ask how it came about that he had written what he had written *before* the tragedy occurred.

He looked at me for a few minutes but I had nothing to hide now, I was nothing at all. Even Annabel had not come into my mind.

"The theme of a storm and a wreck I had dealt with in London. I wrote the music for the film. The theme persisted, recurred. Remarkable this recurrence. For example, there was first the actual doomed ship and the storm, what is called 'the real thing'; then there was the acting of the real thing for the film; then my music for the acting; after that we came here and the theme suffered a sea change into music as an art where the actors are the implications of the themes, reforming and shaping them as though they were so many myths or symbols that come and go, as such things do come and go in that region of shadows to which you may penetrate—if you must, and can keep your head. In that region you will take your old notions with you and expect to be able to answer your own questions in their terms. At first: what is the symbol of a wrecker? Then: what is the wrecker a symbol of? And so on until you are bogged in futility—and begin to realise that your old notions don't apply." He stopped, his eyes in my face. "Then it starts all over again. There is a new storm and a new doomed ship. But this time there is a difference. For example, those who are doomed are different. Recurrence has this seeming variety. Yet what recurrence is a recurrence of does not change. In the region of shadows you have to make contact, if you can, with what you realise does not change."

From this sort of talk I got two quite vivid impressions: the first, that the words were so many noises about something that might be unveiled; the second, that the recurrence of the same tragic theme from its first treatment in his music to Annabel's death on that night of storm was so remarkable, so strangely startling, that a word like coincidence had no relevance and a word like recurrence was as yet only a sound to hold on to.

What could I reply? Because if I said the wrong thing and was found wanting he would dry up and I would have to go. And apparently there was still enough vanity in me not to want that to happen.

"Even recurrence is only a sound to hold on to, a grip on the rope," I said.

"And what about myth and symbol?"

"And totem and taboo," I said, adding to the arid humour. "We find them very useful in my job."

"More grips on the rope?"

"That's about it," I said. "I fancied you gave the words myth and symbol a certain stress, as if they were glib sounds. We may be glib monkeys on a rope."

"And the rope?"

"There's always—the rope," I said. "At least that's the notion—the very old notion." His kind of arid humour was affecting me, and I became aware of a slight enmity in me towards him. Not so much an arid as a searching humour; and the enmity was also in him, if from a different source.

"And where does the rope hitch up?" he asked.

"In your region of shadow," I said. "Probably to one of your bollards," I added hardly caring how he took it. The word "bollards" had an absurd, fantastic sound.

His eyes were glistening and the hard mistrust in his face was losing its edge. Had it been any other man, I would have said he laughed.

He pursued me into the primitive realm of totem and taboo of which anthropologists have made some study, not to mention psychologists like Freud. Here I was on my own ground and I could see he wasn't quite. I had to insist on defining a term now and then. Every expert in his own job knows this difference or difficulty. In music I would be utterly lost in that inside place where the music is made, where the creator works with his material. Even a critic with intimate knowledge of the inside mechanics can get lost here, does notoriously get lost.

Then he startled me. It was over Freud. We were dealing with the recurring Freudian three-in-one: the Father, the Old Man of the Tribe, God. He got going on this "patriarchal notion" in Freud and what it stemmed from, racially and down through Jewish history. Scots bred on the Old Testament had got an idea or two about it. They had been haunted by the same old biblical patriarchs too; had their obsessional viewpoint also.

But I need not pursue this here. His insight shook me; one or two of my own bollards shifted their position and I couldn't noose them readily with the old rope.

"And all this talk about rope and bollard?"

"Is talk about death and immortality," I replied. "Only these two words have become conventional dead stops. They pull down the blinds." With the help of the rum, he had certainly worked me up.

Then I saw he was smiling and I realised that I had at last quite naturally spoken of death and after-death and without thinking of Annabel or him or of what had happened in this house.

I fancy that was the clearing point, or point of acceptance of me, for this night anyhow. And yet it was at this very point that what had happened came upon me most poignantly and in a strangely clarified way. It is remarkable how detachment can affect one in this profounder fashion; probably, I suppose, because what is seen or apprehended isn't allowed to be blotted out by a surge of emotion; it is borne.

One thing more. When I said earlier that Annabel stood in the doorway of my mind, I saw my mind like an inner room and Annabel standing in its doorway with one hand against the jamb, arrested. Much as if she had come into the doorway of this room and stood looking at us.

She did come into his talk presently in a way that no effort of mine at reproduction could make clear. He so somehow took her for granted that her coming was wholly natural. She was not part of him. He hadn't to lay bare his mind. His detachment was quite complete.

It was on a night when he spoke to her of his work at length, a summing up of what he had tried to do and of what he had specifically done in the Cliff Symphony. By this time she could follow the creation of his work from the inside. She loved an evening of this sort. For she knew when he was pulling it off and she communicated her delight, her excitement. For sometimes it was fun, but sometimes it was so deeply moving that her eyes grew bright and she looked at him and looked at the fire, and sat there heavy with wisdom as any old woman, while the firelight danced on her young face.

An evening like that for them must occasionally have had an extraordinary enchantment, actually a feeling of going *beyond* into the place of the music, as if the music were but a recording of what happened in that place and he had brought it back with him. It's an enchanted camera that caught the magic casements and the perilous seas. But this is perilous ground altogether. However, there is no doubt at all that something of this kind happened and that they discussed it to the extent of making, as a game, some sort of programme notes against a score. I can remember two:

Here where deep sea precipices lean.

.   .   .

Down Time's caverns
you can hear the sea
washing the grey feet of Eternity.

He attributed them to her, though he must have been talking beforehand and many a time of leaning precipices and of the sea washing their feet far down. And they have, for me, just that touch of grandiloquence which is fun's solemn frolic. After that they become thoughtless in an odd hypnotic way, at any rate on the edge of cliffs for me.

But this night he was summing up and that made her look at him once or twice. Then finally he came away with it. For he was not such a fool or dodger as not to know that their cash resources must be running pretty low. So he asked her what the position was. She had no hesitation over dodging, and replied that they would be perfectly all right for another year. But he could read her least expression easily enough and one question led to another. In short, he got into his relentless mood and would have nothing less than the exact position.

Annabel put up a good delaying action. He knew by this time of course that she was going to have a child, and now she told him all about her fear of returning to London for the birth. Accordingly she had been extremely economical. She totted up the few shillings she gave weekly to Mrs. Maclellan for so much, and, after adding the few shillings she traded at the grocer's van, she said that was all. It came to so little. There were no big accounts ahead, in fact only three over a whole year: the occupier's rates in January and the half year's rent in May and November. The whole rent was only £18. She often met the district nurse in her small car and liked her very much. Nurse had introduced her to the doctor. Everything was splendid and she was so happy.

This moved him, so much indeed that she thought she had sidetracked him. She should have known better.

"You'll tell me now every penny we possess down to the last one," he said. He had come out of his dream and was taking charge.

It was a difficult position for Annabel because she had not told him about the money she was getting from the magazine. He was making nothing, and were she to tell him of her earnings it would amount to saying that she was running the household. That would have been perfectly natural if he had been ill or was working with any certainty towards getting cash later on. He would never be finical over the conventional male position in such a situation. He had been pleased when she had made enough to buy her typewriter in London and would have been pleased, very pleased, if she were making money now, because apart from helping, it meant she was interested, had her own stake in the household and that rare feeling of having money of her own, extra money.

She dared not tell a lie about the total sum left because he could make her produce it. It would pay the rates in January, see her through the confinement in February, with enough left over for a month or two on her scale of living. That was all, and the amount of luck it included a man wouldn't notice.

But he had come to the talk from his summing-up. That was the bad stroke for Annabel. He had been taking stock of his own position quite relentlessly. He had done a body of work, true, but there was no money in it. And no prospect of money. Not here, unless he got some sort of local job as labourer or gillie.

So at last she told him about the money she got from the magazine. She told him she might make more. The editor was very kind, and there was a possibility of other contacts, through the editor. She spoke a lot as though she didn't want to hear what he was thinking.

"Why didn't you tell me this before?"

"Because I didn't want you to be troubled. You can't work unless your mind is given entirely to it. You know that. In true creation, that's the way. We spoke about it in London. You proved it here. It's true. You know that. And one day it will be proved in London. All that work you have done, you know it's great . . ."

"We had talked about harmony, integration," Menzies commented at this point. "Words like that. Quite true. The condition the artist has to get into for real creation."

The fellow could blast me at any moment with his irony. Only something else was taking place now. I saw it in him.

Annabel had misjudged him. She could not see past her contrivances, her deceits, her cunning. Even her possibility of "other contacts" was at least an exaggeration, for she had not mentioned it to her editor, as I found out.

I was misjudging him, too. It seemed inhuman that

the fellow could go into certain detail as he did. Annabel might have been something that he was analysing objectively in its more curious or dubious parts.

She must have got a shock when she saw how he took it. In London he would have grimly accepted the situation, have said nothing, or said the few words that leave desolation in their wake, and set his own course.

Now he saw, not her goodness or high-minded helpfulness or any overall quality of that kind, but the shifts and the contrivances, the way she got things for nothing from Mrs. Maclellan, the painting of .the picture in subtle barter, the little business deals and arrangements, with use of charm, the deceits she practised on him which to her would not be deceits until he found out, her fear lest he find out because then he would go all wrong on her, he saw them all, and the reason for them all, saw them running through her, body and soul, as veins of golden ore. In the glancing distress of her eyes he saw the wild horses of her dreams. It was his highest revelation of her.

The half hour that followed must have been earthly paradise for Annabel, for on earth no greater love could be.

And yet, before high heaven, she was not beaten even then.

"It came to her," said Douglas Menzies, "with all the appearance of an inspiration. I had said I had come to a stop in my own work. What I could make of all this time and place here I had made. And she said: You should write about it! At any other time it would have been the last thing to be said; the least forgivable, I think. Even as it was she stopped my thought with her hand. And that was good, because it showed she understood a bit. So I listened. What she wanted me to write was what I had told her, the sort of programme we had made out of my work, the themes. Not a literary parallel to the music because, of course, there's none. Yet in our talk we had created something, and it stemmed from the original doomed ship and the storm. Even if I only strung my notes together, she said, they would be accepted by a magazine like the— the——"

"The *Serpent*," I said.

"Yes," he said, "that's the name." He seemed to wrap the name over in his dry humour, then continued, "That excited her and she said a lot about it. She even had a copy or two of the magazine somewhere. After we left London she had kept in touch for a while with some of her friends. It was impossible for me to do it. Like calling on a man to make the last hellish sacrifice to his own failure. And in another medium at that. She struggled to believe it would refresh me, between the phase that was past and the next one. Only when the full enormity of it struck her did she hesitate, and it was an extraordinary moment, for she saw every implication now, beyond what I saw, for she saw me, she saw the born and the unborn, and she was in the middle of it, in the middle of the storm, and she had to hold on to me to keep me from drowning and her world from going to wreck. So she held on."

He reached forward unhurriedly for his cup. I lifted mine and drank though I didn't want to, because I felt the rum in my stomach as though it hadn't been digested, as can happen when the mind or emotions are overtaxed. That curious cumulative run of words at the end, with the sudden introduction of the image, was characteristic of the piece he had written. But when you heard him speak it, as though he was watching an action which he admired, critically, the effect, coming from what was not spoken, turned the rum over in the stomach.

But I did my best to hold on. "So you wrote it for her," I said.

"I said I would write it for her. That gave me the way out."

I could see it was the only, the perfect way. And it explained——

"I could see," he said, "it wasn't a possible way, even when I promised. But I shrouded that over. I had lived too long with the creative moment when it *seems* to flower not to appreciate the perfect moment when it *does* flower. It was a good night we had. And out of it a secret flower did blow: I would not only write it *for* her, I would write it *about* her."

More and more what was behind the scene could suddenly come up, the other vision. Each was so authentic that, when the other appeared, I had to stare or blink.

To write it *for* her would be worse than failure should the magazine reject it; to write it *about* her would be his ultimate tribute to her and, once she had read it, the magazine could scrub its precious spine. He could let himself go, too, because in the piece or story it would be a woman with a different name. But Annabel would know. That would be, for her, its inexhaustible surprise.

I tried to think back to what was in his writing, but I was beyond thinking. Thinking is a matter of abstract thought and tidy care. I was in the place where mental images make their impact. It is perhaps the primitive way of thinking. But I am aware of a deceit in that sentence even as I set it down.

The impact of his love for Anna, as he called her, was beyond any image anyhow. It was an absolute and an immanence like God, when God is beyond the image of the Father. It was whole and forever unchangeable.

Perhaps my anthropological insights were being wonderfully sharpened, though it's no good pretending I was even capable of that thought then, with its ironic relief. There was no relief for me. What was coming had to be borne.

So there they were, busy in their days. The weather was wet and blustery, for though the year had turned, the worst of the winter lay ahead. He did all the fetching and carrying, filled up his drum with paraffin and ordered a whole ton of coal and a bag of oatmeal. This recklessness troubled Annabel with a sort of fearful relief. But after the money order had gone with the account for the rates, it seemed the worst had happened.

Occasionally he wandered about the cliffs, jotting a thought down in his notebook. He was interested in what he had undertaken to do, but he couldn't somehow find a way of putting it down. Simple narration seemed incredibly bald and thin. He read two copies of the *Serpent* and found them a bit cerebral, without guts. His eye brightened when he saw a certain kind of effect coming off. But the writer wouldn't follow up, as if he were frightened of going too far. The "high translunary things" were out of fashion—that was it. My God, they were too! It was somehow an amusing, an enjoyable thought. Old Beethoven would hit the sky whenever he felt like it, with an abruptness, more-over, that knocked the wind out of it and you. He would bombard the place and keep the bombardment up.

Then one night he had a vivid dream of Annabel sitting on a grassy mound by a cliff-top. All the golden afternoons of summer were one afternoon to the farthest horizon, and she sat on her mound, upright, her eyes far-sighted, and all the summers were memories in her eyes. Her eyes—they were beyond all changing love-liness because Annabel herself dwelt in them, and her

108

cheeks were warm. Then he saw her eyes focus, saw the troubling that comes to the brows. As her eyes began to travel down the sea from the horizon he became aware of his own terrible knowledge and the shock of it was so great that he could not stop her, could not move nor cry, and her eyes found the body on the rocks below. When the body was turned over it had his face.

Only the following afternoon, when sitting on the wall of one of the two ruined cottages, did he see that his dream held a good idea. It introduced the kind of vivid image he wanted, the theme that could spill out over a lot of narrative construction. Perhaps there was a musical parallel of a sort after all! But it would serve his purpose admirably because it would permit him to express what the woman felt when her man was gone. And it would allow him to express it with a dream's vividness—if he could. But as it was only a dream Annabel would not be affected. And the man and woman in the writing could even have some fun over the affair.

But for balance there would have to be what the man felt about the woman when she was gone. Of course! Because that was the whole intention of writing the piece. But he couldn't have another dream. That would be creative bankruptcy. So he would have to find another device.

And, there and then, in pat came the idea of the doomed ship. This excited him. Though he could not see how it would work out, he realised that he was now on the way towards bringing in all the themes. It was so interesting, so fascinating, that when a dark premonition threatened to gather meaning he choked it off and got up from the wall.

For three days that premonition dogged him and he fought it with his toughest thought and language. He wanted a happy ending. The idea that now the woman must *in fact* be dead was absurd. That was Fate's bankrupt device, that was the Wrecker at his one and only trick.

Besides it was only a bit of *writing*. It wasn't music. In writing you could do any old thing, twist any situation. Look at the critics, at how they treated a piece of responsible music. Points of view to suit the occasion, to work off a private grudge or prejudice or bit of learning, to inflate the wit and wonder of the writer's ego. And even when it was "good", what the hell!

And this wasn't even criticism, it was just fiction.

Had it been an epic poem it could have progressed —it would have had to progress—cumulatively, like a piece of great music, remorseless as mathematics, to the inevitable end.

A man doesn't write epics nowadays, said the dark premonition, just as you don't write music of the epic age. Man has become more involved, his harmonies have become more involved and his disharmonies. You express this complexity in your art form of modern music. The writer expresses it in his art form of modern fiction. His is the only form in words that can express all the involvements and complexities of his age, cumulatively, remorselessly, to the inevitable end. As it does—when he's an artist.

He got beaten in the end. Inevitability had him like a tyranny. Had it been music, he could have made the very acceptance of it great. He would have tried to, anyway. Cornered, he searched around for a way out.

The idea came to him all complete as he stood on the Head looking down at the Cormorants Rock. The doomed ship. We were all on a doomed ship. There was no dodging the inevitability of death. Fine. They

110

would *both* be on the ship, returning to the land of their hearts' desire. Not much symbolism here, because it had all the detail of a real place, where their roots were, a known land, where they had blossomed.

Enter the Wrecker. The storm. The ship is cast on the rock and broken up. It is everyone for himself now, so he is all for her, to save her, not to lose her. The desperate struggle with the sea. The crawling onto the rock that the rising tide would drown, but not before he told her, in defiance and tenderness, her head in the shelter of his heart, that he would be with her, and that if they got separated he would find her, that nothing would stop him, here or hereafter, nothing ever.

Standing there on the cliff-top, he was moved, and moved, as he knew, by a creation beyond what he could achieve, as if the creation or vision came from its own place, the unimaginable place beyond, glimpsed for a moment, before it fell away.

All art is the same art, he thought, and laughed with delight, and that night he started writing.

I seem to be taking a long time to tell this, as if in some way I had become à victim of the "tyranny" we discussed. The irony of it is that I am condensing, stringing together such glimpses as I had over the hours of talk. He had a way of taking you to the cliff-top and letting you look down. The implication is the terrible thing that is not spoken. But it is remembered.

Let me set down the last few facts quickly. It took him some time to do the writing but he got it done. Annabel's reaction surprised him. Admittedly she could get wrought up easily at this time, even abnormally, because, doubtless, of her condition, but he had not expected her to be moved so deeply that she was silent. He heard her tears fall on the paper. He was afraid that

111

she was taking it too literally, that in some way she had pierced through to that initial feeling of guilt which had dogged him when he had fought for a happy ending. For he could see now that there had been guilt, the guilt that is at the heart of Creation itself, the Wrecker's guilt.

But this wasn't what moved Annabel. And when in time she spoke of his devices, she thought them wonderfully good. For, of course, as a moment's thought showed him, they could not be on any doomed ship, not literally. That was the last conceivable place. It was all a creative fiction. For tears and the heart's most intimate beat.

She typed it, got it all ready, addressed the envelope, and he promised her faithfully to post it. The following morning was wet and blustery and she wasn't feeling too good. "Overwrought with happiness" was the way she put it. He thought they should get some woman in. But she had made all her arrangements. Nurse would be looking in that evening.

He did not go to Balrunie, where he was to post the script and buy a few things she wanted. The sky grew dark and lowering.

That evening the nurse didn't come. She had one or two urgent cases on hand as Annabel knew. They went to bed. The fury of the storm shook the house. Some time during the night she awoke him. He heard the knocking on the door. A man had come with a lantern.

He knew he should not leave her, but when the emissary comes about a doomed ship, you go. He quietened her. A ship in distress off the Head, he told her. She clung to him—and sent him. They got as far as the two ruins when the man said he was afraid the ship was going to pile up on the Cormorants Rock.

Menzies stopped then. The man had said, just before, that he hadn't meant to call at the white house. He had been going to Dan Maclellan's, but had seen a lantern there already, and, as he was near the white house by this time, it occurred to him to call—"because you know the cliffs".

Menzies stood, unable to move, but above the howl of the storm he cunningly cried, "I'll go back for my big electric torch—for the cliffs."

In a moment the man was alone and Menzies was going headlong back through the fierce dark night to Annabel.

What happened was terrible beyond telling. God knows how much he told me, not much. I knew. I would have stopped him. His face was white, and his eyes . . . and his voice, the same voice, the same manner, but, as it were, licked up, as if the rum had burnt the dross away from feature and thought. I felt sick, and when he mentioned the word "recurrence" I cried out in protest. The window was grey and as I moved it moved. The whole place heaved and went black out.

7

I came to myself in a strange room. A picture on a wall, then another picture, bright colours, as from a modern art show. Articles of furniture, woven colour on a chair back. I was lying on a couch, under a travelling rug of subdued checks. As memory seeped back a pulse beat in my head sending out a dark flush.

Annabel's room in the morning light.

Bewildered, shivering and horribly disgusted, I made to get off the couch and saw the stuff on the floor. I lay back and let the pulse hammer.

Once on the middle of the floor I was nearly sick again from shame. I gaped round for something with which to wipe up the mess. There was nothing. I listened and heard the stillness beyond my beating blood. As I strove to move on tiptoe I overbalanced. I reached the other front room, where we had talked, for I could now remember my cap, which I would use. I heard the low rumble in the dog's throat, that threatening sound which precedes the growl, the attack. Then I saw the brute, head lowered, stiff.

I backed away to the entrance door. I had a memory of huge rags sagging from the roof of the steading, but I found they weren't rags; bits of boarding and stiff felt, high up. The floor was littered with sheeps' droppings, but from a jutting wooden arm hung brown rotten sacking, old bags.

As I returned, the dog was outside and moved round in an arc. That brute would stick at nothing, but I didn't care. On my knees I wiped up the mess as best I could, using my handkerchief for a final rub, though for moments I could hardly see. If only I could get away before Menzies appeared.

I got away, carrying the filthy bundle, and as I slowly turned my head to make sure the brute was not on my heels, I saw the gay clean colours, the freshness, like an apparition, of the tall stocks in the weedy garden. The dog was following but keeping his distance. I passed the steading, heading straight for the hotel.

When I stopped and looked back, the brute was standing at the corner of the steading. I went out of sight, buried the rags in the first ditch, went on a little farther and sat down. The cold shivers were gone. I was hot and sticky and when I wiped my forehead I found it cold.

The cliffs and the ruined cottages were well to my left beyond the rising ground. Near me, on my right, the ground dipped into a hollow or dell, rose again and flattened out over broken ground to a fence, then sloped up to the road. Beyond the road, the land stood back in a slow lift to the hills where the fishing lochs were. Ahead somewhere stood the hotel. I looked at my watch. It was exactly seven o'clock. I put it to my ear. It was going. My fingers could not wind it without first taking it off my wrist.

In a bad way! I thought, picking up heart. My God, how Menzies would hate me! I laughed silently at this utter certainty and all that it meant and beyond what it meant. He would hate my guts, I thought, and heaven knew they were not very stable at the moment. But when I had to try them out, nothing came up.

It was a rare summer morning, chill and sweet. A

115

morning for standing grasses and still bushes, wild flowers and a piquant air, earthy and sharp, elusively scented. Hopping slowly, a hare appeared round a bend below. When it saw me it stopped. Its ears went up. Pointed ears of the morning. I could not remain still long, and when I moved it vanished back down the dell.

The hare's world. The innocence of the morning. The freshness. The forgotten, the secret landscape. I was light-headed and liked it. No more thought, that dark inner disease, that cancer. Then there was a beat in the earth, another, and I slewed round to avoid what was coming at me. An ass! He stopped three yards above me, astonished. His pointed ears were bigger than the hare's. They solemnly waggled, then came to attention again. Curiosity was now in his eye. It said he had had a lot of dealings with humanity but was still prepared for a surprise or two. The sky was behind him and he looked carven where he stood, a grotesque of the moor.

I got up carefully and went towards him. He sniffed and found nothing and swung his head front, the way I was going. I expressed brotherly affection and got on his back. He started off along the rim of the dell. I patted him and told him he was sent. One ear came back in acknowledgment and then he sent me flying down the slope.

I disentangled the bundle of myself and slowly sat up, letting the flashes of pain from the brain-anvil die down before I opened my eyes. In a flat green bay stood a small tilt cart, its shafts aloft, and a humped tent. An old woman's head appeared. Just the head, stuck on the canvas. It was more disturbing than if it had been done by Picasso.

"Good morning," I said and bowed as I passed. There are times when one is moved by a great politeness.

When I looked back a man, clad only in his shirt, was standing outside the tent beside the head. I went on round the bend and up the dell. There were many things in the world, and worlds within worlds, and I was feeling damn shaky. Still, I hung on to the freshness of the morning and when I staggered it was no inconvenience. So long as you don't think, the world of appearance is inexhaustible.

That tinker man would come after me for my money. I heard the dark eager thought in his head. I saw a patch of bracken by a bush on a gentle slope against the sun. I made a dog's bed in the bracken and fell into a deep sleep.

I awoke out of a dream of fishing on a loch with bright water lilies at one end and a low golden mound of sand in the middle. It was one of the freshest awakenings I had ever had and I wanted to prolong the dream. The air was so clean and pure that I still heard its faint fairy whistling in the line that ran up my rod. I shivered, and as my head turned my eyes opened and the sun smote them.

So here I was, feeling much better and a little more disembodied. The former hammering in my head had welded the bone into a tight band, which was reasonable enough. Some water for my mouth would complete my toilet, so I moved off and found it, and as I held its strange foreign coldness in my mouth I tried to hear it sizzle but couldn't. I remembered an official report on gipsies who had been apprehended for being drunk and incapable on methylated spirits. When they awoke sober in the cells in the morning they were given a drink of water and got drunk all over again.

There is a grey humour in the eyes of God when he is not the Wrecker. The morning of the earth has

117

pointed ears. The Wrecker, the bloody Wrecker, has only the one trick.

My thoughts were lucid as the dew drops that hadn't fallen last night to be caught in spiders' webs. So I wasn't letting them stray back to what I had left, to the white house. I wasn't even letting them think of straying, for the bitterness of death is an elixir on which a man can get drunk and incapable in a fashion swift and blinding as it is hellish. His hands knot in his memories and the knuckles stand out and his throat growls like a dog.

My body was suddenly caught in a spasm and out of it was squeezed the cry, "Ah, Christ!"

But it's no good being ashamed of that. It leads nowhere, except back.

I kept going on. Presently I saw the hotel in the distance against the upsloping land, and then I saw figures moving about and a car going off. I looked at my watch and decided the day's sport was on the move. As I had no desire to meet that group I sat down, smoothed my hair, put my tie straight and couldn't find my handkerchief. My cap, too, was missing. . . . What if they thought *I* was missing?

That made me lower my head. Search parties. . . . He was last seen going in the direction of the cliffs. . . . I scanned the ground carefully. Even if I had not been missed last night, this morning the chamber-maid . . .

The chamber-maid was a thought.

When at last I circumspectly approached the hotel there was not a soul about. I entered on light feet, went lightly up the stairs, and in my room there was the chamber-maid surveying the bed that had not been slept in. Her astonished face lost none of its astonishment when she looked at me.

She was as fresh as the stocks in the garden. She stood

arrested like a hind in a dell; she was warm with life and what she felt was pointed. She would have fled if she could have got past me, but I couldn't move, for she was the sun and moon.

As she was the only one in the world I wanted to speak to I no doubt said so in my sensible way.

As she slipped past I nearly caught her hand, but she was too quick for me.

At the top of the stairs she threw a glance back and I smiled my invitation and beckoned her to return. She should not forsake me like that. She went downstairs with dignity, though dignity is not the word. It's not dignity a hind in a dell has.

My heart was choking. Could I conceivably have lost some modicum of good sense or normal behaviour? Surely it was not possible that, somehow, turned upside down, I was seeing things the other way? Yet I was not deceived.

I sat on my bed for a while until the nothing I stared at began to make shapes. So I got up and took my clothes off and went to bed.

There was stillness in the hotel when I awoke from the sleep I had at last fallen upon. Afternoon was the hotel's dead time so I shaved in the bathroom and had a bath. I felt purged to an incorporeal lightness; otherwise I seemed all there. The only craving I had was for a whole pot of tea and when I came downstairs I caught a glimpse of Johan on the way to the kitchen and called her.

"Yes, sir," she said and vanished for the pot. But her momentary look had been peculiar. The news would be all over the place.

They would have left the front door open last night and assumed I had returned late and gone to bed. It was that kind of place and the landlord that kind of man. When I hadn't appeared for breakfast I would have been left to sleep on. Then the chamber-maid . . . I felt hot. But it was good tea, rich and strong. I saw the landlord stroll past the window. He would be waiting for a casual word with me, so to speak.

But I had no desire to speak with anyone. What could I say? I couldn't say anything to myself yet. Gossip would be hellish, even as a feat of endurance. So, when I saw the way clear, I went for a stroll, wearing the felt hat I had arrived in, towards the hills. In a hollow I sat down. Douglas Menzies must have carried or dragged me from one room to the other, laid me on the couch and tucked me in. And left me.

It was the enormity of my intrusion that kept on getting the better of me. Had I known what I knew now would I have gone near him? I didn't know what to do. My heel kept hitting a futile hole into the ground until I stopped it. I didn't know what the blazes to do. I had forced myself on him, forced the conversation, then came the rum and my momentary enmities forcing the issues, until he was talking and taking it out of me, stripping me, until he could tell to what was left of me how he came to write his piece of writing. It had been an infernal detachment. And then, towards the end, detachment still, but . . . Lord, how he would hate the memory of me this morning!

The certainty of that hatred struck an understanding so deep that it got translated into a momentary wonder, and in that wonder, through the lightness of aftermath still in my flesh, I wandered into the strange country where he was and had my visions.

I lay over in the heather and the harsh stalks crushed my face. I smelt the heather, breathed it and came to myself, quietened.

When I entered the dining-room all the guests were seated. "Good evening," I said to the Major. "Evening," replied the Major, but this time there was a short general silence. The ladies were having a particular look at me as I sat down at my small table.

Talk came on about the lack of wind in a windy place. The barrister told of an old sailor he knew who did in fact stick a knife in the mast when he wanted wind.

"I told Lachlan to whistle for it," said the Major.

"And did he?"

"No. Even when I threatened he could whistle for his drink. So I whistled myself."

"You should try the dry fly," said Mr. Sneddon.

"I whistled myself so dry," said the Major, "that if there had been any of your trout about they would have caught on."

It was one of his happier scores over Sneddon and the barrister enjoyed it.

"Who was that man in the grey car who left as we came in?" one of the women asked. "I seem to have seen him before."

"The factor they call him here," answered the Major. "Maclean from Balrunie. Collects rents."

"Not at this time of year, surely?" said the barrister.

"Any time," said the Major, "if the rent is not paid."

"You don't mean our habitat is in danger?"

"Not at fifty shillings a bottle," said the Major. "No, not this place."

"What place?" asked the widow.

"A house occupied by a man who has shut himself off from the world. There is reason to believe that he may not even open the factor's letters."

"Oh—that man!"

"That would be, let me see—May," reckoned the barrister.

"Yes," said the Major.

"How you know everything!" declared Mrs. Sneddon.

"Anthropological interest," said the Major, with a dryness lost on Mrs. Sneddon, perhaps, but not on me, for whom it was no doubt intended. But even the Major could have had little inkling of its effect.

"Is he taking proceedings or what?" the barrister asked.

The Major did not reply and the subject was dropped, as if my last night's absence had been suddenly remembered. The tacit moment was enjoyed by all.

As I sat alone with my coffee I took out my cigarette case and found it empty. So I had smoked through the whole case last night. No wonder my mouth had been hot in the freshness of the morning!

But the humour did not help much. Legal proceedings? That would be humour out the other side of the mouth, with a vengeance. Johan, who was clearing the table, fetched me a packet of cigarettes. I would have to do something about this.

Quite possibly, too, that was not the only account he was being dunned for. And I had thought, somehow, that I had been last night in an oasis of secrecy. How innocent I was, how naïve! "That man"!

My cheque book was in my bag. Sums like £9 were easy, as it happened. I might even include my hotel and travelling expenses in my Income Tax return as expenses necessarily incurred in the pursuit of my "anthropological interest". Even the coffee tasted bitter, as if it had been boiled too long.

Either that or cut and run now, I thought. You can interfere with a man's soul but not with his creditors. That's going too far. Unless you could so do it that he never found out. But even then. . . .

It was nasty. However, one could at least find out more. And the man to find out everything from was the Major. He rejoiced in the bitter detail. It kept him afloat.

It was dark before I returned to the hotel, but the Major had not gone aloft.

I asked him if he would join me in a drink and he said he didn't mind. His manner was off-hand; it suggested he had not been waiting for me.

Johan brought the whisky and I asked him about the fishing, how many lochs, beats, and so on. He found out where in my time I had fished and I suggested he should try a dry fly. That set him going and he was amusing about Sneddon. As he moved to the sideboard for his

123

own bottle I insisted on ringing for Johan. It was my night and I was going to have no more than two.

"A heavy night last night?" he suggested.

"Not really," I said. "Though very interesting from an anthropological angle."

He blew through his nostrils, "Hmff!" and eyed me.

I laughed. "I could not help overhearing your use of the word at dinner. And it struck me afterwards how much this hotel is in fact the centre of the local pattern."

He knew I was sidetracking him off Menzies, but he was getting set for a night of it and his diplomacy was long. And then, in fact, he became extraordinarily interesting. He not only knew everyone about the place but also those who had no direct dealings with the hotel, like the roadmen and the postman. I began to see the community in its working habits and personal relations, the married and the single, the children. I asked him questions about schooling and amusements. He knew all the answers, not merely in a generalised or statistical way, but illustrated by the personal instance, and he puffed and pouted before coming away with some devastating or enlightening comment.

I had met this kind of interest before. It is becoming, I suppose, a lost relic of the squire's interest in his tenantry, of the "county" in the folk. I am thinking of southern England, the Major's country. In the Highlands it used to be the chief and his clansmen; even if the social divisions and relations in the two cases were very different. The old instinct was still at work in the Major. To call it "gossip" would be very wide of the mark. He must have seen my appreciation for when I asked him what happened in the wintertime, when there were no sportsmen at the hotel, he rather enjoyed himself. The landlord had run "a sort of sing-song dance affair, ceilidh they call it, before Christmas. Bag-

124

pipes inside this room. Extraordinary hellish noise," he
said with interest. "Though I rather think that Lachlan,
who was playing the damn things, rather liked to stand
near me to give me the full blast. He rather thought, I
think, that he would shift me. But I stood them, and
when he had finished I stood him a large drink. Much
laughter, even cheering," said the Major, "for on such
occasions they have a considerable sense of humour."

I laughed with delight.

"After that, there was a concert at Balrunie and the
landlord here, whom they call Sam Mor—Big Sam—
approached me as a deputation to act as chairman. A
local charity. When I refused he said he would put
my name down. 'You want me to buy myself out of it?'
I said. He was so offended that I apologised. He bowed
and withdrew. I had to follow the damn fellow into the
kitchen. There I bowed to him and said I would be
deeply honoured to act as chairman. He thanked me
on behalf of the committee. 'On one condition,' I said,
'that you don't open the proceedings with Lachlan
blowing his bagpipes in my ear.' Then a light came into
the fellow's eye. 'I wouldn't say, Major, that that had
been part of the intention.'"

"And was it?" I asked.

"There are three pipers in Balrunie, so it wasn't
Lachlan. But when the piper finished I said I hadn't
enjoyed such piping since the hotel ceilidh. After that
I couldn't say much wrong. They get to know everything in a primitive spot like this."

But I was not put off by the Major's use of "primitive". It was not consciously meant to be "superior" or
disagreeable, even if there was now and then that kind
of flavour or smell about. These people were not his
people, and the Major had got into the way of living
with his own primitive reactions.

125

So we came back to the hotel and those depending in some measure upon it. Dan Maclellan, for example, could not live off his small croft alone, and his fish found a local market at the hotel, which also provided in the season those daily fees from sportsmen like the barrister. The same with the gillies. At most points the hotel appeared in the picture. It provided directly or indirectly in some measure that extra employment which the small crofter needed for a simple livelihood.

"It goes farther than that in the odd case," said the Major. "Take Lachlan next. He has a small croft—nine acres—a couple of cows and quite a few sheep on the common grazing. Actually about thirty ewes. But still not enough to bring up a family on. In the season here he picks up quite a bit. So does Catherine."

"Who is Catherine?"

"The chamber-maid. His daughter."

"You mean—the chamber-maid here?"

"Yes."

He looked at me. "Haven't you seen her? Rather good-looking, I think."

"Yes—I have, I think." The way my heart had started to pound on its own was troublesome, but after appearing to remember the girl I looked back at him and lit a cigarette.

"She'll make about three pounds a week," he said. "So all told there's a considerable amount of cash going into Lachlan's household from this hotel at the moment."

"Very interesting."

"Fills in your pattern a bit," suggested the Major.

I smiled. "It does. So they make enough in the season here to carry them on, with the help of the croft, through the rest of the year, the winter."

"More complicated than that."

"Oh?"

The Major seemed now to enjoy a sort of esoteric humour. "The outside world comes in with grants—for education. It assists also."

I nodded, wondering what on earth he had up his sleeve and said, "Also Old Age pensions, insurance and so on."

"Not very specific, are you, for an anthropologist? We have not finished with Catherine. In October she goes back to the university in Glasgow."

The Major must have got the effect he played for. "Thought that might astonish you." He was pleased and finding his glass empty went for his bottle. As I got up he said, "Too late now. In bed. You must get your own bottle—if he'll give you one, which I doubt. Fifty shillings. And he reckons he loses on it."

"What's the normal trade price?"

"Thirty-five shillings. But he makes four pounds by selling it in drinks."

The Major had more to say about these complications and I could see how interested he was, if not mean, when it came to spending his shillings. Yet when it came to pouring whisky into anyone's glass he was gushingly generous. He would travel first class. And so on. But all the time my mind remained suffused with wonder.

"Rather surprised that your chamber-maid should be at 'varsity."

"I suppose I am," I admitted.

"The way they do things here."

I did not care for the gleam in his eye. "You would call it a primitive way?"

He looked at me. "What would you call it?"

"Indigenous," I said. "Though it's now becoming more general. The student who works his passage is

not unknown even at what are considered more celebrated seats of learning."

"Hmff!" He reckoned he had got me going. "Very
nice girl," he said. "And the only singer among the lot."
He could take his time. His diplomatic ways were
devious.

But I was sick of drink, didn't want to get involved,
wanted to get off. I would go in a minute, too.

"She got a bursary to the county academy. From
there, another grant or award of some kind. But not, of
course, enough, even on the Scotch level of student life.
So—here she is. Your pattern becomes rather involved,
uh?"

"It does," I said.

He looked at me now for quite a time. "Of course a
chamber-maid is not needed here after the season. Johan
can do the lot. That's how she supports her mother all
the year round. When Catherine was home for the
Christmas recess, last winter, she gave a hand, I believe,
down at the—at Menzies' place."

It took me a few seconds to realise how this old
diplomatist could knock me about and have me where
he wanted me. But any kind of counter was beyond my
power now.

"How's he doing?" he asked.

"All right," I said.

"Is he?"

"Yes."

"Hm. Not drinking, were you?"

"We talked a lot. To tell the truth, I haven't had
much sleep lately. Feeling pretty tired. So if you'll
excuse me, I think I'll really get to bed." I got up.

"Hm. All night at it, were you?"

"Not quite."

"Some of them wonder where he gets the drink."

128

"What drink?"

His gleam was more than sceptical. "Some think he goes off for a day or two and leaves his dog in charge. A vicious brute."

"Seemed all right to me."

"Hm. You knew him before?"

"I knew of him, yes. A distinguished composer."

"Distinguished?"

"Many thought so, in London."

"Never heard of him, but I suppose one gets out of touch. All I wanted to say was, if he's a friend of yours, he's heading for trouble."

"What trouble?"

"Not paying his rent. Cash." The Major, recognising I wasn't going to tell him much, was becoming abrupt. His mood was changing. The pout in his lips was a trifle ugly.

"I'm afraid I don't know about that," I said.

"Perhaps not," said the Major.

Somehow I didn't like leaving him like this. "Some of them think he should clear out."

"Who?"

"I gathered that locally."

"Locally!" My lack of precision was now an insult. "*Locally* they wouldn't like him to go to hell his own way."

"Good night."

The Major's response was no more than a mutter and I left him with his mounting anger and his bottle.

As I went upstairs I was sorry. In another minute he would have turned on me as he had done on Lachlan. At that moment I wouldn't have minded if he had. I would have let him call me what he liked, let him spit it all out.

And this mood did not even surprise me. Not that I

would have been as mild as all that, I suppose, had the Major got going. Yet I wonder. For I was full of wonder, but it was vague, like the sense of pleasure that accompanied it, mixed with, vaguest of all, an uneasiness. I set the candle down on the dressing-table and saw my face in the mirror. It stared at me as if it had some knowledge I had forgotten.

I was very wide awake and knew I wouldn't sleep. I sat on the bed, then got up and pulled down the blind because I didn't want to be stared at from the air. I could quite see how I had insulted the Major. At barely thirty I was a young pup to him, and this young pup had not only pumped him for the information he wanted but, when it came to giving some information in return, had dried up in, of all insulting ways, a cool polite way. It was too much. Nor could it help that we used the same language from the same "celebrated seat of learning". He would be finding all sorts of insulting tones and meanings in the words I had used. Not that it would matter if he were only feeling murderous. But— did he go beyond that—wonder if he was going to bits —say to himself he was going to bits—on the awful sickening way to the hell of self-pity? Probably.

I could do nothing about it and only stopped moving around my room when I heard my own footsteps. Not much use in disturbing the guests who slept so near. And not much use in disguising any longer the fact that this vague state of wonder had been induced when Catherine had been mentioned. I had heard every word he had said about her with an abnormal acuteness. "The only singer among the lot." I had seen her singing on a platform before his words had died. He might have been talking about no one else all the time. At that moment it would have been difficult for me to remember what else he had been talking about. The wonder kept ballooning up out of my head as if I were away alone on some cliff-top in halcyon weather with the sky the limit.

As that image became conscious it pulled me up. Catherine and Annabel. Odd that neither Mrs. Maclellan nor Douglas Menzies mentioned Catherine. Yet, of course, not odd at all. I knew that. There was something intimate and personal to Annabel in Catherine's visits. Even the Major had only said that Catherine "gave a hand". Whatever he might have wished to imply he could not have *said* that she got paid for it, not in cash anyhow. It wasn't that kind of relationship. I remembered what Mrs. Maclellan had told me about Annabel's early life and realised that they were girls from the same background, same kind of struggle, same sort of secondary school, and the very same university. Completely unlike in appearance, Catherine being fair and vivid, Annabel dark and comely, yet they met in that mutual place behind the events of the world where life is a joy. Their intimacies would have been bright-eyed, grave or full of delicious fun. And I could bet, too, that if Catherine's father and some of the other gillies had managed after their fashion to get some venison in the dark months, Catherine wouldn't have turned up at the white house empty-handed. She sang too. Annabel had hummed gathering primroses. So had Catherine, making my bed. She was starting off on the same path as Annabel. . . .

That word "same" kept recurring, until it changed into "recurrence" and hit me a blow. Then I took it and looked at it and set about knocking the lights out of it. For of course there was recurrence. Thousands of girls from the Highlands went through the same process. In Glasgow and Edinburgh, St. Andrews and Aberdeen. Same talk, same degree, teaching, marriage. The recurrence of porridge for breakfast. One mustn't really become absurd.

And then at last I got screwed up to turning upon Douglas Menzies' "recurrence". Just as absurd; every bit, I thought. For, after all, what did it amount to? Sea films always had a ship in distress, often a fleet of them. Unless there was a ship being swamped or piled up there was no story. But ships did get into difficulties, were wrecked. That's why lifeboats were all round the coast. And you could not live on a stormy stretch of it for years without some sort of tragedy happening. That was the plain truth of the matter.

But somehow it did not help much and, hot and angry, I was full of misery. For I did not know why I was hot and bothered, had no idea why the sudden squall had blown up. Then something inside me, as that face of mine had been inside the mirror, suggested that I had been defending Catherine.

Defending Catherine! From what? From a fateful parallel with Annabel?

But that shadowy face inside one never does answer the straight question. It smiles, if a smile it can be called, for I doubt if there is any expression of half-veiled omniscience more utterly infuriating. If I had seen my face in the mirror at that moment I think I would have spat on it. But probably not. One is so rarely equal to the occasion.

I would have said I never slept at all, but I suppose I must have, because I had frightful dreams. They were fantastically dramatić, and as a dream got carried over into waking thought, thought and dream were of a piece. I smelt fear. At one point I looked about my dark room for what had been happening in the dream. I still know what the smell of that fear tasted like. It was not all fear. But the fear recurred.

Daylight is a relief as it washes the body lying exhausted on the shore. At first I heard the light footsteps coming and the knock. Catherine. I listened to all her knocks and to her footsteps with a sort of greed, it was so good to think of her going lightly and healthily about her business. And when I couldn't hear her she was suddenly outside, I fancied, with the wind in her hair. Fair hair, not so dark as mouse-coloured; it takes the light.

After breakfast, Johan brought my sandwiches. I watched the ongoings through the dining-room window and listened to the high voices as I lingered over a third or fourth cup of coffee. My clay, with lack of oblivion, had certainly gone dry, but I didn't see the Major. He hadn't turned up for breakfast.

Extraordinary the things a fellow will do. It was another fine day in this spell of halcyon Highland weather and I had actually taken my hat off the peg and turned towards the front door when I decided I had forgotten something. I pressed my pockets. No, it wasn't there. What it was I had forgotten I apparently didn't know and it even annoyed me that I couldn't think of anything. Up the stairs I went and the climb set my heart beating. But there was no one in my room and I stood listening until my mouth went dry. Then I became afraid that Catherine might actually come so I left the room hurriedly.

Outside, the landlord, standing by the garage, returned my salute. I knew by the solid way he stood that he was expecting me to go and speak to him, but I was just far enough away to keep swinging on towards the hills. Why I was avoiding the landlord I hardly knew, for if anyone would be sensible and helpful, he was the man. Perhaps he was coming to the conclusion that I was a bit queer, too. And, begod, he wasn't far wrong, I thought, with some pleasure.

For it was a lovely morning in a beautiful world. One has to be wakened up to see it, to be cleansed as clean as a leaf or a grass stalk. Though even then one can't leave it alone. In a heathery hollow the scent of bog myrtle had such a clean invigorating tang that I broke off a tough sprig, crushing the leaves in the process, staining, almost cutting, my fingers, and then inhaling the scent like a drug. There are worse drugs, I thought happily, putting the sprig in my pocket.

After that I took things easy and wandered up into and through and round places I had never seen before, the places that are always at the back of beyond, waiting. This strangely familiar air I simply accepted, this stillness of waiting. The golden plover and its cry, the blue gleam on the loch, were its "memories". But I refused to think that one out. Just as I refused to remember my dreams. For if I went burrowing into my dreams I would end up by evoking a professional interest in the deeper or earlier levels of mind, where the primitive tribes are, with the Major like a looming witch-doctor. The best of us have become intellectual burrowers, like whole-time moles. Then into the scene, moving along the path in the distance, and below me, towards the loch, came three human figures, small, going slowly in single file. First the gillie, with the rods and the game bag, then a man with his head thrust forward and slightly down to accommodate the years on his rounded shoulders—Sneddon, beyond a doubt—and behind him his wife. Even if the place hadn't been waiting for them—or for anyone—it bore them patiently. And patiently they meandered on. They had come here. I was moved. They were the sensible people and I thought highly of them.

But I didn't want to be seen, so I got up and slid away, moving now fairly fast, in a definite direction, like one with an overdue appointment.

When I came over the last crest and saw Loch Runie, I stood and wiped my face. Land and headlands; the blue, the glitter; breadth and length to the sea's remote rim. That sort of scene doesn't "wait"; it is in front of you, not behind. Birds fly upon it and ships go over its rim. Hang it, I had forgotten my field glasses again! And I had gone upstairs too! And I smiled as I went striding down to have a look at the village of Balrunie, for I could afford to let myself realise that I had gone upstairs on the off chance of seeing Catherine. The church was below the road, before you come to the village, and the school on the right, just as you enter. Some fair-sized houses stood back in their own garden ground with small weathered trees. The cottages were strung together, facing the sea. A red van was in front of the post office. Some of the older folk greeted me, "Fine day." The fineness of the weather was in their voices like a gift. Then I saw a house standing back a little from the village street, its flower-plots overgrown with grass. On the lower opaque half of the window to the left of the door was inscribed in tarnished gold letters ESTATE OFFICE. The rusty iron gate was open and I suddenly went up to the door.

No one answered my pull on the brass knob though I heard a bell ringing. I stood there reluctant now to turn away, but at last I came down the stone-flagged path. At the gate a man who was passing said, "I saw him go north in his car this morning." He glanced up the road and said with a smile, "Well, you're lucky: here he is."

The car drew up at the gate and a genial reddish-faced man in a brown plusfour suit got out and hoped I hadn't been waiting long.

"Not at all," I said, and explained I had walked over from Dalaskir Hotel and should like, if he didn't mind, to discuss a small business matter with him.

Genially he invited me in, regretting, as we went, the absence of his clerk. The office was hard and bare, though it had a safe, deed boxes, cupboards and ledgers. Perhaps the dingy effect came from the worn brown linoleum, the dusty varnish on the wood.

"Well, what can I do for you?" He was warm with life up to the reddish hair in a thin swirl on his temples.

"It's rather a delicate matter," I began, "but I gather that Mr. Menzies, who lives in the white house at Dalaskir—you know whom I mean?"

"Yes." He nodded.

"By the way, I am right in assuming that you are the factor for the property?"

"Yes, you are."

"It's the matter of rent. I gather that something may be due—or am I wrong?"

"Well——" As he leaned back he pushed some papers together on his desk. "Excuse me, but may I ask if you are acting for him?"

"I should like to," I said frankly.

"But you're not actually." He nodded thoughtfully. It seemed a troublesome business for him.

"I gather the rent for the May term is still outstanding," I said, for I saw now that his eyes were narrow and acute, "and if it could be arranged that I could pay it without any bother, I hoped we might manage that."

"You are a friend of his?"

"Yes."

"But you don't want him to know?"

"That's about it."

"I see." He looked through the window. "As a business matter, it's not just too regular, is it?" He nodded thoughtfully to the window.

136

"But as long as the rent was paid, would it matter to you?"

He smiled at the papers on his desk. "Supposing Mr. Menzies were to turn up with the rent after you had paid it?" He looked at me.

I saw the difficulty quite acutely.

"I have written to him more than once," he said, "but he did not seem to think it worth his while answering. Are you sure your—ah—good intentions would be welcomed by him—or—even—accepted?"

He was very acute indeed and as I in turn considered the gold lettering on the window I was uncomfortable over the awkward way in which I was interfering. Still, he wasn't helping an awful lot.

"I just thought," I said, "I might be able to square the matter, for the meantime, anyhow. However, if it can't be done in this way, I suppose that's that."

"It's a matter of procedure. I don't want to be personal, but are you sure Mr. Menzies couldn't pay his rent himself if he wanted to?"

That made me think, too.

"My last letter to him explained the position fully. I'm afraid he would have to appear in person or, anyway, reply to my letter. There are a few considerations, apart from the rent. Condition of the property and so on. He hasn't made it easy."

"I see," I said. "He has been through a lot, of course."

"Very true."

"Men of genius are not too good at business correspondence, they say. I thought I might have helped. But my own business insight doesn't seem to have been too bright." I got up. "Thank you very much."

"I'm sorry if I appear to—but——" As he pushed his chair back with his legs, he suddenly looked at me directly. "Might it not be the best thing for him if he were to leave that house?"

Why that sent a lash of anger through my head I didn't know, so I controlled myself, but when it looked as if he might pursue the suggestion I knew it was time to take my leave before I made a fool of myself.

I left the village street by a path that went down to and along the shore, for I could curse there in comfort. I did. And it wasn't altogether at my own inept interference. The hard office with the wooden corners, the genial good fellow with the wintry blue eyes, the intolerably acute intelligence that knew the cunning sore points, that wouldn't accept even cash in order to—God knows what! I knew I was being quite irrational so I let it rip and consigned them all to hell, deep down, all of them who thought they knew "what was good" for Menzies. In another couple of minutes that factor fellow if I had let him would have been deep in gossip's sweet intimacies, prepared to sacrifice a half year's rent, the noble fellow, if only Menzies were heaved off somewhere else—for his own good. Sacrifice a half year's rent my foot! I thought, and my foot promptly let me down for the path was petering out. As I arose I saw the cemetery on the slope above. The ridge of the church was now some distance behind. There were no houses about, even the village was shut out. It was a peaceful scene and reflections among the tombs might ease my humour. Too lazy to go round to the iron gate, I vaulted the stone wall. And then I thought of Annabel.

I read the inscriptions, I looked for her everywhere, but her name was not there. Two or three narrow grassy mounds were without headstones, one quite recent, with withered flowers. Lichened flagstones lay on ancient graves in one part.

She must be here, I thought, so I searched for her

138

with my best detective skill and finally settled on a grassy mound that was not very old—I parted the new grass along the sides—though it looked old at a glance because it had been completely neglected. All the old graves were neglected.

So this was where Annabel lay, I thought, far more dry and acute than I had been in that blessed office. Of course, it mightn't be; she might be buried somewhere else. Still, I felt certain this was the place. Then all at once I was walking to the wall, which I leapt, and continued on over the rough ground, hardly seeing where I went, I was so blinded.

An hour after that I dived into the sea and then sat on the rock to dry.

In the late afternoon, as I drew near the hotel, the landlord, Sam Mor, intercepted me accidentally. The sea and certain thoughts had set me at a cool easy distance from most things and I was able to assure him that I might yet make use of his fishing tackle if I could also make use of his bed for two or three more days.

Apparently one of the hotel party had been taken ill just before coming north and his room, now mine, was available for another week. As I thanked him he asked, "What did you do to the Major last night?"

"Why, is he in bad form today?"

"A bit dark," he said.

I explained that I hadn't felt like another late night and he nodded, reckoning that that was what was wrong. "Sometimes he is just a little touchy. We don't pay much attention to it." He was not so much discussing his guest as giving me a hint which, his smile suggested, I did not seem to need.

"That old diplomat was trying to find out things," I said.

"I'm sure he was." He waited, expectant.

There was something delightful at that moment about us being all diplomats together, and I turned its humour into a description of the excellent walk I had had. "I landed in Balrunie and suddenly thought I would call on the factor, Mr. Maclean. I had heard the Major refer to him."

"Oh, did you?"

"Yes. I gathered from what the Major said that a certain rent had not been paid."

"Indeed," he said. As we eyed each other I saw that the landlord knew all about it only too well, and let me know he knew.

"He didn't help much," I said.

"The factor?"

"I suppose I shouldn't have called on him and I don't want the thing talked about." The landlord nodded with the understanding that was already silent. "It was after hearing the Major last night," I explained. "I thought I might arrange the business quietly, meanwhile."

"And the factor wouldn't?"

"No."

Sam Mor nodded slowly twice. "Excuse me if I seem inquisitive, but you actually offered him the rent?"

"Yes." And I gave him a short résumé of what had passed in the Estate Office.

"I suppose he had you there, seeing you weren't acting for Mr. Menzies."

"What do you mean?" With Sam Mor your question did not always follow on what he had *said*.

"It's none of my business," he said. There followed the mutual look in which confidence is reasonably established. "I rather think you had put him in a bit of a difficulty." I waited. "It might not suit him to have the rent paid."

"Why not?"

"Well, he might have an offer for the house." He paused again but I deliberately waited. "An offer from someone to buy the house."

"I see," I said. "That would pay him better."

"Take, say, nine hundred pounds for a house like that and what's the rent worth in comparison?"

"Not much, I suppose."

"Especially when you take off the owner's rates—and the repairs."

"So he's been offered nine hundred, has he?"

"So I believe."

"I was a bit of an innocent," I said, keeping the smile going.

"Under the rent restrictions a tenant can sit on, so no one would buy the house for a moment unless he could get vacant possession."

"I understand perfectly," I said. "He wants Menzies to clear out."

He looked at me. "Yes."

"What do you mean?"

"I'm thinking your visit was timed just a bit on the neat side. Mark you, I don't know anything about legal procedure but things can be set in motion."

"What things?"

"Well, if you don't pay your rent I suppose they can get an order for your ejection."

The sunlight darkened in front of me and I had the sensation of hounds on the hunt. It was almost visual, but I managed to break off our conversation reasonably enough in the sense that the landlord must have seen he had given me something unpalatable to chew and that I was going to chew it.

But up in my bedroom I couldn't chew my thumb. I was a simpleton all right. In the twilight of the world the hounds hunted and the hunters went in for the kill.

I was positively being affected by Menzies' way of thinking, I thought, with arid bitterness. I swore and sat down.

And I had come back, too, with the intention of reading his script, of trying so to understand that some glimmering of a notion of a way out might be revealed. I had been affected on leaving the cemetery. Annabel had become an extraordinarily real person in my mind. Not only in appearance but somehow in essence.

On that rock where I sat, Mrs. Maclellan's face and expression had come back: "Ach, she's lovely." I had at first attacked this, the emotion, the sentiment that is cloying, the sentimentality even. But all the attack did was liberate the essence, almost pure. In Menzies' dreadful dream, Annabel sits on the cliff-top with the golden afternoon about her. In the dawn the moment would be silver. But there was no way of doing away with these moments, any more than with the afternoon or the morning. No good my trying to hunt and kill them. So why try? I thought. Better face up to it. I accepted violence and death and damnation and bombs. We all did. We wallowed in them, feeling safe and sensible, with no flies on us. Not a bloody fly. Malevolence, too; the neurotic malevolence that hunts in order to destroy; and to make sure it does a real job we put extra teeth in it.

Oh, the old argument, the world stuff. We all knew about that. But at last, at last, it was really getting beyond itself, this hellish destruction, beyond tragedy and becoming a bloody bore. If anyone mentioned gold or silver it had to be in hard cash. Otherwise you were dodging the column. Nine hundred pounds worth.

Wallow in that and you're sane and safe, you're a knowing fellow. But the gold of the afternoon or the silver of the morning—don't mention it. If you do you're crackers; the higher critics wave the banners with the strange device: Schizophrenia. Paranoia. Or even Escapism.

And now that I was in the midst of the hot bout I even remembered Menzies' expression when he used the words: integration, harmony. The irony as he looked at me. . . .

He was in his own twilight, hunting God's beasts, or the Wrecker's beasts, if there was any difference.

I gradually cooled down.

What was I going to do?

9

That evening, after dinner, I was sitting in a hollow when I saw Catherine coming towards me along the path. Her appearance was so utterly unexpected that it was magical in the sense the old primitive hunter must have experienced when the totem beast materialised in the wrong place.

When she saw me she involuntarily stopped, in the dead stop that is action suspended, like a hind. But only for a moment.

I was now on my feet and greeted her.

She was not superior or haughty. That was not her kind of defence. She was simply wary, ready for flight but not showing it, contained, leashed. Even her breathing was better controlled than mine.

"I am glad we meet like this," I said with the wonderful aptitude of a chairman to his committee. "I mean here," I added. "I should like to explain," I said, "that when we met before I didn't mean to—ah—intrude. Nothing could have been further from my—ah——" I felt "intention" was a long word so substituted—"from what I had intended." Heaven knows what my temperature was now but it felt about as high as it could rise, in my face anyhow.

Her eyes had the remarkably vivid capacity of flashing from one thing to another, including my face, in an instantaneous way. But she said nothing. And what choked me all the more was the certainty that if I didn't say all I had to say quick she would be off. So I gathered myself like the formal ass whose committee know him well and, after saying what I had said already, contrived to add, "I didn't mean to be rude." I then made a remarkable leap and asked, "Did you think I was?"

She reserved judgment. I felt that was just.

"I came on you so suddenly," I explained. "That was all it was. You surprised me." These last three words were like a trickle of wit coming from far away into my dry sand, and though it may be difficult to hang on to a trickle I did my best. "You surprised me very much." I tried to smile next.

She gave the ghastly affair one of her flashes, and her body twisted slightly, and she glanced down at the earth. I saw her hand and knew it might have plucked a grass if there had been one tall enough. I even thought her hand astonishing, that it was there. I looked up from her hand and met her eyes and she looked away.

"You see, I really wanted to speak to you." For the lie had come full blown into my mind, a lovely one, a beauty. It steadied me like a sail on a boat. It knocked weights off me and several years. I became rather solemn and looked away, too. "I knew you had been a friend of—the Menzies."

Her eyes came full on me now, but I did not meet them for I was preoccupied. I hadn't, of course, known anything about her at all when I had previously seen her. And that morning, in particular, when I had returned from the white house and must have looked like a drunken rake of the palest dye ready for a head-on attack—hadn't I beckoned her back to my bedroom!— was something that in the ordinary way would have needed some explaining away. But I had explanation enough now and, sadly, to spare.

"So I wanted to talk to you," I said. "That was all."

I turned my innocence upon her and now she looked into the distance, then again for the tall grass that wasn't there. It was a hazardous moment for it almost seemed as if she were becoming embarrassed at having misjudged me so wrongly.

"I can quite see," I said, "that you—that appearances were against me. How could you know what I wanted?"

I got the impression that she thought I was taking a long time, so desperately I said, "I would like to speak to you. Do you mind?"

"I am late," she said. "I must really go."

"I should like your advice. You knew them. And things are getting pretty desperate."

Her eyes grew troubled. A breath of wind deepens and darkens pools on a moor. I had no idea what on earth to add, so I said, "Today I called on the factor in Balrunie. He wasn't very helpful. In fact—he wouldn't take—wouldn't do anything."

"The rent?"

"Yes. But that's not what I meant to talk about."

"Did you offer to pay?"

"Yes," I said, bogged in embarrassment. "I had no right to."

"He wouldn't take it?" Her voice was light and clear. I felt like an absurd kite on the end of it.

"No. He wouldn't. It seems he has darker intentions." With this effort at lightness I took my courage aloft and looked at her with considerable normality.

I got a surprise then. She stood exactly like a hind in a dell hearing something in another dell. In some mysterious way I had stopped her.

"What intentions?" she asked quietly.

"I have gathered that he wants to throw him out on his ear," I said with confident humour.

146

Then she was looking at me quite steadily. It was confounding, but I did my best to show that men had the odd habit of throwing each other out on their ears. She needn't be surprised at that.

She wasn't. She was quite still.

"Do sit down for a few minutes. Have a smoke." I found my cigarette case.

"No, thanks."

"You don't smoke?"

"Sometimes." Her smile was slight but it was wonderful at that moment.

"Can't I persuade you?"

"No, thanks."

"Won't you sit down?" And I made to sit down myself and stopped just in time.

Then she simply sat down.

I sat down, too, and there we were.

"Have you been for a walk?" I asked sensibly.

"I was home," she said.

"Oh, is that your place round the hill from Loch Dubh?"

"Yes."

"A lovely situation. You'll be able to go home quite often?"

She could pull a grass now and did. "Do you mean the factor is going to make him leave the house?"

Only now did I fully realise that I had been talking about Menzies. "That's his idea."

"When?"

"I don't know." Then I began to tell her quite simply, with a sense of extraordinary relief, of my interview with the factor and subsequent talk with the landlord. "So you can imagine the sort of knot I was in before I saw you coming."

"Couldn't you tell Mr. Menzies?"

147

"That's just it. Could I?" I was completely freed at last for this was obviously what I had wanted to ask her. She must see it now. "What do you think?" Inwardly I was so pleased with myself that I thought her shy and tentative in a delightful way, her human concern so natural and simple.

"Why couldn't you?" she asked.

"I don't know," I said, doubtfully. "I don't know him very well. We talked most of the night, but, as a matter of fact, that was the first time I met him."

When she looked at me direct she knocked most things out of my head, including Menzies.

"I thought you knew him well, in London."

"I knew about him, of course. I actually had some business with him. That's what started us talking." I wondered if I should tell her about the script.

"How is he?" she asked.

"Quite fit," I said. "In fact, tough." I would tell her when I knew her better.

"He's got such an extraordinary power about him that I would feel very awkward barging into his personal affairs. Not that I would mind his resenting it if I thought it would do any good. You see what I mean?" I asked.

"Yes."

I turned my face to her. She was sitting a good two feet away. "I should like to be quite frank with you."

She waited.

"I resent these people who think they know what's good for Douglas Menzies, like the Major and the factor and all the rest. Damn them, they don't understand. Forgive me, but I could see them far enough. The Major tried to pump me about the night I spent at the white house. He pumped in vain, I can assure you."

If I was suddenly filled with wrath it didn't disturb

148

her. I even contrasted the world he occupied with theirs. It was such a relief letting the cork out of my bottle. And after all I had some knowledge of what the men of art have meant to human culture all the way from the pictures in the cave of Altamira. But for them we might still be baboons. "Or do you think that's overdoing it?"

"No," she said.

"You are fond of music?"

She looked at the old earth. I pulled a long grass and silently presented it to her.

She took it without thinking, then threw me a flash.

"About the music—there's something I would like to know. These old Gaelic songs that you and Annabel used to sing together sometimes. I have wondered."

"Who told you that?"

"You did, didn't you?"

The slight flush that had come into her face when she hesitated over throwing the grass back at me increased if anything.

"Has someone been talking about me?" At last she was curious.

"How could anyone help it? You were fond of Annabel."

"Yes." But she was growing restless, though she hardly moved.

"Mrs. Maclellan thinks she was lovely. Ach, she was lovely!"

"She was," said Catherine.

I was deeply moved and felt she would be off at any moment. "I think so, too."

"You met her?"

"No," I said.

The first faint dusk was on the earth and a greeny afterglow remotely beyond a hollow in the hills.

"I have been haunted," I said. "It's good of you

149

listening to me. I have no one to talk to. When people don't understand you can't talk to them. If only I knew more. . . . Would you tell me about these songs?"

"What?" It was quietly said.

"Tell me this first, and then I'll tell you why I'm asking you. Do you remember when I came into my room that first time and heard you humming something? What was it?"

"I don't remember."

"Please try."

"I really don't. I often hum things."

I felt if only I could get her to sing to me it would be a tremendous step forward and I pressed her as if something really important depended on it. I think she knew there was deceit somewhere, for her instincts were remarkably clear and acute, but all at once, without a movement, she started humming an old air, and, like a true artist, she hummed the whole air through. "Is that it?"

"No," I said. I couldn't say any more. I was frightened to tell this girl what she and her singing could do to a human being at such a moment. Enchantment is a superficial word. It doesn't get tangled in the dark roots. And the word love isn't any better. Something moved then beyond us. "What's the name of it?" I asked for something to say.

"Land of Heart's Desire," she said.

"O God," I said.

She looked at me then. I hardly knew how to go on. "It's something he said, about music or about life. There were times when I hardly knew which was which." Then I remembered quite vividly. "It was about two persons coming back to the place they knew, on a ship. But they were coming back after their wanderings. The old place was bright in their minds, and now at last they would make things of it. It was fresh with the extraordinary freshness of art. After experience the dream you had when you were young becomes a new dream. But old, too, and remote as the morning of Creation, which is any morning you find it. I'm getting mixed. But he must have known your song. For he said they were coming back to the land of their hearts' desire." I didn't even feel I had said too much because I couldn't mention the irony in Menzies' face.

There was no irony in Catherine's face. She could hardly have understood the muddle of words, but perhaps she understood something more. I realised in a moment that she had made the whole thing personal to Douglas Menzies and Annabel.

"That actually was a story he made up. I'll tell you about it sometime. But it really had to do with his music also. Am I making sense at all?"

"Yes."

"He was interested in the old songs?"

"Yes, he was."

"You knew them well."

"Yes, I used to go there often." If she could have flown away at that moment she would. I knew I wouldn't get her to speak and I was sick of my own voice.

"Were you there—when it happened?"

"No. I had gone to Glasgow over a week before."

I could not break the silence.

"If you'll excuse me, I really must go." She got up. It was getting dark. "May I come back with you?"

"No, please." She smiled and her eyes shone and she walked away, quickly, yet holding herself. I stood watching her until she had disappeared.

It occurred to me again that since coming to Dalaskir I seemed to have been going through a process of getting skinned. Eyes and all. Something very odd was happening anyhow. I stood like one not knowing where to set off for next. I sat down again in the intimate night.

She had sung to me. And though I knew that it was quite a natural thing for her to do, yet there had to be a time for it or wild horses wouldn't have brought forth the song.

I got up and began wandering back.

Presently I found myself sitting again like a fool in the twilight. I could not help laughing under my breath at my astonishment, and when I realised I was laughing I had a look around. Menzies affected me no more than the man in the moon. There wasn't a moon. It wasn't just a girl. Heavens, girls were free and easy these days. A fellow couldn't live in any city without knowing that. Girls just knew what it was all about. And when things got too tangled up, one did not use the talons of one's ingenuity to untie the desperate knot, one snipped the connection. It was laughable and delicious; like imps of the night dancing in a ring. Nothing was quite real. There was *something more*.

Excruciating how callow I had been! My God, it was wonderful.

After wandering heaven knows where I at last approached the hotel like a sleuth, for the Major wasn't going to trap me tonight. I listened, opened the door, hung up my hat, grabbed my candlestick and went aloft to my room, feeling like a miser with a secret hoard of gold which he could proceed to count at leisure.

10

The following day any notions of angling for trout were far from my mind. I felt fresh as the morning and slipped away with my sandwiches in an unobtrusive manner. Dalaskir was growing on me. Nature had laid it out with that careless abandon which achieves so rare a balance. It has everything, I thought.

The morning would be a very busy time, preparing lunches, clearing up, making beds, and generally getting the hotel shipshape. Not until the afternoon would any member of the staff be able to have an hour or two off. And, again, after dinner. So much was obvious. One thing Catherine could be quite certain of was that I would never again embarrass her on the premises. I knew only too well what that would mean, especially as gossip among the guests. I could think of the ladies going into a small huddle; and even funnier, of Big Sam being concerned about the reputation of his house.

I was quite confident now of being able to deal with Menzies—with Catherine's help. Alone I would have been able to do nothing. But guided by Catherine, I could hardly fail. That, however, meant more consultations. It certainly did. She was so sensible, too; I had only to hint about the rent and she was on to it. The more I had thought about that the more wonderful it had seemed. That she could have had a deep concern for the practical realities, too! Remarkable, a girl like

that, setting out in life, winning her bursaries, not afraid
to turn her hand to anything, yet remaining vivid in a
way the sophisticated would think naïve, yet singing
the profound issues in a way that tied the listening
heart in ten knots. It would take a few consultations
to fathom all that.

So I was extremely cunning and wandered away
from the hotel and the white house in the opposite
direction to Catherine's home, until I got among the
hills. I had my binoculars and enjoyed some extensive
views. It was astonishing country and I had always
been interested in birds. Through the forenoon I
worked my way back towards Loch Dubh, for my main
aim was to make quite certain of all possible paths
Catherine might follow between the hotel and her
home and the best spot from which to command them.
Naturally Catherine did not wish to be seen in my
company, and, if we were going to have a real talk,
the best spot would not be bang on the path along
which anyone might come at any time. That had probably worried her last night. Besides, there was the
factor, and a lost day would be a lost day. I had thought
it all out.

I lay in the heather for a long time looking at
Catherine's home through my glasses. It was a simple
stone house with a slated roof, a small porch, and out-
houses. I saw her mother come out of the house with a
dish and the hens running towards her from all direc-
tions. I liked the scene very much. I could not at the
distance get any impression of her features but I did
get an impression of herself, the way she stood, scat-
tering the food, the bountiful provider. It was she who
would be behind Catherine. In such circumstances, as
I knew well, it generally was the mother. For one
moment I had a wild impulse to go down and talk to

her, as a stranger who happened to be passing. But I controlled that folly. I hardly knew Catherine well enough yet!

The croft lay facing south-west with the hill behind it. I left it and came back round the steep shoulder towards Loch Dubh. I began to understand now my first evening in the hotel, when the Major and Lachlan had had the verbal conflict which had so annoyed me. To save Lachlan walking all the way to the hotel in the morning and then back to the loch, the Major, the night before, would have arranged to meet him at the loch. He would certainly have had that kind of consideration for Lachlan, and anyway it would work in with the Major's uncertain hours. He wouldn't mind keeping Lachlan waiting long enough. He could always pay him. They had been a long time together and had developed peculiar foibles and no doubt a reasonable way with the cash. The Major did what he could to keep himself out of the bog of boredom!

Amused by such fancies I began to wonder who would be on Loch Dubh today. The shoulder grew steeper, then all at once the southern end of the loch was just below me and two men were standing by the boat, whose square stern was towards me on the edge of the water, having an unholy row. Their voices volleyed up the hill. Lachlan and the Major!

"Shut up!" roared the Major.

"I can shut up if I like——"

"I'll murder you." The Major staggered.

"Murder is it?" cried Lachlan, and as his head tossed he saw me.

I backed out of sight at once, blasting the Major. He would go too far one day and Lachlan would let him have it. Serve him right, too! I was angrier than I had been that first time and as I walked on felt more murderous at each step. If only Lachlan hadn't seen me! Like looking on at his humiliation. He was Catherine's father.

I went a long way before I cooled down. By a stream I ate my sandwiches. I knew about the Major's rages, how at a certain point he went round the bend. Lachlan knew, too. Still, that was no excuse. There was a limit. I would analyse it for him some night. By God, I would.

Presently I found myself laughing, for there was something oddly monstrous about it. The Major was in life's black shadow. Possibly he could never be yanked out of it now. Lachlan was probably the real danger. I wondered if the Major ever realised how near Lachlan must come in temper to sticking the old dirk of his race in the Major's bowels. I decided that he probably did and enjoyed the perverted savour of a danger he was damn certain he could always dominate. Then I had a short peculiar vision of the Major carrying his own death-stroke with him.

So it was high time to forget about them and lie back and see the tips of the budded heather against the sky. How lovely and cool, rare and exquisite! In a moment the vision of Catherine was near. There was something of her in the wind that cooled the pale budded tips. I gave way to my fancies.

Annabel's image was still, caught by imagination in the door of my mind. An extraordinary contrast between them.

Catherine was alive. That was it.

Catherine was here in life, and remembering Annabel, we were not so far away from her. That peculiar notion I had got since coming here of the other landscape touched me again. That it should do so in daylight was what made it uncanny—and so strangely familiar.

156

I hesitate here lest I should seem to be implying too much too obscurely, when in reality what I felt was clear, simple and delightful. The wandering wind, the light, the buds of the heather. The very skin is bathed and all the congestions and knots of living are resolved. The vague dim pall of concern, of violence, of guilt, of remorse, which accompanies us, perhaps unconsciously, like our shadow, fades away, as the night mist under the sun, and the high clear blue is there, and the clouds wander. Here is release, without thought of what the release is from. It is delightful, and if thought is foolish enough to intrude at all it is to wonder if there may be an order of being to which this delight is natural. And one knows that *there may be*. There may be the other landscape which the delight inhabits. If the thought is a little startling and holds the breath, it is also strangely familiar; as Annabel would be familiar if I saw her at a little distance in the daylight.

Banish the thought and the delight remains, more exquisite than ever, with its own rare order of humour.

Catherine was real anyway, like a hind in a glade, and for me carried this delight about with her. Vision has its amorous moments more intimate than one may care to tell, but how lovely, how delicious, they are!

However, the image of the hind in the glade must have remained, for the glade in which I had seen the gipsy wife's head stuck on the tent was suddenly evoked and I thought I would like to see it again in my sober senses. In particular I remembered the ass, as though between that ass and myself was a peculiar affinity.

I went down by the small burn until I saw it was the one which passed the Maclellans' cottage, left it to go along a hollow, came round a knoll, dipped down towards the road, then having spied out the land, for somehow I did not want to be seen or interrupted, crossed the road, leapt the fences and found myself near the foot of the dell by an old stone sheepfank.

As I wandered slowly up the dell it narrowed. Small birches were on the rather steep bank to my left; the weather had dried up the stream on my right, leaving clear little pools that scarcely trickled from one to another. A sally bush here and there, an alder. The bank beyond the stream overhung in places as if in times past the water had eaten it away. Ferns, starwort, campion, grass of parnassus. A beautiful spot to be tucked away like this. Only romantic man would think of it as hidden, secretive. It was open to the day, in its own place, a haunt of small singing birds. I watched a greenfinch. Bird families grew up here. Willow warblers. Here and there intrusive bracken had been slain by the tinkers' tilt cart. Trust them to find a spot where pitching a sheltered tent was easy and an ass could eat unobserved! The young migrants were practising their flights. I thought of north Africa, the lands and seas between, and then saw ahead of me the blackened stones of the tinkers' fire. They had gone! Beyond a thick clump of hazel and round to the left would be the flat grassy bay and the steep slope down which that ass had thrown me on my head. I moved over the noiseless turf, rounded the clump and saw sitting at the foot of the ·slope, side by side, Douglas Menzies and Catherine.

The kind of emotion I experienced was curiously blinding. I lost my bearings, lost myself. I could not move. And they stared across at me without any emotion at all on their arrested faces. Catherine's face was pale and different from what I could ever have imagined it. It was responsible, quiet in a world of meaning where her vivid movement was lost.

Awkwardly I turned away, for my footing was none too sure, and went back down the dell.

I don't remember much about that walk, but I possibly returned fairly exactly by the way I had come from the spot in the hills where I had had my amorous fancies. What can still make my chest cave in was the awful attack on me, as from outside, of swarming black thoughts. They attacked *me*, not anyone else. My folly! My utter abysmal idiocy! What came into my hands I twisted and tore. Occasionally I got locked in a bodily spasm, my teeth gnashing on oaths. God, how I could have been such an ass! I laughed and staggered on. Perhaps someone saw me. I have no idea.

Even when I got back to my lair in the hills, I rolled on the heather and bit it, like a wounded beast.

Black as this was and hellish beyond any experience I had ever had, it was yet only superficial. It had only to do with my folly, my vanity. That I could have so blinded myself with my fancies, that I could have imagined, what I had imagined, about Catherine and myself——! And without one atom of reason for it! How could I have done it? How? It was incredible, it was fatuous beyond what I could bear. It was terrifying. I tore the heather out by the roots. I spat the crushed buds from my mouth.

Then little by little the sunlight went out in my mind.

As I went over the conversation I had had with Catherine it got cleansed of my infatuation and its meaning became quite clear. I saw the kind of fellow I had been, how my own feelings and desires had vividly coloured everything to a degree that had created complete illusion. Every movement she had made, every word she had uttered, should have destroyed the illusion, but I simply wouldn't let it. There was something

shocking here beyond all human folly and for this reason
that I didn't know I was performing any illusive trick.

She had never even spoken until I had mentioned the
Menzies, had never properly looked at me. And when
I stumbled on about the factor, she had her swift
definite question about the rent. In no time she had
found out all about the rent and the factor's intentions
quite precisely. No cross-examining lawyer could have
been quicker on the kernel. Then I had asked her to sit
down and she had hesitated. But suddenly she had sat
down—because she had wanted to find out more. And I
had thought I was getting on like a house on fire.

Then I had asked her to sing.

And she had sung to me.

All else I might gloss over but never that. It was too
terrible. And she had hummed the air right through to
the end, as beautifully as any siren in the Land of Heart's
Desire. And on the back of it had asked: Has anyone
been talking about me? And with my astonishing wit I
replied: How could anyone help it?

She had wanted to know if Menzies had been talking
about her in our long night at the white house.

Earlier she had found out all I knew about him, had
found out in particular that I might not care to mention
the matter of the rent to him, and, having understood,
pressed it no further.

I would not have believed it possible that illusion
could ever have blinded me so utterly.

Even when she asked: How is he? I could see now
that it was not a real deceit: she merely wanted to find
out what I, as a man, thought of the peculiar condition
he was now in. It certainly would be worrying her.

For she would know he was drinking, not eating
properly. I confess that I had never before really
bothered about how or where he had got the rum. The

Major's reference to his drinking had simply irritated me. Compared with the profound issues which appeared to have Menzies in their grip, the matter of drinking was incidental, temporary, and the source of the drink of no particular consequence. When discovered it would be a simple fact like any other.

I wondered now if Catherine was the source. Nor did the notion shock me. I had had enough of illusion. Where she could get rum of that strength I couldn't readily imagine. Had it been whisky it might have come from a smuggler's still. Could it be smuggled rum from a fishing boat somewhere on the coast? But it didn't matter. Even thinking about it was only a temporary relief for my mind.

I thought of them, meeting. How often? Because they couldn't meet in the daylight without its being found out. In the dark? That might be possible, but difficult in the short summer nights, without a lot of explanation by Catherine when she got back in the early hours.

Once you have shed all illusion, the stark outline of truth is never far away. Catherine would have her day off. She could sleep at home. Where she slept any night almost would not matter, so long as she was back on her job in time. For to the hotel, she was sleeping at home. To her home, she was sleeping at the hotel. It was very simple. One night a week would be fairly easy.

Those I had met, from Mrs. Maclellan at one end of this district to the factor at the other, had said or implied that it was high time Menzies was out of the white house. The only one who had made no such suggestion was Catherine. I had thought it wonderful of her. The depth of her understanding, I had thought!

I saw now how deep it was and I got a profound view of her, simple and stark and essential as the pattern of truth itself, at last so clear to me. I may have

161

been infatuated before. It went deeper than that now.

It was not bitterness that took the brightness out of the sunlight. I don't know what it was. For the truth is that I was still trying to avoid taking the last look into the abyss. I was still somewhere about the surface trying to hang on to the tatters of my illusion. Though that is not perhaps the right way to put it. I simply could not bring myself to think of Menzies.

Off and on I had thought of that night we had had in ways I have not cared to mention. He was at the back of my mind, even when I wasn't thinking of him. He was a force. I find it difficult to define even to myself what I mean by that. I know it before I start to define it, then it gets lost among words. It's not force of character, as we usually think of that phrase. It's not—but there I go, bogged in the old difficulty of trying to define by negatives, when the whole point of the reality is its positive drive, like a miner's drive into the dark coal-face.

So I go back to that something relentless in him, which, once it got going, had to go to the end. It did this, not for himself in the usual selfish sense, but because it had to be done, for reasons which we cannot know, as we cannot know why life is here and what it is driving on towards. To say that it is driving on to-wards nothing is a particularly futile kind of negative, which means no more than it says, which is nothing. But one can drop out of the drive, or appear to drop out of it. This, however, was just what I could not conceive Menzies doing. It was not in character, unless his force had collapsed, and during the talk I had had with him I not only found again what had excited and disturbed David and myself in his script, but found it strengthened and given a shift onto a new plane. On this plane his force was more single, more relentless, and immensely more disturbing. And I don't mean a "higher plane". In the curious visual trick—or image trick—that seems to accompany this kind of effort at understanding, it has the appearance of a lower plane, where the shadows are, where the answer is not heard, where the face is not seen.

This was in him so naturally that it was instinctual, part of his force. When writing his parable about Annabel and himself, the parable which was to let her understand how much he thought of her, he conceived the image of the ship on which they were both wrecked, so that, between the wreck and their death on the rock, he could tell her, her head in the shelter of his heart where she could hear him, that he was with her, and that if they were parted he would find her, that nothing would stop him, nothing ever, here or hereafter. It was like a "second sight" of his own essential nature, a prevision of what he would inevitably do, committed to writing before the event.

More than that, though I hesitate now, for I am reluctant to say that I felt Annabel's presence about the house. If she appeared it was in the room of my mind, not in the room of the house. It may be that in his search he could visualise Annabel so acutely that I was affected by his "projection" of her. I turned over such psychic possibilities, but they were curiously unsatisfying, and always left me with the feeling that there was *something more*: for, as we know, in any rationalising process the vivid nature of the experience itself, its spirit, is lost, as life is lost when any germ is physically analysed into its chemical elements. The best any psychologist can do is analyse, like his fellow seekers, the biologist and chemist.

In short, I had thought I wasn't fooling myself.

163

Further than that, I saw this search by Menzies as more than a search for Annabel, though it was primarily that. I saw it as a sort of warfare into those regions which (to call on the image) the Wrecker inhabits.

There could be only one end to that search, that warfare: tragedy. That was my problem. And the problem, for Menzies' creative plane, only began there. Beyond that I couldn't think, except in terms of my "interference".

Lying there in the heather, I could hardly bring myself to look at all this—and the much more that surrounded it, for to tell the truth it had induced in me not only this matter of understanding but also a deep and quite involuntary loyalty to Menzies. There's nothing I wouldn't have done for him. When I had left the estate office in Balrunie my cursing may have seemed excessive, but it was not the mere matter of rent that had given it pith.

There are illusions one can let go.

There is a deep life illusion, so tangled with the roots that one can hardly tear it out without tearing the lot away. Menzies had got tangled somewhere down there.

I became utterly wearied, exhausted. Anyway, all this was out of my hands now. All I had to do was go back to the hotel and pack up. I stretched out and lay over, letting myself sink, but I couldn't sink. So I got up and wandered back to the hotel.

As I approached I thought there was an unusual commotion about the place. Afternoon is a dead time, when in the normal way it is difficult to get hold of anyone. I looked at my watch and was surprised to find it was just turned five. Still, that was early, unless some sort of party had arrived for tea. Bus tours avoided the district with its narrow roads and awkward bends. The landlord and Ian the gillie were hammering away at something by the old-fashioned grindstone beside the garage. Sneddon seemed to be putting up his fishing rod, his wife hovering about him. The widow, in earnest colloquy with the Browns, made a dramatic gesture. I heard her high voice. The kitchen maid, Ina, a young girl, went across from the kitchen premises to the landlord, spoke to him for a moment, then ran back. Ian saw me approaching and said something to the landlord who turned round and kept looking.

I went up to him. "Planning an expedition?"

"We are," he said in a reserved peculiar way. I glanced at Ian who has a dry humour. There was no humour in his tanned face.

"What's wrong?" I asked.

"It's the Major. He's missing," answered Big Sam.

"Missing?"

"Yes. On Loch Dubh."

The short scene by the boat came back to me with the Major in his murder staggers. It had been a dark patch on the daylight then.

"What happened?" I asked.

"I don't know. We only know what Lachlan told us." I could see Big Sam was reluctant to talk; he was secretive by nature and now was being very careful indeed. I looked at what they were working on and realised that they had been putting the final touches to what could only be primitive grappling irons. "They'll have to do," he said to Ian.

"They should," said Ian. "You'll feel with them whatever," and he set the curved iron fingers at a raking angle. Willie, the slim gillie, came up with a coil of rope over his shoulder.

"Right. You be going then. Hold Lachlan if you see him," ordered the landlord.

"We will," said Ian.

165

As the landlord turned to the hotel I went with him and asked again what had happened.

He stopped and, having no witnesses now, said with a simple impressive dignity, "Lachlan came back a little while ago and said the Major was gone. It seems, by his story, that they had a row. According to himself, Lachlan then said to the Major that he was through with him and went away off home. But at home he thought better of it, for he has a sensible wife, a nice woman. Still, he was thrawn and had his lunch at home and only some time after did he go back to find the boat adrift on the loch and sunk to the gunnels, with no sign of the Major at all."

Lord, had Lachlan done the Major in! I was seeing a lot of raw stuff today.

"It's no laughing matter, I'm afraid," said the landlord.

I hadn't laughed, still he has an acute eye in him has Big Sam.

"Tell me this," I asked. "Have the Major and Lachlan ever had a real quarrel before?"

"Oh, they spar away, but only once did Lachlan give it him straight. That was the year before last."

"What happened?"

"The Major went to his house afterwards and apologised so they made it up. But lately—I don't know what's been happening to the Major . . . he is taking a drop too much. I have had to cool Lachlan down more than once, for beneath his talk—well, he's a piper. None of us wants trouble."

"One thing more: how did the boat get sunk?"

"According to his own story, Lachlan was at the loch in good time because the boat has been leaking a bit lately from a bottom seam. And that's true enough. Last night I asked Lachlan to repair it first thing this

166

morning and he got some tow from Ian. There was a good drop of water in her and she was heavy to handle. He took the cork out of her to lighten her and get her dry at the leaking seam. Then he put the cork back, he says. When he had done that he took the chance, he says, to have a look at other parts of her bottom. She's not a young boat. He had done about all he could when the Major arrived. Then they had their row and Lachlan left him, without, he says, putting a foot in the boat."

"So no one knows what really happened after that?"

"No. No one saw them at all."

"Where's Lachlan now?"

"He's gone back to the loch to search around for the Major. He cannot believe he's drowned, he says."

I looked at the landlord and the landlord looked at me.

"I believe Lachlan completely," I said.

"Would you care to come with us?" I could swear I saw relief in his eye.

"Certainly."

"We'll take this car so far. It saves a bit. Just a minute." And off he went.

It looked like a fool-proof story, the way the landlord had told it. Quite a brilliant story. It might even be true! To control my expression I started for the front door. Sneddon was actually whipping a big hook to the point of a fishing rod.

I nodded to him and his wife and was almost run into by the widow in the tiny hall. Under the stress of her emotion, she drew back involuntarily, as though I were something objectionable she might have touched. Never had I got my character in such short compass. I bowed and proceeded upstairs. Then the little corridor, the bedroom, and it was all Catherine.

167

Things were certainly getting a bit complicated for that girl. The landlord would have phoned for the police. I had better, perhaps, think this business out. Lachlan would be put through his story in fine detail. As I went through it again I saw blank spots. The ground by the loch would be inspected as carefully as the boat. The Major's body—— A car siren hooted and I left the room. Big Sam was at the wheel, with Sneddon beside him and the parts of his fishing rod. Behind, Brown was holding some gear on his lap to help make room for me beside young Charlie, who worked about the garage and gillied occasionally. Brown was dark with a hawk-like nose, and probably forty. He and his wife had a certain reserve that guarded, I fancied, a private life of some felicity. No one spoke and very soon the car drew up in a bay by the roadside from which the footpath went to Loch Dubh. We all got out and young Charlie, carrying the bag of gear, started off, followed by Sam Mor, Sneddon, Brown and myself.

One thing I tried to puzzle out was why Lachlan had not told the landlord that he had seen me. I could hardly believe that he hadn't seen me. Where was his point? For he had admitted that the Major and himself had had a row and all I could do was confirm it. Lachlan must have some reason, so again I decided to say nothing about it.

As I looked back over my shoulder I could see the countryside that I was getting to know so well. Always that white house, like a beacon that had got shoved ashore. And, on this side of it the almost concealed dell. But no one moved there.

I had already decided that Catherine had taken the risk of meeting Menzies during the day in order to tell him about the rent, which might indeed be a very urgent matter. Had she gone to the house? That surely would have been the simple thing to do. In a couple of minutes she could have told him all that was necessary, then left at once as if she had gone with a message.

Unless they had a private arrangement of signals? Because that seemed fantastic it seemed dead right. It had the intimacy. The secret world within the ordinary world!

Already Charlie was well ahead of Sam Mor. It was a silent solemn procession which, being last, I could enjoy in my fashion. For it was a relief to be dealing with the ordinary world where normally decent folk did each other in. Something homely about it, where one could play one's part in a practical way. No illusions, only the exercise of shrewd detective powers. Brown's grey tweed, with the suggestion of a dark check, was rather fine in the weave for a plusfour suiting, but it was well cut. His stockings, however, were the real thing, plain, hand-knitted and a rough help for his rather thin legs. The dark brown boots were quietly expensive. I suddenly missed the barrister, but he wouldn't be back from sea yet. Charlie had probably done a quick round up of Ian and Willie, hence Sneddon and Brown. It was perhaps as well the barrister wasn't here.

Charlie was far ahead now, and soon out of sight. We came on the four figures standing in close colloquy by the edge of the loch, Lachlan, Ian, Charlie and Willie. A gathering of the clans, I thought, in final strategy. Ian was the sort of lad who would see that Lachlan was fool-proof. They separated quietly and Ian turned to Sam Mor as though he had been waiting for his orders. "I think I'll reach her," he said, "with the anchor."

We all stared at the gunnels of the boat awash some twenty yards from the shore. One oar and a bottom board were afloat quite close to her, the other oar several yards away. I had a stealthy look at Lachlan.

169

He was very straight and still, drawn within himself in a way I hadn't anticipated. I had somehow thought of him dancing around full of excuses. He was not speaking now until he was spoken to, and it was obviously Sam Mor's inclination to ignore him in a human decent way.

"Have a go, then," said Sam Mor to Ian, then he told us all to stand back.

A light three-pronged anchor was tied to the end of the coil of rope. When Ian had the rope arranged to his satisfaction, he turned his back to the boat like an athlete at a Highland Games about to throw the hammer. Charlie had a surreptitious look at Willie whose left eyelid flickered in a solemn wink. Ian had at least two critical judges as he grasped the rope a yard or more from the anchor. After a final glance at the boat, Ian gave the anchor a first swing round his head, a second faster one, then into the third he put what strength and judgment he had, his body flexing like a rooted birch tree, and let go. The anchor started off as if to cross the loch, but the drag of the rope checked it, and when the rope got the water the anchor fell plonk! just over the middle of the boat.

"Good shot!" said Sam Mor.

"You haven't lost the art," Willie allowed.

"I was thinking of Charlie having to swim," said Ian slowly.

Charlie smiled but didn't like to say anything.

"Canny, now," said Sam Mor, as a fluke of the anchor appeared over the gunnel. Gently Ian persuaded the anchor to fall into the boat.

"Hold!" said Sam Mor. "If you come down this way a little bit a prong will catch under the after thaft."

Ian did not say anything but he glanced at Charlie as he moved along a few yards. They were getting a lot of orders from men who knew this day!

170

At this sou'-west end of the loch the land came down steeply and the water was deep. The slipway for the boat (there was no boathouse) came in between two irregular rocky ledges and into this opening Ian and Willie slowly pulled the boat. When she grounded they went in to the thighs in the water and Charlie and Lachlan followed them.

"If you give us the head rope," said Sam Mor, "we'll give you a haul."

Ian, who had already been fishing it out, handed it to Charlie after a moment's hesitation, and Charlie brought it to dry land. Sam Mor got an end of it and I took it from him. Brown followed me on the rope, then Sneddon and finally Sam Mor stood with it in one hand, as captain.

"It's uphill," said Sneddon anxiously, "but that should help."

"It should help to lift her head indeed," Sam Mor agreed.

"Take the strain," said Ian.

"Heave!" cried Sam Mor.

We all heaved, the rope parted and we tumbled in many postures because of the slope.

I lay with my face in the short bents, choked with laughter. Ian had seen it coming. I controlled myself, wiped my eyes as I lifted my head, and below my nose observed a cork, whisky-bottle size, with a slight bulge at one end.

"You're not hurt?" called Sam Mor.

I got up at once, leaving the cork where it was, and joined them, rubbing my face.

The gillies were heaving at that boat as if their lives depended on it. She was canted well over now and three-quarters empty. Sam Mor was examining the rope with some surprise.

171

"It hasn't been too good for a year or two back," said Ian drily. Then taking a deep breath, he cried, "Heave!"

Sam Mor looked at him. Charlie's face was like to burst from all the heaving that was going on.

When she was drawn up, Ian was the first to see that the cork was out of her. He said nothing. Neither did Willie nor Charlie when they spotted it. Sam Mor said "Ha!" generally as he gripped the gunnel and looked about the boat. They were obviously bothered.

In the absence of the bottom board the hole was now quite visible. The water left in the well was already beginning to swirl above it. Lachlan alone stood gaping at it as if it fascinated him. Brown and Sneddon could not help following his eyes to the hole and so they saw it too. Sneddon exclaimed, then pointed out the hole to us all. Brown took another look at Lachlan.

"All I can say," said Lachlan, "is that I certainly put the cork back in her." His feet moved a little but not excitedly.

"Do you think you pushed it in tight enough?" asked Sneddon.

"When I put a cork in I put it in," said Lachlan.

"We can all make mistakes," said Sneddon in dignified reproof.

"How true that is!" said Sam before Lachlan could say anything.

Ian gave Lachlan a look that should have pulled him off any high horse. Brown saw it; he was full of intelligence.

"I think we should wait for the police before taking any further steps," said Sneddon. His smooth butler's face had a sudden pallor that gave it quite an aristocratic air. The gillies stood empty-handed and looked anywhere but at Lachlan.

"Well, gentlemen," said Sam Mor, "it's whatever you say."

"When will they be here?" asked Sneddon.

"I couldn't be sure," said Sam Mor. "It might be a while yet."

"But what did they say when you phoned them?"

"That's just it," said Sam Mor. "It was the policeman's wife that answered the phone, and she said he was out on his rounds just now, but I told her to be sure to send him over to the hotel whenever he came back."

That shook Sneddon who had no doubt been thinking of a detective inspector's squad flying to the scene.

"Seeing we are here," said Brown, "I think we might as well find out what we can."

Sneddon turned to him. "You think so?"

"I do."

As Brown was the other gentleman present, Sneddon had to consider his suggestion. "I'm not at all sure," he said. "We may be destroying evidence."

"Just as we destroyed the rope," said Sam Mor gravely.

"Exactly," said Sneddon, confirmed in the mastery he had assumed and leaving the impasse to speak for itself.

Brown gave it voice. "I don't mind," he said reasonably to Sneddon. "Only I don't quite see what evidence we can destroy."

"That's a matter for the police," said Sneddon.

"What do you think?" Brown asked me.

"It seems to have been the general idea that an attempt should be made to recover the body. What do you think?" And I looked at Sam Mor.

"I only want to do what's right. I just thought it was the natural thing to come and see what we could do."

173

The idea of crime, liberated by Sneddon, began to seep deep. I rather think it was Lachlan's reply about the cork that had set him off, made him fully realise that the gillie remained and the guest was gone. The gillie had deserted his post. He had left his gentleman to drown, by his own story. Almost a capital offence in itself. The investigation of that story certainly was a matter for the police.

I could see that Sam Mor had lost the initiative. Any step now might be the wrong one. No one even looked at Lachlan. Sneddon ignored him, for to question him would be incorrect.

"What police station did you ring up?" Sneddon asked.

"Balrunie."

"I think you should get on to police headquarters at once."

"They're a long way off—on the other side of the county."

"Doesn't matter," said Sneddon. "Must do the correct thing."

"Very well," said Sam Mor.

"Will I try to get hold of the oars?" asked Ian.

Sam Mor looked at him and then at Sneddon. "What would you say, sir?"

"I think nothing should be done until the police come."

"I was only just thinking, sir," said Ian, who was Sneddon's gillie, "that a boat without oars wouldn't be much use to the police. If the wind gets up they'll drift fast."

Here was a tremendous difficulty for Sneddon. To stop everything was easy. To make a decision on a positive act paralysed him.

After a glance at him, Brown said, "To have the oars in the boat would, I think, be a help for the police."

"If you think so," said Sneddon. "I don't want to——" He drew his palm across his forehead.

"Before you put her in the water again," said Lachlan, in a clear almost ringing voice, to Sam Mor, "I want to show you what I did according to your orders."

Every head turned and looked at him in astonishment. His expression was drawn and hard and his eyes were glinting. Internally he was excited but it was a deadly excitement. I had fancied he could be like this; now I knew. At once he went into action and Sam Mor obediently stooped down and examined the caulked seam. He nodded, "Yes. Will you look at it, Ian?"

Ian got on his knees and fingered the seam, picking out a few strands of the tow with his nails. "That's the fresh tow I gave him," he murmured.

"Then here," said Lachlan. And when the inspection of her port side had been completed, he ordered them to turn her over. On the starboard side the inspection proceeded, and Ian agreed that a certain bit of planking was spongy and would be the better of a patch.

Rubbing his hands on his hips, Sam Mor at last said, "You certainly did a good bit to her."

"I put the cork in her, too," said Lachlan, "and what happened after that the police can find out—and welcome."

The thrust at Sneddon was so direct that Sam Mor said soothingly, "That's enough, Lachlan."

"It's enough," said Lachlan, "when I say it's enough."

Both feet were on his native heath and he was giving us, in the old Highland phrase, the back of his hand. No stag at bay had ever turned more royally upon the hounds. A queer dry thrill went to my heart. The real man was coming out.

175

"Have you anything to plug the hole?" Sam Mor asked Ian.

Ian looked at him and had to think of what he had said, then he moved with a drugged reluctance, but not before I had seen the hard light in his eye, the fighting light, that Lachlan had roused. Charlie and Willie stirred in a slouching manner. Lachlan might be their butt many a time, but what they wanted to rouse in him might have surprised themselves.

With his knife, Ian whittled the round bit of stick which held down the forward bottom boards, wrapped his khaki handkerchief round it and rammed it into the hole, while Willie got two boards ready to act as sculls. The boat was launched and Ian and Willie set forth, paddling slowly but quite effectively.

I saw Ian, as they approached the first oar, glancing over the surface of the water and realised that he was looking for the cork. If he found the cork there, it could mean that the cork had come out while the Major was afloat alone. It would be the Major's affair. Lachlan had only to stick to his story. That, no doubt, was why Ian had suggested retrieving the oars.

But I knew the cork wasn't there.

That the Major had gone so far from shore alone without noticing that the cork was out of the boat was possible but hardly likely. And, anyway, the flow of water into the boat wouldn't have been so fast but that the Major, when he did notice it, would have had plenty of time to row ashore before the boat filled. Unless in a startled scramble he had lost an oar and then lost his head.

From the police angle two points were clear: first, Lachlan and the Major were known to have rows, and on this particular occasion Lachlan admitted they had had such a row that he had told the Major he was

finished with him and had stalked off home; second, if
it had come to a struggle by the water's edge and
Lachlan had drowned the Major, here was as near a
fool-proof way of covering up as could readily be
imagined. But why did Lachlan admit they had had a
row? Because that was his only possible reason for not
being present when the Major was drowned. It was
known they had rows and Lachlan was cleverly making
use of the fact.

However I thought of it, it looked bad for Lachlan,
though difficult to prove if the Major's body, when
recovered, bore no marks of violence. The police would
grill him, though, pretty hot, and when Lachlan was
hot the words came.

Ian and Willie were rowing back and Sneddon, after
his taste of command, was a trifle restive. He had
begun looking around as if to impress all possible detail
upon his mind. He probably read detective stories;
there were a few paper-backs lying around in the hotel.
I saw him look from the parts of his rod, with the large
hook on the tip of the point, to the rocky ledges. If the
Major had got back so far under his own steam he
might easily have failed to haul himself up the foot or so
of rock—a very difficult thing to do from deep water.
Sneddon must have thought of this before starting out;
the long rod would be a sensitive gaff. I saw his eyes
wander. He followed them, looking at the ground for
marks or tokens of any kind. At that moment he was
disturbingly like one of those simple pertinaceous
characters in a detective story who make astonishing
discoveries. I felt it coming. I saw him stop, then dart
on the cork. And I could have palmed the thing with
the utmost ease.

There was no stopping him now. His strangely naked
butler's face assumed a masterful dignity. He had the

177

boat drawn up and tried the cork in the hole: a tight fit.

"You see that?" He turned to Sam Mor. "Try it."

Sam Mor tried the cork in the hole. "It would do," he said.

"Would do?"

"I didn't know the cork," replied Sam Mor.

"I know it," said Lachlan. "Will you let me see it, please?"

Here was another difficult decision for Sneddon, who had put the cork in his pocket. He took it out as if it were alive and might escape. Lachlan took it from him, examined it, tried it in the hole, then handed it back. I could see he was puzzled. He said nothing.

Sneddon could not resist asking, "Well?"

Lachlan maintained his silence.

"Most of the corks are all the same," said Willie.

"That can be investigated," said Sneddon, made confident by his own surprising success. He turned to Brown. "You think we should continue the search?"

"Seems human to me," said Brown.

Sneddon thought for a moment. "All right." He addressed Sam Mor: "You and Ian could try out there below where the boat was."

"Very good, sir."

I could see Sneddon was really anxious to have a go with his gaff, and when the boat was under way he put up his rod. Willie and Charlie moved off for a few private words. Brown strolled after Sneddon to watch the gaffing operation.

I was amused at the way Sneddon felt for the bottom as if he might be into a monstrous fish at any moment. His beam stuck out roundly.

I had to glance at Lachlan and found him looking at me.

178

"Think he would make a good poacher?" I asked quietly, glancing back at Sneddon.

I heard Lachlan shift on his feet as if he had been released.

"I want a few words with you after," I said. "Wait for me round the corner of the hill." I spoke casually without looking at him.

Just then Sneddon got into something.

"Not beginner's luck?" I muttered and walked towards them, for they were only twenty yards away.

Sneddon was excited. "I feel it giving," he said to Brown. But it didn't give very far. I could see he was stuck in something that felt soft. He struggled away for a long time, risking more and more strength on the pull. When as a last manœuvre he tried to release the hook by pushing it back, the point snapped.

"Hard luck!" I said.

He looked at me. I took off my hat and smoothed my forehead for the hat was inclined to grip it.

"Hallo!" said Brown looking at the boat. "They're stuck, too."

They had been for a little while, and no matter in which direction Ian pulled the boat the irons held the bottom. They tried every angle and every length. I have never seen two men so reluctant to give up. Sneddon grew impatient. "They'll have to cut it," he said in quite a loud voice. Sam Mor looked across at us, then he went into a long conference with Ian who finally tied the end of the rope to some bottom boards and dropped them overboard as a marking buoy. They would have another go yet to save a good rope. Then they rowed in and pulled the boat up.

"I'm sure we'll all be the better of something to eat," said the mild hospitable landlord.

"It was folly trying without the proper implements," said Sneddon.

"It's a foul bottom," said Sam Mor. "Very foul."

"Let us go," said Sneddon.

"Will you be going home for your food, Lachlan, or——"

"Yes," said Lachlan.

"Well, you boys better be off then and when you've had something to eat we'll be seeing you."

"Very good," said Ian, and with Willie and Charlie he set off on the short cut.

Sneddon, Brown, Sam Mor and I took the track to the car. Nearly half way there Sam Mor said, "Where's your hat, Mr. Urquhart?"

"What!" I said, my hand to my head. "Hang it!" I turned back annoyed.

"Will we wait for you?"

"No," I cried. "I'll take the short cut."

I hurried back, found my hat where I had left it and Lachlan round the hill.

"Sit down," I said, for I was winded. "I didn't want anyone to know about this meeting. I haven't got long. I want to help you all I can. Things are not looking too good."

"I can't help that, I told the truth."

"Did you tell them you saw me?"

"I only saw your head for a moment. It was none of my business."

That stopped my breath. I looked at him for he wasn't looking at me. Good God, it couldn't have been in his mind that I might have been with the Major *after* he had left him?

"Did you tell them yourself?" he asked.

"No," I answered soberly. "Please listen to me. I only saw you both for that moment, then I cleared off.

I never liked the Major when he behaved like that, so I beat it. The trouble, as I see it, is the boat, and the trouble with the boat is the cork."

"I put the cork back in her."

"Yes, I know, but the cork wasn't in her when they brought her ashore. Mr. Sneddon has it in his pocket now. You know that?"

"That may be. But I put the cork back."

I wiped my forehead genuinely. "Look! My evidence may be very important. Now I'll tell you exactly what I saw and heard in these few moments." As I told him, the scene came back so vividly, for I was trying to be absolutely precise, that I not only saw the boat but saw her stern inshore. At once I questioned him.

"In the end I had to slew her round to get her stern high and dry to get at the seam that was leaking."

"When I saw her the stern was still out of the water?"

"Yes, just ready to push off, for I had done about all I could to her."

I let out a huge breath. What had worried me was this: if the boat was wholly in the water and the cork out of her she would simply have filled before anyone went aboard. But with the hole out of the water and the cork out of the hole, the Major might have pushed off and rowed quite a distance before realising that the old tub was leaking more than usual. The explanation was perfect, the truth obvious, and with some excitement and all the lucidity of which I was capable I laïd it before Lachlan.

"I put the cork back in her," said Lachlan.

It would have been maddening but for an air of rectitude about him that made his expression remote and cold, not in a stupid but in a sensitive way. It was almost, I fancy, an instinctive reluctance to be mixed up with crime, as with certain diseases. Positively tribal.

Sticking a dirk in the Major would be quite a different thing. He plucked a piece of hill grass and put it between his teeth, then dropped it, and I thought of Catherine.

"All right," I said. "We'll all be cross-questioned by the police. In describing what happened you'll tell them you saw my head for a moment. I'll tell them exactly what I saw and heard. Is that clear?"

"Yes, thank you, that's clear enough."

Then I knew that he saw it all. "And as for that blessed cork, all you can honestly say is that *as far as you remember——*"

Catherine stopped me. She was standing at a few yards, like a wan apparition of herself. We were sitting in a small dip of ground and I had been so concentrated on getting Lachlan to follow me that I was certainly startled. I got up at once. She had come in on my right shoulder and might have been there for some time. As Lachlan turned to her I saw her eyes dwell on his face. She obviously knew the whole story and her quick shallow breathing was tremulous.

I told Lachlan I would have to hurry, nodded to Catherine, and off I went back round the hill. I stumbled along at a great pace, wondering why on earth I hadn't been able to go on talking coolly, why I hadn't brought the girl into the talk, for she would have put some sense into that father of hers. I should have spoken to her anyhow. Heavens, I could have shown her by a certain detached cool behaviour . . . I heard a swishing behind me and swung round. It was Catherine with my hat.

I took the incredible piece of headgear from her. "Thank you." I could not say another word.

She swayed for a few moments as if caught by the feet. Choked with tumult, I looked at her, and she gave me a strange wild glance. Then she turned away.

It was humiliating to an excruciating degree. I

paused several times on my way to the hotel and once at least sat down. What I called myself could hardly have been improved upon. Coming from her meeting with Menzies, that meeting with Menzies . . . to find her father. . . . And me, without a word. . . . She would have read me like a book.

And I had been so detached over the simple matter of the Major's drowning that I had thought myself in touch with real life at last, that nothing could upset my ironic appreciation of the human comedy.

I didn't amount to much, and by the time I had washed my hands and entered the dining-room I was cool enough to appreciate the subdued air of those who were awaiting their soup. As I sat down there was complete silence.

The silence grew to an intolerable pitch that no one could break, not even the barrister. Then the footsteps began coming down the stairs. I must confess my skin caught a slight shiver. There was never any mistaking the Major's tread. In comparison Sam Mor, though nearly a head taller than the Major and heavier, was light on his feet. Down the stairs and towards the door. The door opened and the Major appeared.

The widow screamed. Everyone got up. There was, for such a company, a most unusual commotion.

The Major seemed taken aback and wanted to know, with a well-chosen grunt or two, what all this was about. "Drowned," he replied to Sneddon, who had managed to stutter the word, "who said I was drowned?"

"Lachlan, your gillie—he came—he said——"

"He sometimes says quite a lot," admitted the Major. "Are you implying that on this occasion the wish was father to the thought?"

The Major always could get the better of Sneddon.

But the women were clamorous to know—— The door opened and Johan appeared with four soup plates

on her tray. When she saw the Major the tray tilted
and the plates slid to the floor. The policeman and Sam
Mor passed the window.

The Major handled the situation with skill. I could
see he was enjoying himself in his fashion. The policeman never appeared, and all Sam Mor said from the
doorway was, "Well, well, is it yourself, Major?" He
was beaming over the backs of Johan and Ina who were
cleaning up the mess on the floor.

The story the women got out of the Major seemed
natural enough. Lachlan had apparently been showing
the Major what he had done to the boat and the Major
took the opportunity to reply that it was high time
something had been done, that they were a damned lazy
lot and would let property fall to bits under their feet
before they would take their precious hands out of their
greedy pockets—"or words to that effect," said the
Major. "He had the temerity to question my accuracy,"
said the Major. He supped his soup. "So I became more
categoric. He developed his line of argument and
presently departed in high dudgeon. He has a considerable capacity for high dudgeon." The Major broke
bread. "After that I had to fish on my own or not fish
at all. I decided to push off. The stern of the boat was
just out of the water, so I pushed off. It took me a
little time to notice that water was pouring in from
somewhere below, and I decided the cork wasn't in the
boat. Unfortunately I moved rather quickly and knocked
an oar out of the rowlock and it slipped over. I reached
for it too far and, well, there I was in the water. It wasn't
far from the shore and I managed to land, but pretty
blown."

"How awful!" said the widow.

"It was wet certainly," agreed the Major. "I wrung
my clothes and put them on again, then kept going.

Must keep moving. When I got here not a soul about, no one answered, so I went to my room and had a stiff rub down. Took a drink and a couple of aspirins, then got under the blankets to work a heat up. Didn't fancy pneumonia. I simply fell asleep."

"How extraordinary!" said Mrs. Sneddon.

"How do you mean, extraordinary?" asked the Major.

"That you should have been asleep when we were nearly all off our heads."

"Of course when I found the cork," Sneddon began.

"What cork?" asked the Major.

"The cork of the boat. I had a pretty shrewd idea by then that something unusual had happened. As a matter of fact——"

"What sort of cork?" asked the Major.

"Out of a whisky bottle, that size."

"Did you smell it?"

Sneddon took the cork out of his pocket and smelt it.

"What I don't understand," said the widow quickly, knowing the Major's playful moods, "is how one never thought of going to your room."

"Possibly, ma'm," replied the Major with a charming glance, "an excessive modesty."

The widow smiled in an almost skittish way.

The old Turk had all the strings in his diplomatic fingers and what might have been a flat anticlimax developed into a lively discussion of lochs, boats, gillies, corks, leaking seams, local characteristics, personal idiosyncrasies, with some mimicry of Lachlan and Sam Mor. The Major and the barrister rather fell foul of each other in an analysis of laziness, the barrister sustaining a plea of *genius loci* and the Major of genius my foot, but it was well argued and in longer sentences than are normally acceptable at table or, for that matter, anywhere else by such a pleasant sporting company.

As they trooped out the Major did not, so far as I could see, even glance my way.

When Johan brought my coffee her hands were still inclined to tremble. I wondered how she hadn't heard the widow's scream and the commotion before arriving with the soup.

"Their voices are that loud always," she said, "I never thought."

I was surprised to find she was quite inclined to talk, and when it occurred to me that had the worst happened it would have been bad for the hotel she said it would have been bad for the Major, too.

"Not to mention Lachlan."

"Awful," she said. "Poor Catherine got into an awful state."

"I'm sure she would."

"Yes. She doesn't like it sometimes." Then, as though realising where she was, she murmured "Excuse me," and withdrew. She was certainly upset.

Catherine wouldn't like the wordy conflicts between the Major and her father. Everyone would know it was a sort of game, but when the Major went round the bend, he was too forthright, too brutal.

It was difficult not to laugh when thinking over the whole incident. It had seemed so absolutely certain that the Major was a goner. Yet how simple and natural the explanation! The afternoon was a dead time and even had the old cook, who was probably lying down, heard the Major she wouldn't have answered. They would be used to his ring or his bellow down the long crooked passage. Besides, the Major mightn't have bellowed as loud as all that. There would be no harm in leaving Lachlan to get the fright of his life. That was a thought. The ironic devil!

The irony came seeping in with the evening. All at

186

once I felt flat and miserable, as though the anti-climax to the Major's adventure suddenly released what I had unconsciously been keeping under. Heavens, had life got any sort of pattern? Everything changes as you look at it, everything is an illusion, like the Major's death by drowning. And even if he had been drowned, what the hell, I thought quite irrationally, and got up.

I found the landlord round by the garage. Behind his smile I could see his relief. In fact only now did I realise what a terrible affair the Major's death would have been for the hotel, the landlord, for everyone.

"It looked damn bad for Lachlan," he said, with a touch of awe.

"Has anyone gone and told him?"

"Yes. He did wrong. If he wasn't going to carry on with the Major he should have come to me, not gone home. That was his only mistake."

"Do you think you could let me have a bottle of whisky? The Major has been so generous with his and I should like to stand him one."

"Our quota is not that big," said Sam Mor with an expressive mixture of doubt and innocence that was very intricate. "Well now, let me see, it's not easy."

I appreciated his difficulty so much that I said I could not take the bottle unless he charged me for it at the rate of individual drinks.

"I won't charge you that," he said, "but maybe we could compromise at three pounds."

I thanked him very much and accompanied him into his small office off the passage. When I asked him to join me in a drink, he poured out two but would not let me pay. In his own room the first one would have to be "on the house". Somehow I was greatly taken with Sam Mor and when he accepted a drink from me it was with the remark, "Och, well, it's not every day

187

we raise a Major from the dead." I could see he was a fairly abstemious man, but this might well be a mellow night before the cock crew. We talked about the day's happenings, and some of his observations were so unexpected, yet so utterly natural, that I laughed until the whisky shook out of my glass. I was safe in a cubby hole in the dark centre of an old world and when he casually asked me if anything was doing around the white house I could not, did not want to, reply.

"Not much," I said. "Do you ever see him?"

"No. I haven't spoken to him for many's the month."

"Does anyone?"

"No. Even the postman, if there ever is a letter for him, pushes it under the door. That dog is not safe."

"Tough-looking brute."

"You got on all right with him?"

"We had a long talk. An extraordinarily brilliant man."

"He's all that, I'm sure. But I liked him."

"Did you?"

"Yes. There's something in yon man."

"You think so?"

"He doesn't need to bother about little things, so he's good company. He was whatever."

"What can anyone do?"

"See him again. It's the only way to bring him back."

"Why?" I asked. "Where do you think he is?"

Sam Mor looked at me and apparently was doubtful of my shift of expression. "God knows," he said. "His wife was a lovely woman and if you don't bring him back he'll follow her. That's about it." There was a slight hardening in his voice. He took a bottle from a case and said, "I'll have it sent to your room."

I paid him and left.

The twilight was deep and grey-glimmering and I

did not want to face it. As I wandered off I was suddenly assailed by an extreme bitterness. None of them knew about Catherine, I thought, about the intrigue that was going on under their noses. It was the first time I had let the word intrigue sound in my mind; the ordinary common intrigue, I thought; perfectly natural, of course. Finding consolation elsewhere for the loss of his Annabel. And comfort. All the comforts. Who would blame him? Not me. If there hadn't been so much humbug about searching for Annabel it would have been quite all right. But, Christ, that stuck in the gizzard!

For a short space I experienced what I don't care to remember. Emotion carried on beyond my darkest thoughts swept through me like a river.

No doubt Catherine was the cause of this. Yet all the time I knew she wasn't really. To think of blaming her was unspeakable. I didn't. It was Menzies—and those dark roots where we had got tangled. I cannot explain this. To have it all torn away seemed worse than having life torn away. Heaven knows what something had formed in my mind about it, what had gathered round the roots. To talk of illusion now was silly, thin and silly. And the emotion that surged beyond what I couldn't understand, though yet I felt I knew, was black and drowning.

I had never before entered this shadowy region in person. Something like it, perhaps, I had tried to imagine, for primitive religion was an aspect of my work that had long fascinated me. Here the usual academic "explanations" I had always mistrusted as products of, in particular, last century's rationalism. When the rational mind out of a well-bred tradition of liberal thought and evolutionary "progress" attempts to account for the manifestations of a primitive religion

189

by trying, in effect, to extract from inside itself its lowest or most primitive modes of thought and then attributing them to the savage, it misses the reality by more than a mile. Apart from the unscientific nature of the complacent process, the dynamic element is completely lost. When Darwin, after almost a lifetime of research, of supreme exercise of the rational faculty, tried to resurrect his early appreciation of Shakespeare and music, he found he couldn't. Such subjects bored him, so he realised that atrophy had been going on. All Freud's speculations on God, with reasons annexed, left me dissatisfied. What appeared so objective and rational was so often, it seemed to me, a concealed subjective process. Not that I would mind such a process if I could trust its subjectivity. But where the capacity for deep subjectivity has itself become atrophied what can it achieve in the way of activating, and thus understanding, forgotten modes of being?

When Catherine moved me so profoundly by humming a traditional air, whom could I trust among rationalists to explain me to myself, when I knew that they do not know how I am being moved? And, if that be true for a simple tune, what about death and God, here and the hereafter?

I was putting some such bouts of thought and feeling off my bows like a boat in a stormy sea, when I saw Catherine coming. That she should be there coming towards me through the early night was the eternal lonely miracle. It affected me in an unforgettable way.

We had to stop.

"You'll have heard about the Major?" I said.

"Yes."

"Very glad."

It may have been an effect of the deep dusk that turned her face, her expression, the vivid quality of life in her whole body, into a witchery that could be borne only by gripping it physically; either that, or by clearing out. Again she had the quality of being arrested in flight.

"We are pleased," she agreed and smiled, glancing away.

"Went to his bed and slept!"

"Charlie told us."

"Your father will be relieved."

"Yes." She hesitated. "He was grateful to you."

"For nothing! We may get our own back on the Major yet."

Presently I saw her making her effort. "I told Mr. Menzies about the rent."

"Good. I needn't do any more about it."

Her features troubled. "I don't know."

Only then did all my wits come back. She was going to ask me to help him, to help them both. I was able to look at her and see her as she was.

"If it's money, I could manage that." I actually experienced relief at being able to control my voice.

"He doesn't seem to mind about the factor."

"He'll have to, I'm afraid, if he doesn't want to get thrown out."

She understood that.

"Mrs. Maclellan thinks it might be the best thing for him if he did clear out," I said, watching her closely now.

Her eyes flashed onto my face and surprised my thought. I held her eyes. Her colour mounted, her brow gathered, her look went over her shoulder along the path. I had made their relationship too naked, but I didn't mind.

"If I can help in any way," I suggested.

191

"I'm very late," she murmured and began to go, then suddenly went.

"You didn't come well out of that," I said to myself, amused. Remarkable how a woman will make use of a man for her own ends, and all the more when she knows he is interested in her. No conscience about that.

Menzies wouldn't give a damn about the factor. Anyway, she wasn't quite sure if he would go through the act of paying the rent and thought that I might prod him on or something. Her feminine contrivances and anxieties wouldn't be too clear to Menzies. Even Annabel's had been beyond him for long enough.

Then I suddenly saw Annabel in my mind, but I couldn't look at her.

11

By the time I got back to the hotel, all the guests were aloft except the Major. About to enter the dining-room, he returned my cheerful greeting with a throaty mutter. On this night of defeat he was my elder blood brother.

"If you would care to join me in a drink," I said, "I should be honoured."

"Bit late."

But the bottle was in my bedroom and in no time I was pouring him a hefty one.

"Hm. What did he charge you?"

"Three pounds."

He nodded and grunted, but seemed secretly pleased.

"Robbery."

"Still, he could make more out of it by selling it in drinks, and if his quota is small——"

"Bloody robbery."

"Anyhow," and I raised my glass, "I hope you will permit me to welcome you back. We were very upset."

He gave me a shrewd look then drained his glass right off. He had had a good nap in the afternoon and seemed in finely destructive form.

Of course he had not forgiven me for my behaviour at our last meeting, my reticence and sudden departure, and with the long memory of the elephant he was going to balance the account. I was all for paying up, with interest.

"So you took part in the dredging operations?"

"I watched Mr. Sneddon while he gaffed you, driving the hook well home, in ten feet."

"Sneddon was solemnly begotten." He made of it a ponderous utterance which he yet contrived to savour.

"He rises to your dry fly."

"Hmf. Broke the point of his rod, his precious rod. I thought he had a steel centre."

"With his deductive powers he dominated the scene. In fact, he found the cork."

The Major eyed me. "He has probably taken it to bed with him."

As I laughed the Major indulged in somewhat lewd comparisons with short words.

It was going to be a rich night in which much could be forgotten. I had even a sudden inspiration of what had probably happened at Loch Dubh.

"You pumped me the other night and then scuttled," said the Major, like an elephant dealing with a photographer at the right moment.

"You were very interesting."

"Really?"

I told him I had been disturbed.

"What about?"

"What I wouldn't tell you I wouldn't tell anyone. Besides, I rather fancy they want to sling him out of his house."

"You're astonished?"

"Aren't you?"

"No. They cannot help trying to stop a man going to hell his own way."

"Going to hell?"

"Are you one of the interferers?"

There was a distinct pause.

"You think I should go with him?" I asked.

"You know better than that," said the Major. "You are that kind of fellow."

With, I hope, less obvious satire I thanked him for his high opinion. We were getting on, and the Major was getting a lot of his own back. Which was fair enough. He did me the honour, moreover, of dealing with my bottle without any tedious polite preliminaries.

Going to hell was a subject on which he had decided opinions. Not going to hell was a parochialism which he characterised acutely. If occasionally and abruptly his language was lurid it was also colourful, fulfilling the useful function of emphasis. More than once the school-boy word resurrected the schoolboy in him, and this shift in time could well make one wonder if any of us ever really did grow up. It made me laugh in the wrong place, for at such a moment the Major was sweepingly serious, yet this odd shift in the planes of appreciation was something he did not misunderstand, for his eye had the cunning of the serpent that curled its length in the bottom of his chest.

He sold the contents of that chest lock, stock and bottle under various guises. Much of it, I realised, was old rubbish of a hankering kind. And the local people he spoke of were not always those he inwardly saw, so that "they" and "them" were a motley crew in far-flung places. As I was the nearest concentrate of them all, he had something to work on, and his sense of grievance, to which I had so recently and unintention-ally applied the spur, fed on itself as presumably an elephant's wouldn't. So he would never stop taking it out of me, if only to prevent the indignity, the give-away, of his own descent into self-pity. It had all the makings of a good party.

And I took my opportunity when it came in order to keep things going. When he declared that he would not trust certain people as far as he could throw them I suggested that the distance involved would be less than that to which he might well have thrown the cork.

"What cork?"

"The cork of the boat," I replied smilingly.

His mouth caught its ugly pout. "What are you trying to say?"

"Pure theory, based on the notion that you thought Lachlan was due a lesson. You pulled the cork out of the boat, chucked it away, then launched the boat upon the waters with a mighty heave which sent her over twenty yards before she settled down."

"Clever, aren't you?"

"It took a bit of working out," I agreed.

"What more did you work out?" Brutality has always a witless air and we had been getting on so well.

"What does more matter? I was trying to be amusing."

"You think an accusation of that sort amusing?"

"Don't you?"

"I think you're bloody impertinent." The explosion was at hand. I would take it in my fashion, as Lachlan did in his. I had a swift intuition of the relationship between Lachlan and the Major. I was now of their company—and beyond the three of us, Menzies.

"I'll admit it and beg your pardon—if I'm wrong." I looked into his eyes and knew I was right.

He looked into mine and asked thickly, "What the hell's wrong with you?"

"When the sunlight goes out death sits in the chest," I said.

"Good God," he said. "Literary!"

"I have heard the beating of a distant drum," I replied, evoking the Rubáiyát once more.

196

"What?"

This confounded mixing of tilting planes and noisy associations plainly aroused his curiosity to the point of inhibiting the explosion. A certain enthralment invaded his fleshy face. "Death sits in your chest?"

"I have carried the burden of it about with me all day. So——" I shrugged.

"So what?"

"So what is one bloody cork more or less?"

He had certainly never expected to be bewildered, and all but laughed. Even his harsh throat could hardly smother the music in a run of liquid l's and a's as he invoked Allah and poured himself a stiff one. There were possible journeys of discovery ahead. He gathered himself richly and swept nothing from the table. "What death?"

"Just death. Enough for one day, surely."

"Anything wrong with your chest?"

"Not so far as I know."

"Parables, uh? Aren't you a bit young to be talking to me like that?"

"You called me an interferer."

"Ah!" He had hold of something now. "So that stuck!"

"It's a thought," I granted.

He looked at me quite a time. "Worrying you, uh?"

"Yes."

"You would save him from himself if you could?"

I had nothing to say to that.

"The magnitude of such impertinence."

"I admit it." From the place where death sits in the chest one gets a good view.

"Well? Isn't that enough?" probed the Major.

"I don't know."

He pushed the bottle towards me and I took it.

"What don't you know?"

"I may not matter, but Menzies the creator does."

"How do you know?"

"Just by knowing. Though epistemology is quite a subject."

Satisfied I was not trying to be clever, he asked, "Why should we create?"

"God knows."

"Do you believe in God?"

"I feel as if I don't and couldn't, but I'm not sure. In my business I have to deal with God a lot."

"It has left your mind untidy."

"Possibly. Do you believe in God?"

"No."

"That makes it easier, tidier."

"Which shows your depth," said the Major.

I nodded. "I know there is a Roman dignity, difficult to come by. But that kind of dignity must kill the worm of inwit or there's hell to pay. So we seem to come back to hell all roads." He could take what he liked out of that. At the moment I wasn't caring; even though I had a vague feeling of having drawn his picture.

If the Major flouted the Roman dignity that was in him, it found itself now and then in the orotund phrase. "A Daniel come to judgment," and his mocking interest crawled like the worm.

"In profound moments it is difficult to get away from the literary. We go on hearing the beating of that drum."

"Boom! boom!" said the Major in unexpected but expressive criticism. I was glad to be able to smile again.

"That's all," said the Major. "Boom! boom!"

Laughter shook me in an empty place. "Ta-ra-ra-boom-di-ay," I agreed.

"Hell's back roads," said the Major.

"And heaven's back teeth."

"And all the rest of the bloody rot," said the Major with a poet's splendid assurance.

"A new FitzGerald." My evocation of the translator of the Rubáiyát was respectful.

He eyed me. But I wanted him to go on, to become more sweeping.

"Do you know why they beat the drum?" His face came forward.

"Because it deafens them."

He drew his face back. He was reluctant to laugh as though the compliment would be beyond my deserts. All the same his body shook like a quaking bog. "And drowns the memory of this impertinence," he quotingly capped me. "H'm." He drank. "They have no intelligence."

I fancied the immediate reference was to his fellow guests, but his field was wide. I wondered aloud if intelligence was the word.

"Costive," he said at large and as his body rolled it emitted a comment on its own. "That for them."

"Gone with the wind," I agreed.

"Huh! huh!" He rolled even more dangerously.

This was talk in its existential moment. From Paris to Vienna went the Major, and from Vienna to Persia which seemed to have a hoodoo on him. Anyway, Persia reminded him of the road to hell and every man's imperial right to go his own way thither, so he came back to where we were. But his clean sweep of the European scene hadn't missed the more gruesome corners, for a paragraph in his posted *Times* meant more to the Major than to most and kept him up to the minute in a remarkably post-dated fashion. When

199

it came to characterising hell he was ready with all the horrid minutiae which could not be gainsayed.

"Hell," he started off, and as though the light had been patiently waiting for this moment it began to gainsay him with a peculiarly dramatic aptness. "Hell!" muttered the Major to the white globe as it slowly dimmed to its ghost.

"Shall we wind up the universe?" I asked him.

"Hmf!" He tried to move, then thought better of it.

"I think I'll manage it," I said.

"Candles," he ordered.

As I brought the two candles from the hall the Major was sitting upright in a deep gloom like Pluto. I had never encountered a scene at once so infernal and classical. Around his glassy unwinking eyes the candle flickers danced. I turned off the gas tap and sat down.

"So you wanted to wind up the universe?" He could not let me off even with a trifle.

"We are all God's deputies."

That shook him, but he managed the word "Anthropology!" with unfaltering enunciation still. His classical learning even prompted him to a final criticism: "The two-faced. Janus."

I agreed. "Good and evil in one."

"Good and evil," said the Major, like one sampling mildew. "Christ!"

"Christ was good only. That was the marvel."

"What hellish logic!"

I looked at him and slowly nodded.

"If you put good and evil in, they're there," said the Major, "and you can't opt out of them when it suits your fancy. God and the Wrecker. The Wrecker, uh?"

"God when he wrecks."

"The wreck. Hmf. What's he doing in that house?"

"Hunting the Wrecker." I felt my own mouth pout wryly.

"Going mad?"

"Far from it."

"Can't you speak plain, damn you?"

"I would if I could, but good and evil is a difficult topic whether you like it or not. How can I follow where he hunts? So how can I tell you? If you think I'm hiding anything, you flatter me. What are you hunting, for example?"

"Trout," said the Major.

It was a peculiar silence.

"Gone all metaphysical. Hmf! An odd road to hell, but one of them," he allowed. His fleshy countenance was amused but in the uncertain light I fancied I saw a gleam going deep into his face where the schoolboy sat, the good schoolboy who had used short words to free him from the mamby-pamby ideal and make a man of him. But I was probably seeing too much. I couldn't look anywhere without seeing too much.

We wrestled over good and evil until he suddenly pinned me down to an exposition. "Very well," I agreed. "Newton was one of the two great Englishmen. For him space was an absolute and time was an absolute, and everything fitted into or was explained by his classical mechanics. Rationalism was satisfied absolutely. The billiard balls clicked and having clicked moved on, while prediction, which is science in action, unvaryingly said: I told you so. Thus it was and would remain, time without end, amen. But it didn't remain quite like that. Queer things happened in and about this blueprint. And to explain them Einstein decided that space and time were not absolutes but aspects of a unity which embraced them in a four-dimensional time-space continuum. All of which I am aware you know very

201

well, so I need not pursue the analogy needlessly. I would merely suggest for your consideration that good and evil may be two aspects of an unknowable unity as it manifests itself to us inside the four-dimensional time-space continuum."

"Good God," said the Major with a faint horror, "you speak like a medium in a seance."

"I feel like it, too. But I don't see any spirits about. Do you?" I looked around on the off chance.

The Major took up his glass. I took up mine and assured him I felt as if I spoke in a glass darkly.

As he drank he muttered deep about words.

I remembered Shakespeare, but all I said was, "I had only begun."

However, I seemed to be holding my own with him and this suggested a pleasure fine as a thin wine of which the bouquet could hardly be remembered and the dry aftermath was delicately ashen.

As for the Major he was clearly experiencing a curious dichotomy, for his Roman dignity wanted to be itself in all its crushing weight but the worm of inwit, horribly fascinated, wanted to see what might yet crawl out of me and my words. I was amenable to suggestion and when he ordered me to proceed I proceeded:

"As children we had puzzle pictures, drawings of trees, for example, in the branches of which was a face, if only we could find it. At first we searched and searched, turning the picture all ways, but could not find the face. There was no face, we decided. There could not be because we could not find it. Then suddenly, in a flash, we saw it, composed of twigs, and it was so obvious now that we stared at it and wondered how on earth we could have missed it."

"Is this a parable," asked the Major, "with esoteric reference to the face of God in the tree of life?"

I realised I had stopped talking and, looking at his face, saw the congestion of interested contempt.

"That's an idea," I admitted, "for I hadn't been thinking of God. It had merely come upon me that I had given a short account of the history of science."

The Major could not speak for a moment, then he said, "Come upon you?"

"One can become either too finical about words or word-drunk," I allowed. "But if they proceed out of a sudden apprehension of clarity, as in the case of the face in the tree, they may usefully be taken, I suggest, with a pinch of salt."

"Are you trying to be infernally funny or are you in a bloody trance?"

The tragedy of the Major was that he couldn't forget himself and I saw this with a certainty that moved me strangely in his favour. How he reviled me did not matter. That was not what mattered.

"Perhaps it's the whisky," I said.

But this annoyed him, too, as though I were now deliberately suppressing thoughts which I could not expect him to follow. He wanted it all roads. He had to be the dominant chord. I really did my best to let him sound so for a time, but at this point I must confess that while all this was going on there was something of me following its own thought. Just as, when a boy, I had suddenly seen the face in the tree, so when I had spoken of Einstein's physical system, if I may so call it, I had had a glimpse of a psychological or mental system that interpenetrated the Einstein one and yet stood back from it or beyond it, much as the unity which embraced time and space as aspects of itself in the four-dimensional continuum stood behind the continuum. Though "stood behind" is meant much in the sense of the reality, whatever it may be, that "stands behind" the mathematical symbol. Was the *ultimate* unity a *mental focal point?* Not that I asked myself the question. I simply *apprehended* the focal point as I *saw* the face in the tree.

I would not have launched upon these verbal flights had it not been for what followed after the next question. If the basis, then, of Einstein's or the physicist's universe is very different from the ordinary physical world as appreciated by our senses, might it not well be that there is a mental universe different in its ultimate workings from the ordinary workings of our minds? It was at this point that the words spoke themselves in my mind: "God has a different system", and I remembered Menzies using them, and I saw his face.

This had a silencing effect upon me.

It shouldn't have been before time from the Major's point of view, but he was in a very complicated predicament. I was resolved, out of deference, not to make a move to bed until he moved, but movement was now his difficulty, and I dared not offer assistance. However, he got up and, like his servitor, I bore both candles. My head was preternaturally clear and my feet like thistledown. I went before him, tacking a little as I half turned to shed light upon his course. Solidly he reached the first step and laid hold of the rail. I stood off as he took the companionway and mounted step by step, rolling a little with the ship but holding fast and proceeding steadily. As he reached the landing I was behind him, so he had to come about to hail me.

Now there was a narrow spindle-legged table against the off wall, which was yet all too near, and upon this table sat a glass case containing a stuffed trout of, originally, 11 lbs. 3 oz. As the Major came about he shipped a heavy one and yawed. At once I set the candles on the floor, but thistledown is a light material to stand on and before I had deployed my resources the

Major was pitching straight at the table. My tackle was low, but when the trout leapt from the surprised table, I was there on the floor, spreadeagled, and the glass case was fielded intact upon my yielding stomach.

"Well held!" said the Major as he slewed up to a sitting posture against the wall. He nodded with Roman recognition and did me the honour of accepting my help once I had got the table and the trout in position.

"Damn good night." He made a gesture which handsomely abolished reservations. He shook hands with me. "You'll make hell of it yet." Then he passed into his room.

In my own room what had thinly covered me fell away and I felt like death and freedom. Catherine was more remote than a hare in the grey twilight of a morning. I felt cold. All day through daylight hours and evening, recognition had been inwardly gathering of what had happened in the dell. Without form and void, and I was excluded. I had not thought it would mount like that, unobserved and stealthy, like a sickness in the chest. But more than sickness was the void beyond, without shape, where there was nothing to be looked at ever. What I had thought of Menzies was now less than a cry echoing down a far cliff. The shiver passed over the still water and the grasses nodded. The extreme bitterness of misery is haunted by the beauty that will not be seen and is only half remembered. I pushed my braces off my shoulders. That old Roman! I thought. Fancy his being bothered about his old ego still! It was wonderful. I got into bed and the cold sheets made me shiver like an aspen. But I hung on to the Major. He had been on his road a long time now, and God alone knew what was waiting for anyone like myself entering on that road. So he had taken the cork out and chucked it away. The very distance he had chucked it, the undeliberate short distance of a sudden uncaring anger, showed the mood he had been in, evoked him in the impulsive act complete to the ugly pout and the cunning in the eye. The cunning was for his story. Inevitably a schoolboy story; and a beauty! As he could not have slept all the afternoon, he must have heard the voices and the preparations. He laid low and said nuffink.

I did not want to leave go of the Major, who was companionable, for to leave go is to be more vulnerable than before. So I shut my eyes and wondered if he had actually wet his clothes in his room for his story's sake. You should at least have wet your trousers, old boy, otherwise Sam Mor may get slowly thinking. But just then, I decided, the Roman might well have interfered with the schoolboy. It would be beneath a Roman's dignity to wet his trousers. Ah hell! I thought, tired of his trousers. So I thought of hell. But the basic trouble with the Major's hell was that he didn't believe in hell. He didn't even believe in retribution on the way to the hell that wasn't there because he was a dominant chord. Having chosen his spot, he could command what destiny was left him and tread Lachlan underfoot and in fancy. And Lachlan would in the usual way just go away off home. Even retribution was an illusion. I made myself so tired thinking of what didn't matter that, wide awake as I was, I fell asleep and dreamt of hell.

12

Hell had a dominant chord; this developed into a truly remarkable cacophony, with dark bowed figures yelling like the lost souls they were and an occasional glimpse of a wolf's jaws that howled until hell's roof shook. The tempo and pressure increased until hell as a bomb blew up the universe and I awoke before the hurtling masses of the spheres could fall on me. Then I wondered if I was awake, for the terrifying hullaballoo continued. It was outside my door. I got out the wrong side of the bed, because it was the right side for my home bed, and hit the wall a stunning crack. I got off the wall and found the door and pulled it open.

Ay, it was a scene, that. The Major's room was a belching fiery hell, and darkly silhouetted against the flames was a dancing figure with a tail that Ian the gillie tripped over. In his wild lunge Ian clasped Willie round the waist and thus they grassed each other in mutual embrace even as they sent young Charlie reeling. Before the figures of pandemonium on either hand, assortedly garbed and half garbed, could close the breach I went in, lightly clad, and tripped over the tail but saved myself a full toss by knocking Ian flat again. Strange indeed were the yells and screams and screeches in this horrifying milieu, for those coming from the stairs who wanted to see the fire blocked the ladies and gentlemen from the principal guest rooms behind who wanted to escape, while all the time the widow raised a weird wail of what may well have been mixed motives. With my hand I followed up the cold hairless tail to the fork of the dancing figure and then I heard its voice, and then I knew with a wild amaze that it was Lachlan upon his peak of derring-do. From him amidships proceeded water at a terrific speed as though jet propelled, as indeed it was, for the brass nozzle was narrowed to a small jet and the whole force of the hotel's gravitational water supply was ramming itself through this orifice with the hiss of a snake pit. As Lachlan's tail resolved itself into the garage hose I came somewhat abreast of the proceedings and perceived that the seat of the conflagration was the Major's trunk whose lid stood open above the exploding matchboxes and the rolls of candles. Smoke and steam, married by Lachlan's jet, belched in a convoluting honeymoon that threw a passionate tongue of flame up a window blind, but if it did, Lachlan, like the expert shot he was, caught the flame on the wing and killed it dead while the window panes drummed to his jet like a wisp of demented snipe. It was excellent work and I could afford to take my bearings, if such could adequately be taken in that infernal gloom, for of the candles only their flames could be seen flickering as in some Eastern embassy where the Major had had his thousand and one nights and was now resuming them in a single impression for the diplomatic bag. It was then that the Major's voice was heard.

I inclined left and there like a Roman half risen from his sarcophagus sat the Major in his bed. His solidity was strangely enhanced by thin veils of smoke now curling about him and by the bared chest which his unbuttoned pyjama jacket disclosed. And the Major had hair on his chest. I have observed that such a

208

phenomenon will draw the human eye, male or female, before the facial expression above it is rightly appreciated. On this occasion it drew more than the eye, for at the sound of his master's voice—though no, that is a public phrase and Lachlan, as a Highland crofter, admitted no man as his master—at the sound, then, of that well-known voice Lachlan pivoted, taking, very naturally, his nozzle with him, and the jet hit that mat of hair for a bull's eye. The jet spattered. It spattered loudly, dead on the mark, and radiated in a spitting spume which veiled the Major's face. At such a moment a curious helplessness, perhaps induced by surprise, seems to deny a man the exercise of that impulse which, in this case, might well have swung the jet off its mark. It was only when the valiant Major had to give way and lean back against his pillows that I turned to Lachlan. But already the jet had waggled and Lachlan, swinging it as he did his twelve-bore shotgun, caught the chair on which the Major had dropped his clothes and tumbled it like an overgrown rabbit; then, after pausing for a moment to reload, he continued his swing and got a couple of candles with a beautiful right and left before once more knocking fumes out of the now smouldering trunk.

This marksmanship was too much for Ian who was his deadly rival at the annual clay pigeon shoot.

"Gi' me a shot," said Ian, and I could see now that he had drink taken.

But Lachlan would not give him a shot. "Shoot you on your own shoot," he said and I perceived that he had drink taken also. They were about to settle down to a stand-up argument when Charlie nipped the nozzle from Lachlan and, after giving the far candle too much of a lead, got it so to speak with the second barrel and sent it spinning. Among all three a slight fracas then ensued. As they swayed or staggered towards the door, Lachlan emerged victorious with the nozzle held aloft like the ardent prize it was, for its stream, hitting the ceiling, fell back upon them in a drenching rain which they, being well bred in their climate, did not observe. But as Lachlan, whose back was now to the room, brought the nozzle down, the jet caught Mr. Sneddon, who with recently aroused desires for leadership had been pressing close to the mark, fair between the eyes. Perhaps he could not fall backwards because of the human press behind. In any case, he collapsed as if pole-axed, and then followed a slight misadventure for which Lachlan was always a little sorry. At one moment there was Sneddon's face; the next moment it was gone and there was the widow's. Most unfortunately her mouth was open, for she tended to be vocal, and, to get the horrid matter over, the full jet at close range dislodged her dentures in no uncertain manner. She went down with a choking gargle.

It was then that Sam Mor, mellower than his oldest dram, hove in sight and Lachlan turned back into the room and was confronted by the Major on his two feet. Perhaps the Major did not trust his feet; trusted, rather, a terrible immobility, as he glared at Lachlan.

Back glared Lachlan, his nozzle at the ready by his hip, its jet passing so close by the flank of the enemy that anyone of less heroic mould than the Major would have been buzzed.

"You fool!" said the Major. "You blurry ass!"

As Lachlan's hand jerked in a well conditioned reflex, the jet caught the Major below the belt.

Yet the Major did not even perceptibly bend, much less double up. Stoical was his stuff.

Realising what he was hitting, Lachlan raised the nozzle and the jet travelled up the Major's person until it reached his mouth. It steadied there, as though Lachlan realised he had at last a cleansing operation to perform of long standing.

"You can put the cork in it now," he cried aloud.

And at that the jet fell as if slain, and we all stood bewildered, spent and nonplussed while the drooping nozzle dribbled its last. Sam Mor entered, having (as we later learned) turned off the bathroom tap to which Lachlan had fixed the hose, for the hotel was his property, bought for an old song, which he had considered very dear, when the estate was broken up. "Well, well," he said, choking a little for he was fresh to the fumes. Then he saw the Major. "Dear me," he said, as he went and put a friendly hand on a half nude shoulder. "Why, Major," he declared with mild concern, "you're quite damp."

The Major did not reply. Perhaps shock supervened. After a few gentle words Sam Mor led him to his own room and there stripped the pyjamas off the now sagging figure, rubbed him down, and turned him into his own warm bed.

It had certainly been a good night, an outstanding party. Even as a Highland ceilidh it had probably had unusual features. And it was not over, for in some measure now I was a host, with strangers over my doorstep. I turned to Lachlan who seemed rather directionless without the hose that Charlie was looping back to the bathroom while craning heads peered at the scene of the mêlée before retreating in loud undertones. "You'll need one after that noble service," I said. "Come with me."

There were quite a few candles bobbing about to light our way downstairs. And then I saw Catherine in a green robe with negligent hair and a white throat. Corks, drowned Majors and burning hotels vanished like the bard's insubstantial pageant before eyes that scattered me with their concentrated concern, their strange affright. I never even thought of my pyjamas, neither the scarlet nor the black frogs (presented by a female cousin in the country for a service rendered) because it was not my pyjamas which held her regard, it was my face.

"Get some warm water, Catrine, and a sponge," said Lachlan her father.

She turned away and I stepped on space, but with the help of the rail and Lachlan I recovered my balance. My God, I thought with profound humiliation, she'll think I'm drunk, too.

In the dining-room I found my bottle and the two glasses where the Major and I had left them. The bottle seemed light as I shook it against Lachlan's candle. I perceived it was empty. I thought this very strange.

"Never mind, sir," said Lachlan. "Bottles have that way with them."

From the sideboard I took a bottle which had a sup in it, and two tumblers.

"That's the Major's bottle," said Lachlan.

As I poured the contents into the tumblers Lachlan cried, "Hold! hold!" when it was too late. "It will go to my head," he said with humoured doubt but taking the tumbler.

The door opened and Ian's head appeared.

"Come in," I called hospitably.

He came in, followed by Willie, and both declared they were only wondering where Lachlan had gone. But there was no more whisky in the sideboard, so I brought out two glasses and began distributing what was in my tumbler, whereupon Lachlan insisted on sharing out his, and four sizeable drinks were on the table and some comments of a jocular nature when the door opened and Catherine's face appeared.

"Come in," said her father, and she entered with a steaming basin. After looking doubtfully at the polished surface of Johan's table she set the basin on the floor and was turning away when her father told her to hold on. He then wished me the best of health, and so did Ian and Willie, and we all drank the Major's whisky in health and good fellowship. Then Ian muttered something occult about Sam Mor and went out, followed by Willie and his thanks, and by Lachlan who offered the hasty remark, "Just one minute." Clearly there was a tacit agreement that this was not the diplomatic spot for an interview with the landlord.

"What's wrong?" I contrived to ask.

"Your face," answered Catherine.

I had never thought of my face as indecent but my fingers found adhesive flakes below my nose. Blood! I was utterly bewildered until I remembered the crack I had given the wall on getting out of bed.

This was amusing. "How amusing!" I declared. "Must have stubbed my toe."

Catherine's lashes withdrew her eyes as she turned away.

"Am I supposed to wash myself with this?"

"Yes," she replied generously.

"I can't see," I said. I got down on my knees before the basin and lifted the full sponge to my face and the warm water ran down me in a stream and I didn't make matters better by trying to stop it below my throat with the soppy sponge, not that I could be wetter than I was, and the warm water was encouraging for I had begun to shiver.

All this was too much for her and she took the sponge from me, dipped it in the water, squeezed it, and then

213

with a touch light as thistledown began to dab and smooth my upper lip. It was strangely maddening, like being kissed by her eyelids, and her eyelids were very near as she bent over me.

Because I couldn't trust myself I merely said, "You are very beautiful."

She regarded my mouth critically, dabbed at one corner of it and at the nick in my chin, then at a cheek bone. To stop my making a fool of myself, I murmured, "Have you ever seen a slender grass bend over in the grey of the morning?"

The door opened and Sam Mor's head appeared.

"Beg pardon," he said and closed the door.

I caught Catherine's left hand. "Don't go," I pleaded.

"Hsh!" She shook her head at me, withdrew her hand, lifted the basin and said coolly, "It's clean now." Then she walked away, leaving me on my knees. I stayed on them for some time.

A man rides his folly as an ass. The toss has to happen to be believed even by himself. Deeper than ever plummet sounded. *Plummet.* What a fantastic word! Like *bollard.* Boom! boom!

A prey to such annihilating reflections, I got to my feet and with cold indifference, for bitter chill it was, passed upstairs and observed inside the Major's room Ian and Charlie mopping up, and over by the bed Sam Mor and Catherine feeling the mattress.

"I'm afraid it wasn't the fire your father was aiming at here," said Sam Mor.

They saw me but I went into my room and removed the gay if sodden rags my country cousin had sent me as evidence of her sophistication. She had been in temporary difficulties conjointly with the curate and the local banker, "though how I cannot imagine."

My main trouble was with my teeth, for though I rolled myself in the bedclothes into a papoose, they clattered like castanets. I knew what was wrong with me now, what it had all been working up to: a pneumonia.

Let it come, I thought. But no, though hell should explode into carbon molecules I would not be an object of self-pity. Let it come if it must, by all means.

What came was a gentle knock on the door; the castanets stopped as by magic.

"Come in," I whispered.

The door opened and Sam Mor came in with a candle in one hand and a large cup of tea in the other. "Something to warm you," he whispered.

"How kind of you," I whispered.

"Take you that, now, and excuse me, for I have them on my hands yet." And having lit my candle, he withdrew.

Whispering so that his guests be not disturbed, this big-hearted man whose hotel had been all but ruined. Such greatness was beyond any plummet of mine, or bollard. If only Catherine had not looked more ravishing the closer . . .

I drank the tea and resigned myself for good to my penitential bed. Then I arose, dressed, opened the door quietly and listened. But the passage was now deserted of all sound except a snore with a broken valve. I stole along to the infernal room, went downstairs in a dusky gloom, and then step by step along the crooked way. Murmurous was the distance and as I stood by the kitchen I heard Ian's voice: "Just one more small song, Catriona, before we part."

"Be quiet!" said Catherine.

"No, no," said Sam Mor. "It's high time you weren't here. Off you go, now, all of you!"

I retreated, and back in bed once more did not even wonder how this strange night had arisen. The grey of the morning was in the window; its loneliness I knew, for even the pneumonia had deserted me.

13

The inquiry took place after lunch in the dining-room. Sneddon had brought Sam Mor in to the barrister and Brown, and though Sneddon looked askance at me, I sat on at my small table. The Major had not so far appeared that day. The ladies were in the sitting-room, awaiting the result of the court's inquiry.

Sneddon led off but quickly became involved, and, in short, asked the defender to explain how so shocking an occurrence had occurred.

"It was just a celebration," said Sam Mor sadly.

"Celebration!"

"Just that." Sam Mor shook his head. "I am more sorry than I can say, gentlemen, if any of you were inconvenienced in the smallest way——"

"Smallest!" repeated Sneddon. Then in a rush it came out, including the widow's lacerated gums. "Drunken, damnable, we might all have been burned to death. As for that two-faced gillie, Lachlan, I unmasked him at the loch. Because of that he used the hose in a way—in a dastardly way, which I cannot overlook. I warn you now that we take a very serious view of what happened, and you may as well know it."

"Well, well," said Sam Mor, "I can only say I regret it. As for Lachlan, I am afraid the simple truth is that but for his prompt action we might all have been burned to death indeed. And if in his excitement his hose waggled a bit it may have been as he says that there were that many lights about it was difficult for him to know with all the smoke that was in it what was a light and what a fire and he only tried to make sure by extinguishing what he saw when he could. Moreover, as for the passage-way behind Lachlan—and you may be sure, gentlemen, that I cross-questioned him very severely about this, for I have run my hotel in a way that has never been called in question before—as for the passage-way, he says, and you can judge of the truth of what he says yourselves, gentlemen—he says that such cries and screeches came from the passage-way that he wondered more than once if fire had broken out in it. He was only doing his best. And if he wet anyone he couldn't have wet them more than he wet himself; and he was so happy, so pleased, at having saved us all, and saved the hotel, that it was only after difficulty I got him to empty his boots before walking back along that long way to his home in his sodden clothes."

There was silence in court for a few moments. Then the barrister asked gently, "How did the fire break out and how was Lachlan here at that hour?"

"It may look a strange coincidence until you know what happened," said Sam Mor. "And this is what happened. Everyone was that pleased that the Major had come to no harm, for he is well liked generally, that they decided to celebrate. They were also that pleased that nothing was going to get Lachlan into trouble that Ian came to me and asked me if I would sell him a bottle of whisky so that himself and Willie and Charlie could take it to Lachlan's home for the occasion. I was that pleased myself that I said I would give him a bottle at cost price. Now they only just had the one bottle, which was a good thing as it turned out, for some of them when they get an offer like that are not beyond hinting that in that case their money could run to two bottles. One bottle it was, and in Lachlan's house they had a ceilidh. Now in this hotel at the same time the Major was having a long talk with Mr. Urquhart—over there. Well, when the bottle—I mean the ceilidh was finished in Lachlan's house, Lachlan convoyed them back here, for they felt something might be going on. Now about that very time, as Mr. Urquhart is aware, the Major and himself decided to go to bed, having finished their talk. Well, I am not going to answer for the Major, but from such words as I had with him it would appear that the Major had taken his candle to look for something in his trunk and laid it on the corner of the open trunk. He then turned away to do something—I am not sure what, maybe, and he can tell you himself—but when his back was turned the candle, it seems, fell into the trunk which contained some very inflammable material. So you see, gentlemen, everything that happened was perfectly natural and sober. It could happen to anyone. What was so lucky for us all was just this: the trunk was by the window and as the flames ran up, the boys were coming round the gable-end. Of them all it was Lachlan who was the quick-witted one, for he not only got the hose but ran with it to the front door and found it open. The last one into the hotel must have left it open and I think that was Mr. Urquhart. Am I right, sir?"

"Quite right," I called.

"In a word, gentlemen, and I speak very seriously," said Sam Mor, "if it hadn't been for Lachlan, God knows where some of us might not be now."

"Will you chalk him up two large ones from me?" asked the barrister.

"And from me," said Brown.

"And from me," I called.

"And from me," said Sneddon, with cheeks like the hot poker flower.

"Thank you, gentlemen." Sam Mor bowed. "This will not only make Lachlan happy but all of them. It is beautiful of you to be so generous."

"And of you," said the barrister, "for being more generous."

"Sir!" said Sam Mor who had been a sergeant in a World War, an officer in the Home Guard, and had the courtesy of an enemy general but his own smile.

It would have taken anyone out of himself, and some hours later I was able to consider my part in the night's proceedings with less uncertainty. The Major, it seemed, had decided to stay in bed with his swollen throat. The barrister had so much neglected correspondence on hand that he had arranged for the day off to suit Dan Maclellan who wanted to attend a "displenishing sale" at a farm some distance away.

The general disruption of the night had carried over to breakfast, and Sam Mor, in compensation, had laid on a reputable lunch. He had also now laid on a story which flowered in the joy of the Major's return from a watery grave. Really it had been a gala night. And it had cost them nothing.

The sea wimpled to a sportive wind and I had the notion that if I wandered upon it and swam deep enough I might come up clean. So down I went to Dan's cottage and encountered his lady breaking peats. I had to tell her what she didn't know about the fire, which wasn't much. I liked her face more than ever and she had the good manners not to introduce an alien subject into a laughing story. The small boat? Well, she wasn't sure, so away with me she went. The tide was far out but coming in so it would be a long launch. Yet I did want,

I explained, to have a look at the birds on their ledges.

"Ach, I often give him a hand," she said, with a youthful fling. And expert she was with the small wooden rollers under the keel.

Afloat, I gave her a salute.

"Mind," she called, "don't go too near the rocks."

So I rowed away, wondering if Dan realised his luck. He probably never thought of it. Beatitude.

To be sea-borne was a divine suspension. And I was becoming fairly expert at remaining suspended. Indeed it seemed to be about the only way to keep alive in this hectic place. Far as my eye could travel not a soul moved. Not even the dotted sheep and three if not four cows. Peace. Tearing across this scene of primeval good will and summer sleep came a motor car from the gap in the mountains like a large black beetle stung fiercely behind. Towards what end?

How people rushed on for nothing, to miss the tide at the end of it most likely, not to mention the ferry boat that plied to the Land of Heart's Desire.

My perilous reflections were answered by the sea at the south end of the island with a faint: *Boom! boom!* I lay on my oars, listening. It would not come again, and then it came from inside the high dark rock structure: *Boom! boom!* A jut of cliff above me was like a Roman jaw.

With feelings of gratitude I rowed on until I opened the west wall of the island, which soon had shut the land away, and there I was with riven cliff and ledges from which birds took off, guillemot and puffin and razorbill, and the calling gull. But not many. Too early to be home from fishing. The white of a dozen eider drakes yonder where the water swirled about the tangled end of a skerry. A cormorant. Was that a northern diver? It was! My glasses . . . his ardent head swam into my round field, his throat, his striped neck, but the thrust of the head, the wildness, the Arctic seas, oh beyond wonder! . . . and down he went, not head first like a tippeting duck or cormorant but head last, as if the sea in its depths had taken him.

What had I been doing on land with the sea here? And down he came, the fulmar, in the loveliest of curves and up and over . . . and down, without a single wing-beat. Carved out of wood, he seemed, hypnotised and hypnotising, a flying shuttle of the continuum, weaving a spell which held the cliffs to silence. Beyond the spell, cliff and ear listened, and perhaps some ear heard.

Marry, ay; where did music come from?

Then words die away if you're lucky. The sea's breath is pristine. A puffin is a comic parrot in an older than boyhood's circus. With the right change in your pocket you enter in.

So I pulled along the west wall; the eider drakes got up; the light off the water entered my eyes as I followed and lost them. I just pulled along; in time passed beyond the island; and the mainland came back in the distance and the white house. All but mindless now, on I rowed in the direction I was going which was towards the Head, until the white house fell away and here were cliffs again. But the stack made me lie on my oars. It was like a great long loaf parallel to the cliff behind, with a passage between. I turned the boat's nose for the northern entrance.

The passage was narrow, the cliffs sheer into the water on either hand, and as I looked up they leaned over. *Here where deep sea precipices lean.*

"A haunt of seabirds" was an old expression that got its meaning back. When a seagull fell from a high ledge on outstretched wings, and, still descending, lifted its head to cry from a throat of bone, walls reverberated and caverns sounded. There were many gulls.

I rowed clear, and looked back, and rowed slowly on.

Thus I came under the cliff where the white house was and saw its raddled face in bounding descent to a beard of skerries. I glanced from under my brows at the crest where a head might appear, so that if it did appear I need not see it but pull slowly on, watching the birds. But suddenly I was bothered and resented this. I realised I was tired, too, for I had rowed a long way. When I saw the cave I thought I would stretch my legs.

The foot of the cliff was shelving rock, broken and runnelled, that the sea, from obvious markings, clearly covered at high tide before surging on into the cave. The tide may have been half in; anyway, it bore me over a safe passage until the boat's forefoot grounded comfortably and I got out and gave her a heave, then took the painter with me for I was barring all accidents to Dan's property on a rising tide.

The arch was somewhat squat though I needn't have stooped. Inside the height grew, but there were protuberances, sloping strata and a rather slimy footway. As the cave narrowed it took a twist to the left and, curious to see how it ended, I looped the painter round a boss of rock. Old seawrack showed the high tidal mark as the floor rose. Rounded stones now slid noisily underfoot and I wondered if anything alive might hear me. There is always the possibility of a beast, if only a seal: the black body and the two eyes in the dark corner. Even a thought of tusks, for the paleolithic period was a long one in our story. When I saw what I thought was a crouched body, I did not believe it but I was instantly wary. I even fancied I saw the pallor of teeth, low down. I growled. The rotting seaweed had a peculiar stink. Nothing moved and without shifting my eyes I slowly drew out a box of matches and struck one. When the match flared I was so astonished that I failed to shield the flame and it went out. I moved in on the dark mass and struck a second match. It was a rum puncheon.

The match burnt my fingers and I stood lost in the dark for a little while.

I carefully examined that cask all over. What I had thought were teeth was a whittled stalk of white wood used as a spile low down on the near head. A smaller spile stuck up on top of the cask. When I rapped there was a hollow sound. Full, it would hold over a hundred gallons. Wondering how much was still left in the cask, I tried to lift one end but my feet gave. There was certainly a lot in it yet. It was shored up on two sea-worn baulks of timber. How could one man have got it here, even on top of a spring tide?

But under these superficial questions were those that could hardly form.

Perhaps from the wrecked ship the cask had floated free. From that wreck, that night.

Around the rocks . . . bobbing and eddying . . . thrown back by the smashed waters before it could smash itself, borne by tide and wind, knocking now and then, until it came below the white house.

A present from the Wrecker, I thought.

Bitterness is the colour of rum, dark brown. It gets squeezed out and beyond it is darkness. If only the cask had got squeezed and smashed . . . but God knows. Kick the spile out and it would empty. Not that one would. The colour of fate; dark brown, the colour of blood from a deer's throat in the heather. Unlawful things I saw and didn't see, because I could hardly look at them. Every dodge fell from me and, stark, I turned away, seeing nothing until I saw the shape of a man against the cave's twilight.

The shape did not move. Then it moved. It was Menzies.

So the interferer had got caught, the sneak had gone underground too far. God, it was bitter.

"I have been prospecting," I said.

"Been working things out?"

"No. Just bird-hunting."

"Is the cask all right?"

"Seems to be all right, yes. But I confess I hadn't thought of it."

"No?"

"No. I thought it was a sea lion." I couldn't see his face properly because his back was to the light.

"Your boat is afloat."

I staggered as the stones gave and he came behind me. I picked up the rope off the rock and we stood at the cave mouth with the sea almost at our feet. As I pulled on the painter, he sheered the boat's side off a ledge. His face was expressionless, without the suggestion of a mood of any kind. The eyes were clear and alive and for a few moments they rested on my face. I let them move over it and then met them. But they merely had a look at my eyes, too. They had nothing against me in their remote or near curiosity.

"Can I give you a lift?" I asked. And when he had got into the boat I hesitated on the oars, wondering where he wanted to land.

"That way." It was the way I had come, so I started pulling. His appearance like an apparition had not worried me. The simple explanation always turns up. But now, as I had to look over the stern anyhow, I could see the rock wall as it went on past the cave and swung south. Just beyond the cave, the sea came in deep to the rock for quite a distance; again, on the seaward side, along which we were now rowing, were sheer spaces where no foot could pass. His only approach must have been down the cliff. I made myself look at that cliff incuriously but found no possibilities there.

"Are you in a hurry?" he asked.

"No," I said and slowed up.

His expression was tranquil and interested, even touched by a faint wonder which brought the suggestion of a smile to his eyes, as though, in fact, it was rather wonderful to be afloat again. I knew the feeling precisely and it did me a lot of good. I looked about, too, as we rowed slowly on. Now and then his eyes came critically on green swirls round a rocky point or on the flight of a bird. I saw things more sharply than I had done before. When his eyes followed a fulmar their expression went glimmering deep inside him to such old familiar seascapes as I felt might yet haunt myself. This haunting indeed seemed to be something I already vaguely knew, like that earlier fantastic traffic with the other landscape. The absence of talk instead of inducing a sense of strain completely dissipated it.

It was when we were well through the narrow channel that I saw his expression come alive as a man's will when some beloved woman enters a room. I could not help looking over my shoulder.

Where the channel ended the dark edges of the cliffs ran with light. A magnificent gateway. Beyond, the sea floor had a golden sheen from the evening sun and extended to a horizon that ran its fabulously distant line against an ultimate of molten silver. The sea moved under us and we were suspended. The three words he let fall irradiated that seascape with so profound a humour that they matched it. "The slow movement." If I say the moment was translated in some divine way I know I can only appear to exaggerate. I did not look round at him. I could not even be quite certain that he meant the slow movement of his own symphony. Nor did it matter. After a moment or two I dipped the oars in.

When we got out to the open he asked for an oar.

I handed over an oar, shifted a rowlock and asked where he wanted to land.

"Aren't you returning to Dan Maclellan's?"

That was all, and we rowed back along the outer wall of the island, where bird life grew noisy at our late approach.

When we ran the small boat ashore Dan was there. A medium-sized man, stocky, brown and easy on the move. No introductions. We might have been meeting often.

"The wife would like you to come up for a cup of tea," said Dan when we had hauled the boat up.

In the moment's silence I glimpsed Menzies' face and said, "For myself, I must get back or Sam Mor will have a search party out."

"Well, perhaps some other time," said Dan at last.

We both thanked him and as we moved off I saw Mrs. Maclellan trying not to appear beyond the gable corner. Still, that I had Menzies with me was something she would appreciate. And, frankly, I felt I had achieved something myself.

We followed the path near the cliffs, though my easiest way would have been up the burnside to the road. But I could leave Menzies just short of his house, then cut across by the sheepfank, or even go up the dell, for all I could hope for now was a late sandwich in an hotel that had fallen upon such dramatic times.

The dog met us at a combination of ditch and fence. In a recess under a flagstone were the milk pail, a small basket with eggs, and a loaf wrapped in paper. Because of a few awkward steps I took the milk pail from him and we went on in single file. Near the house I stopped and handed him the pail, which he took.

"Like a drink?" he asked.

"Well, thanks." As I went behind him towards the door I was annoyed with myself. I was spoiling everything. His invitation had certainly had no warmth. I suppose I still had to tell him that I was not a spy.

As we came into the room in which we had talked he stood for a moment looking at it. The dim light seemed to emphasise its disorder. Its smell was fairly thick, too. Heaven knows what passed through his mind at that moment, but I felt him grow more impersonal, colder.

"Sit down," he said.

It was too late for excuses to go away now. He went out and came back while I sat there wishing to heaven that I had had the sense to leave him with his slow movement. It had been a beginning. I could have called on him again, arranged another sea outing. However, I would go immediately after the drink, and perhaps turn that into a more friendly way of making the invitation.

He was in no hurry. The two washed tumblers had beads of water on them.

"Can you take a raw egg?"

"Yes, thanks, but——"

"But what?"

"I don't want to invade your store."

Whether he first reduced the rum with water I don't know, but when he had got an inch or more of rum and milk in a tumbler he cracked an egg and dropped it in. The yolk floated whole in the liquid. He added a little more milk. After he had dealt with the second tumbler in the same way he handed it to me.

The yolk filled my throat before it slid down with a

soft elongated ease and, after draining the glass, I was left with a fragrant velvety aftermath that was pleasant. I said so and he asked me if I would have another. I wouldn't and he took the tumblers away. When he brought them back they were rinsed again.

I was on my feet now and thanked him. "The landlord will be wondering what's happened to me. The hotel had a very disturbed night last night."

"Oh."

"Yes. The Major all but put the place on fire. In fact he would have done if it hadn't been for his gillie, Lachlan."

"Lachlan?"

"Lachlan Macgillivray. Catherine's father."

He remembered. "There were one or two Lachlans."

My heart was thumping, for Catherine's name had slipped out before I could stop it. His cool manner was beyond me. I had nothing more to say. The hotel fire did not seem to interest him and I was just about to take my leave when he said, "Catherine told me about my rent. You seem to have been interested in that?" He looked at me.

"I apologise. I had no right to interfere. But I had heard the business mentioned in the hotel and happening to meet the factor, Maclean, in Balrunie, I somehow spoke to him about it. I thought there might be some mistake."

He stood quite still, looking now out of the window where the evening was gathering fast. What he was thinking I had no idea. There was something unearthly about the fellow.

"You offered to pay the rent?"

"Yes." It was humiliating.

"And he wouldn't take it?"

"He asked me if I was acting for you and I said no.

So he wouldn't have anything to do with me. Quite right, I suppose."

"Right," he echoed with a faint undertone of irony. And then I realised that it was the absence of this irony that had so changed him today. He turned from the window and poured out a couple of drinks. "One gets out of touch with the old tricks. Until you came I hadn't talked to anyone for a long time."

Did he mean he hadn't been talking to Catherine for a long time? What on earth did he mean?

"Sit down," he said and I sat down.

He did not refer to Catherine again nor to the rent.

Probably it was I who got the talk round to cliffs and caves for at least I had not been up to any human trick when I found the cask of rum and I wanted him clearly to understand that. I referred to the fire again; explained how the Major and I had been making a night of it and how annoyed the Major had become because I would not tell him what transpired, especially in the matter of drink, during the long night I had spent in the white house.

"Why didn't you tell him?"

His directness could turn my mind into a blank. "Because the drink didn't matter," I said.

But my reply interested him and I realised I couldn't have made a better one. It summed up the whole talk the Major and I had had, and Menzies got it complete. A myth or a symbol or a tail-end sentence: it was all the same. And once understanding is achieved in this way, any kind of sally becomes possible, even companionable.

And the cave in prehistory was a fecund topic. Compared with our civilisations it covered so vast a period of time. Man's gestation in the cave, the long incubation of his unconscious. This was old subject matter for any anthropologist and I thought I knew a lot about it until he drew out of me more than I had hitherto been aware of. Not that he implied he knew more. But he knew more, all the same, of what was essential. The sudden light in a dark corner, the sunlight on a black piece of exposed earth and, if you watch, you'll see something wriggle. That is always surprising. Accumulated knowledge can squeeze out life.

And then, out of some rare need for balance, he began telling me how he salvaged the puncheon of rum.

It was an extraordinary story, a dark cave battle. He had returned to the white house in the afternoon after burying Annabel. They had buried her in the churchyard which I had visited. (And let me say here that the stoneless grave which I had thought was Annabel's was in fact hers.) He had come back to the house alone, and the house was empty. The neighbours had done their duty and now he needed to be free of his neighbours. The house was empty and silent. And the things that had been hers were there, the terrible mute things. In that silent house one empty room led to another, and he saw her shoes and the dressing-gown behind the door.

He went out and saw the cliffs and heard the mournful gulls and he saw the sea with its rim in the west. To the edge of the cliff he went and looked down and he saw the cask bobbing against the cave's mouth. He watched it until he felt himself falling over so he looked around and no one moved anywhere. When he looked down again the cask was there and, farther along, some wreckage, with a human arm and the back of a head. He decided to go down the cliff.

He did not expect to be able to go down the cliff and the fatal aspect of this knowledge was far in his mind. The desire to get away from where he was had grown on him very strongly. If he slipped and fell he would be on the way—or at its end. It was the way Annabel had gone; there was that for company, anyhow. This friendly thought, this warmth in the emptiness, brought all his forces together and freed him and he felt nimble.

There must have been a precarious track down that cliff in olden times and he hit on its beginning. It zig-zagged, using fissures, with knobby handholds for a short drop and sideways movement when a bent knee would have thrown the body off; but not really very difficult, he said, if you had a head and went slowly and took no chances. He deliberately took none and the path suggested itself, step by step. The total height must be somewhere around 150 feet. He reached the bottom.

The tide was flowing, and though the storm was long past and the day calm there was still a dark weltering movement in the sea. It glutted against the rocks and frothed. By timing the sea's impulse he was able to cross three yards of skerry to the cave's mouth without wetting his feet. Then as he waded to the cask he brought the wreckage in sight. It was now in a swirl beyond the skerries and even as he looked it went slap against the sheer cliff. The loose boards were knocked apart and the human arm, a seaman's arm in a dark blue jersey, rose up a little way and then disappeared. He stood there while a couple of waves soused him to the waist, but if the drowned body came up it must have been under the timber. He never saw it again.

The water was icy cold but he struggled with the cask, trying to direct it over a shallow ledge that was in its slewed fashion the cave's threshold. Some timber had been washed into the cave and presently he was able to use a batten as a lever. He worked away like a man possessed and occasionally did have bouts of super-human strength that came from a terrible drive within him to drive beyond himself. "The cask did not matter."

When nearly trapped in the cave he suddenly decided not to be, and, though swept off his feet, he reached the foot of his climb and went up the cliff, the ascent being easier than the descent. The dog was waiting for him on the brink. The brute had been devoted to Annabel.

The darkness was falling. Dan Maclellan came to the door with a creel which contained a warm meat pie, cleaned fish, a loaf of bread, and other foods. "If there's anything we can do for you you have only to say it," he said. He was a little awkward, as though it was not an easy thing to bring such gifts, so he blamed his wife. When he had turned away he said, "If you care to look over, you will be more than welcome." After standing for a few moments where no more could be said, he went off.

So there was the night.

Perhaps of that night he could have made the inmost cave of all caves, but, strangely freed though he was from the personal, he apparently could not face any mention of it. It was late the following afternoon, he said, when he remembered the cask and, taking a hatchet, a gimlet and a torch with him, he went down the cliff.

Being an hour later than the previous day he found the tide in about the same position. The cask was inside the cave neatly held by a batten whose ends he had kicked tight against the rock. The way the water swirled back had helped to jam it, as he had foreseen. He was rather pleased about this and set about wondering how he was going to roll up the cask beyond high water mark. Not an easy job for its weight would be getting on for half a ton. Even had the rising floor been smooth concrete he would not have been able to hold it against the slope, much less push it up half an inch. Where it lay he couldn't budge it. So he inspected the cave carefully and decided that the best place to fix it finally would be well above high-water mark and round to the left in a sort of tiny alcove—in fact in the place where it now rested. As an apparently insoluble problem it might well put in the whole of his second night. He had no desire to sample the contents of the cask.

Before the daylight went he hacked at timber with his hatchet, cleared away slime and rotten seaweed, and scooped out rounded stones. Sometimes he whistled to his job critically like a workman, for as the rising tide came well into the cave it made odd sounds in its swings and roundabouts and tumbles. When he heard himself whistle what was no tune the cold water responded. He wasn't interested, but after a few moments there were five notes. They went back down through the green water to its cold source, wherever that was. Then the cask swayed to the tide and the struggle began.

Very early he nearly lost his leg when the cask came back over the hurried foot that was meant to jam it. But before the bone cracked the next thrust from the sea saved it. After that he became expert with his couple of wooden chocks. With the cask broadside on and a batten under its bilge as a lever to heave when the wave came, he would gain a few inches, ram the chocks home and sit and wait.

It was a slow, cold, wet business, only worth mentioning because it produced a bodily discomfort, a misery, that was almost pure.

A curious detachment comes from this misery, a disinterestedness, and at the same time a commingling with sea, rock, slime. Physical life has reached rock bottom; it has in a mysterious way come home. Something of this can be experienced in daylight, but in darkness, in a cave, there is touch, deliberate conscious touch, a hand grips, even the inside of the head *feels* the near approach of solid mass; while ears hear what is lost in the light and nostrils discriminate a smell into its sources lest there be one dangerous source. It is an elemental traffic which cannot be carried much farther. It generates in time the cold glow of a thin fine delight. That was his first insight.

When he got the cask beyond the slimy rock and among the rounded stones he knew high water was near. The moon was on the wane, but still a few days short of neap tide. He could have done with a roaring spring.

But he had his plan and it was simple enough. From side to side of the cave—about four paces—he scooped the stones away and laid down a couple of battens, a foot or more apart, as rails upon which to roll the cask, with the off end of the rails an inch or two higher than the starting end. On reaching the off end he would relay the rails so that when he rolled the cask back he would gain another inch or two. Back and forth, back and forth, gaining each time an inch or two: the theory was excellent but the practice was fantastically difficult for one man in a darkness that could be defeated at times by a sparing use of a half-exhausted electric torch.

A new country opened up inside his head at this time. Misery and absorption, exhaustion and the effort that went beyond itself, induced an odd conception of static time within endless distance. When he could do no more and slid to his haunch and lay, the awful silence of the empty house would threaten its invasion and then for a few moments he would be given more than his normal physical strength. Of this he was quite certain. And he tried to make it clear by saying that he was aware of using a force which was there, inherent in the complex of the moment, and not gratuitously or supernaturally conferred upon him from outside. I realised that this was his second insight and that it was interesting in a suddenly known and astonishingly way; he was being wary, if not sceptical, of everything except what in fact he actually experienced.

The time came when he admitted to the cask that it had beaten him. "I am going to put you in that corner," he said to the cask, "but not as you are." Considerable relief came from this conversation, if also an ordinariness which carried with it a suggestion of defeat. However, he didn't mind about that now; in a moment he didn't mind about anything except boring a hole with his gimlet low down in the head. By draining the cask of some of its contents he would lighten it. His gimlet went in with a rasping persistence, then suddenly slid through. He pulled it out and a trickle of rum ran into the chimb of the cask. He had expected a spout and was astonished. Off his palm he tasted the stuff. His astonishment grew.

Having shoved his spile into the hole, he began boring into the top of the cask to let air in. To get both hands on the job he put his torch in his pocket. When he pulled his gimlet out the spile was shot from the head and a thin strong stream splashed the stones. It took him a few moments to realise what had happened and then followed a scrambling, hilarious interlude when the bulging cask insisted on giving birth to its rum over the stones and up his sleeves and down his neck, for the torch had dropped from his pocket and he couldn't find the spile. From the urgency with which he tried to stem the stream it might have been the cask's life blood or the cave's. Flat out on the stones, he got a palm against the hole and for a few seconds breathed the heady fumes. After the wild fuss it was an intoxicating peace. Then he had a practical idea: he would strike a match and so find the spile and the torch. His free hand extracted the box of matches from a jacket pocket, opened it against a stone and drew a match out. But in making a slight movement in order to aid the strike his other hand slipped and the stream of rum drowned the matchbox. Only afterwards did he realise that had he in fact lit the match he would have been burnt to a cinder. At the moment it was merely another victory for the cask. Then the cask all but won for the rum hit his face and he swallowed a full mouthful.

Trying to get breath cured him of his concern for the stream of spirit, and in his last gasping roll the torch poked his ribs. After that, phantasy carried matters over into that realm where a stagger is another kind of gesture and responsibility makes way for a new order. This seeming freedom from responsibility was his third insight.

After that there was the cliff in the moonlight.

The vividness of the detail had been almost hallucinatory. But that was the point of the story. Not any dabbling in an extra dimension, not an intrusion from the unknown, but a realisation or evocation of what happened on the spot with the given elements. Only, there were a lot of elements in that old cave and in Douglas Menzies, not to mention the cask, whose spirit was as fiery as that of a man of the Old Stone Age recounting a marvellous hunt. So the span of human experience was long and the implications as many as one cared to make them.

Our talk grew rich and equally vivid outside the story. We took a mouthful of drink now and then, but it certainly amounted to no more than the usual companionable or social gesture. Certain plants don't free their fragrance until the sun warms them. Man finds it difficult to enjoy talking about death and the hereafter until he, too, gets warmed up. But however freed, I might still find it impossible to ask Douglas Menzies how far he had tracked the Wrecker because the question would involve Annabel. Here was an intimacy which I would never dare touch. But the cave was another matter and the cave was "on the way". For the remarkable thing about prehistoric man, even about the sub-man who came before *Homo sapiens*, was that he buried his dead in the cave mouth and believed that the dead lived on. Professionally I could put all this to Douglas Menzies. But the fact, however remarkable (and I confess it has haunted me at times), is still only a fact. What I wanted from Menzies was his—how shall I say?—evocation of the fact, as he had evoked his struggle with the cask of rum, and all that surrounded that struggle, in the sea cave. I wanted him to evoke the cave man in his moment of immortal belief, because already I knew that he had a unique appreciation of other modes of being. Many of us have intuitive glimpses. This man could get the whole field, the integral intuition. He could wander about in it.

And he did wander. He meandered. Sometimes he seemed to me quite illogical and I pulled him up; his words were thickets that obscured the issue so I hauled him back to it. Once or twice, in fact, I wondered if I had been over-estimating the man. There was a lot, it seemed to me, that he only half knew; and many old notions that had been exploded by modern research he would assess needlessly in an exasperating way. For to give the impression that the talking was all on his part would be out of balance. When two are talking volumes the incidence of the noise is both here and there. But I knew more, and because I knew more I wanted to cut the cackle and save time and get ahead to the boundary line of research where a new opinion might be exciting, especially from Douglas Menzies. But no, he would not accept the best authorities; he would loop back and curve on with that extraordinary persistence of his, until with resigned patience I would forget my authorities and pet notions and not only let him go on and on but even listen.

Out of his words something begins to come, something that does not belong inside my closed circle of ideas, and then, in a moment, the face is there in his verbal thicket, like the face in the tree of my boyhood's puzzle picture.

It was as surprising as that and quite exciting.

If I must illustrate this—for mystery is what I would avoid—let us take the simple matter of that ancient hunter at the moment when he has brought down his beast, his red deer, for example, in this very district of Scotland where it is still hunted. The hunt has been a tremendous affair and he finishes the brute off with his rough stone weapon, then claps it on the flank and calls it his dear departed brother. To us this appearance of tenderness and compassion after the brutal slaughter is a form of sickening sentimentality that just can't be borne. It is beyond speaking about, and anyone who goes on and on trying to suggest another point of view becomes irritating if not monstrous. Our circle of sympathy is closed. We don't want to reach an understanding of paleolithic man at that moment, even if we could. All the same, there is a mode of being at work here which becomes, the instant it is grasped, extraordinarily illuminating, and in its light even the concept of the totem animal, the *animal* that is the ancestor of the tribe, gathers meanings which we had not before dreamt of. Much as, by infiltration, we begin to understand the hunting code which the best kind of modern sportsman observes, the man who is shocked to his marrow at the fellow who fires into a covey of birds instead of selecting one bird, the man who will pursue a wounded beast to the end of his resources, who loves his horses and his dogs, and who reacts to cruelty to animals more swiftly and uncompromisingly than any other in the community.

This is admittedly an elementary illustration of a mode of being unusual now but still to be encountered in some degree. It becomes more complicated when we reach the pictures of animals that the Magdalenians painted on their cave walls in the south of France and the north of Spain, a dozen millennia B.C., and that are still preserved in these fantastic underground worlds with their subterranean rivers and chasms. What moved the long-vanished artist to paint the hunted bison with such vivid skill and force in caverns of perpetual darkness? When we have tried to make ourselves feel as "primitive" as possible and have a few labels like "magic" handy, we may think we know.

I found Douglas Menzies difficult here. Actually he did not know much about these paintings and drawings, but in no time I forgot that, because he knew what moved the artist. Here my intuition could only do its vague best. Of course, he had his own experience as an artist, a composer, to draw upon now. When cliffs and seawater are transmogrified into a "slow movement" in a musical symphony odd things have been taking place somewhere. However, I was anxious to get as clear an understanding as possible of specific issues, leaving a larger comprehension to come as and when it might, so I produced the instance of the bison dance, where in a lean time, with no game about, the hunters dress up each in a bison's head and horns and dance in order to compel the bison to come. If the dancers keep on dancing long enough, the watchers on the hill-tops are bound to spot a few wandering beasts in the offing, so the magic, I suggested, may not amount to much.

"I am not so sure," Menzies began as usual. And then we were into that weird realm of extra-sensory perceptions and kinetic forces to which physics so far has no clue. I had to admit that even in our day mani-festations like hypnotism and telepathy implied a means of communication between minds inexplicable in physical terms. Such talk can be commonplace enough and the bison always are or are not, so to speak, appro-priately influenced by the argument, but with Menzies there was always the extra step, that shift into an extra feeling. While telling me about the dancers he was also telling me about something else. The verbal thicket begins to form. I want to pull him back to the dancers, to one thing at a time, but already I know that the unexpected will come and then I begin to feel it coming. This feeling is a peculiarly sensitive condition of arrested excitement. And Menzies was in some odd country now where the tracks in the thicket looped back even on our starting point, which concerned the burial of the dead in the cave mouth, the hunters' belief in an afterlife. The compulsive magic of the dancers takes on an extra significance if not an extra dimension, if dimension can be apprehended as another mode of being. I can see an extra pallor on his face, an extra brightness in his eye. An uncomfortable sensation of movement affects me as if planes of being were tilting, known and unknown. I should do something to stop this, to anchor myself. But I don't; I can only wait for the unimaginable to happen or appear. As I look across at him through the cigarette smoke I see a slight smile on his face; it is the smile that defeats the irony or the impersonal, that makes him human and lovable, and I remember our passage through the narrow channel before he had seen the sunlit gateway to the west . . . and then he had seen it, and his expression deepened in recognition, as if a beloved woman had entered the room. That memory tilts and vanishes before the terrific intensity of what I experience now. But the compulsion to turn, to follow his eyes, is too strong for the cramped reluctance that would defeat it. So I turn round and see Annabel standing in the doorway.

She is different from my mental image of her, much as a living person is different from any memory of that person. I had seen her, I now realise, as a picture, framed in the doorway of my mind: comely, dark-eyed, dark hair and quite still, but with none of the features too distinct. An artist's picture at a little distance.

This face is alive, near, thinner; the cheek bone and the line coming down to the chin are smooth and swift. Her hair is in a natural disorder as though pushed back by a quick hand. But the whole energy of her being is in her eyes. And her eyes recognise Menzies with an intensity that is tragic and beautiful. Yet why write the word intensity when there is a smile in her eyes and why tragic with this ineffable communion between them? I perceive there is also compassion in her eyes, as though a woman at the end bears all. This terrible living quality, this sheer expression of love at its ultimate moment of wordless communion, becomes unbearable and I stir and get up, perhaps, God knows, to make way for her. The movement brings a dizziness to my head, a momentary half darkness, and the door is empty.

When I sit down I feel utterly drained. Menzies is pouring out a couple of drinks. But I don't want a drink. I have only had two or three small ones, well watered. However, my muscles are a bit uncertain and I accept the drink. In fact I take it right off and get up, making my apologies, saying the hotel door will be locked.

He does not try to detain me. He is normal and even considerate, for he says it is dark and he had better see me to the main road. I assure him this is unnecessary, but outside I am relieved at having only to stumble on after the dim figure. Peewits swing up and a curlew or two. The dog is foraging around. The old overgrown farm road has an awkward spot below the sheepfanks and I feel his hand under my arm.

At the public highway I should say something, if only thanks for his hospitality, but I hear his "Good night" and he is gone, so I plod along to the hotel, which is in darkness. But the door is open and I lock it behind me.

As I get into bed I am utterly wearied. I am glad to let go.

14

The following morning I was sorry to disappoint Sam Mor who told me that the Major was having another day off and that I could have Lachlan and tackle for one of the lochs. I should have liked to have done it, but somehow I just couldn't. I wanted to be left alone to moon about, and when I got my sandwiches I wandered into the hills, found a lonely hollow and curled up in the heather. I fell asleep and felt a bit better when I awoke, more alive. The air was cleaner as it sifted around. I observed sky and cloud and the pale tiny buds on the heather and was unaffected by them in a remote not unpleasant way. This remoteness, this not being affected, had its point. An eternity of disinterestedness might be possible. About the only thing that could, in fact. I got up and wandered on.

When I rested among peat hags things were so primeval that I placed my hand against a moist black bank and left its clear impress there. My dearly departed paleolithic brother often did the same. But after starting on again I came back and rubbed the impress out with my foot. I wasn't at all sure that I wished even an imprint of any part of me to last for ever. In fact it was cleaner and sweeter to leave none.

What a tyranny the immortal notion was! Better far to leave nothing of oneself and slip by and away. Everything around me understood this. The mask of conspiracy was perfect and the wind was its invisible messenger.

In the afternoon I drifted back to the hotel for tea. The thought of tea was beguiling, for the long intestinal tract could not as yet be wetted properly by cold water, it seemed.

Sam Mor was in conclave with a gentleman in the sitting-room and as I went into the dining-room opposite, I heard:

"But if the cornice is done up——"

"No," interrupted Sam Mor, "because there is also that small streak—look, can't you see it, coming down there? You cannot just rub that off."

"But that would mean the whole sitting-room, ceiling cornice and walls, would have to be papered and done up!"

"I'm afraid so," said Sam Mor. "We couldn't stop the water coming through from the Major's room."

"You seem to have used a lot of water for all that was actually burnt," said the gentleman.

"You know the old one," said Sam Mor, "about sparing the rod and spoiling the child. If we had spared the water it's not just a few rooms that would have to be done up."

Their voices were so hard and jocular that they must have been in battle for some time. Then they came in and Sam Mor, while he regretted having to disturb me, introduced me to "Mr. Swithin from the insurance".

At once I volunteered my testimony and assured Mr. Swithin that his company was particularly fortunate in the magnificent way the hotel staff had risked life and limb in extinguishing a fire which, but for their instant initiative, would in a matter of minutes have burnt the hotel out.

My grave manner so impressed him that he politely

245

requested my name and address. Even Sam Mor, who had been on the crest of his game, was stilled somewhat to a deeper pleasure. After all, a guest like Mr. Sneddon might have subscribed to an over-indulgence in the use of water, not to mention other liquors, and so perhaps have lowered the altitude of the bargaining level.

"My bedroom," I said, "will also have to be re-decorated."

"I think we have seen all the bedrooms affected," replied Mr. Swithin.

"Not Mr. Urquhart's," said Sam Mor, who could hardly know what was coming.

Mr. Swithin looked at him.

"It gives me no pleasure," Sam Mor explained, "to make out too big a claim."

That one stilled me, too. Then I led them to my room and pointed to some blood stains on the wall where I had bashed my nose.

Manifestly the bedroom would have to be papered because no landlord could expect a guest to sleep within blood-stained walls. The blood was mine; it had flowed as a direct result of the fire. Whether, in these circumstances, I was liable for the cost of redecoration I did not know but I would be obliged to Mr. Swithin for his opinion.

Sam Mor caught the elbow of his left arm in his right hand and the elbow of his right arm in his left hand, gave his stomach and shoulders a juicy uplift and waited.

The argument grew long and involved and only when Mr. Swithin was establishing the primacy of water as the destructive agent in this case did Sam Mor remind him that blood was thicker than water.

"That's beside the point," said Mr. Swithin.

"I'm only trying to judge," replied Sam Mor with a slight air of offence, "between your water and his blood."

Things were not quite so simple as Mr. Swithin might like them to appear.

"I think," concluded Mr. Swithin with a jocular grimace of destructive sarcasm, "that what would meet your case would be having the whole place done up from top to bottom, front door to back?"

"If that would be easier for you," said Sam Mor, nodding agreeably.

Mr. Swithin blew through his teeth. "That's everything, I take it."

"Well, now, you haven't seen the passage below to the kitchen and——"

They went away.

As I was finishing my tea Sam Mor put his head round the door. "He's off."

"Everything satisfactory?"

"Och, yes. Good enough. I left three rooms out and that made it easier for him."

"Which rooms?"

"The ones I couldn't put in," said Sam Mor. "But when I get an estimate from Dingwall and another one from Inverness for what there is to do it will be that much that Donul George from Balrunie will be able to undercut them and do the whole place at a profit. So I'll save the insurance company some money. And the hotel needed doing, I admit."

"You have been considerate."

"I must thank you for being so thoughtful yourself. That one about the blood was beautiful. I haven't enjoyed an argument so much for a long time."

"Do you enjoy the argument more than the cash?"

"It's when you have them both," he responded richly.

We laughed. The Major was up and out, he told me, though his weather glass was low. I assured him I wouldn't tap it, if that was what he was trying to convey.

"There wouldn't be any point in another fire just now." His eyes swam. "It's my first claim in twenty years so I let them off lightly."

"Heaven help them otherwise."

He appreciated the compliment so much that he said, "Would you like a wee taste?"

"I'm finished with tastes for good. Of all forms of indulgence it's the lowest."

He nodded. "The Major might agree with you at this moment, I'm thinking. Maybe later on?"

"Thank you."

We laughed and he went.

The hotel was getting back to normal. I wandered around like one of those beetles that skate about on water. I hadn't yet begun to look down. I wasn't afraid to look down. I simply didn't want to. This kind of indifference I had never experienced before.

Everyone turned up for dinner, even the Major. But the whole affair of the fire had obviously been discussed to that point where no awkward questions were asked. Already it was the kind of adventure that happened in remote spots where natives behaved after their fashion. It would be the subject of letters, of talk over dinner tables in civilised places. The more awkward and annoying at the time, the more memorable in retrospect.

But this obvious aspect was given a jolt towards the end by the Major who could bide his time like the diplomatist he was. Not that he was interested in biding his time. He just bided it. "The Insurance man was here," he said.

"Oh?" said the ladies.

"Sam Mor has been asking my advice." The Major glanced at the barrister. "The water has seeped into many places and left its mark."

"Ah!" said the barrister.

"Yes," said the Major.

"So what?" asked Mrs. Sneddon.

"With such small assistance as he may get from his insurance company, our landlord has decided to re-decorate his premises throughout."

The barrister chuckled.

"High time," said Mrs. Sneddon. "If you saw the faded roses on our walls!"

The Major was gallantly mute.

"There are birds on mine," said the widow, "that must have died before William Morris did."

I stole a glance over my shoulder and saw the Major incline his head towards the widow. The temperature began happily to rise.

"In his anxiety to be agreeable to his guests," pursued the Major, "Sam Mor wondered whether the ladies would be willing to assist him in the matter of decoration by choosing, before they leave, the colours and wallpapers which they might deem most suitable to their rooms and his house."

It was certainly Sam Mor's master stroke, his cat among the cooing pigeons. Flights of wallpaper lifted laughter on their wings into the sitting-room.

I sat on, going lower as everything and everyone else went higher. I felt like asking Johan where Catherine was though I didn't particularly want to see her. I didn't want to see anyone. I felt the abysmal damned depression coming like the storm that takes a day or two to work up. One can't skate on nothing for ever, more's the pity.

I went aloft and sat on my bed and wasn't even

amused by the blood spots on the wall. He drank rum when his depression got too much for him, when it became the horrible nihilism that is a black wind in an empty place, and then even the wind doesn't move. He wouldn't have moved himself but for the persistence in him that went on blind and took the cliff as its highway and the cave as its primeval den.

But I didn't want to think about it. Even the premonition of it was too obliterating. So I went out. But I found no relief even in the way I took, for I wanted to go towards the cliffs, the Head, to look down on the Cormorants Rock: depth and space, whence black birds might take wing. I took the opposite way and even then circuitously, indirectly, as if I wouldn't go to where I was going, but I arrived there and sat down. However, this spot where Catherine and I had met would be the one spot she would avoid. There was that grim satisfaction.

I hung on to Menzies, now that I had been able to think of him again, to save me going farther in my thought. He had begun to form coherently in my mind and that was something. The two aspects of him, the two nights, were quite different. The first night he had been drinking, had been pulling out of a bout of depression, and had carried the lees of it in him, hence the irony and that almost brutal use of the image. The bollard was a weapon, and yet wouldn't have been a satisfactory weapon if it hadn't been something else. For he was driving on then, his persistence was at work, and if I hadn't had a glimmer of understanding I would have been disjointed and left around like a drowned bag. Babbling in upon him about his manuscript. My God!

The second time he had been quiet, quiet and still; standing there in the cave, looking at me. My heart had missed more than a beat. He had come from nowhere and said nothing, while I was searching out his secret in what must have seemed a sneaking way. But he had said nothing, hadn't even been sarcastic, as if the affair flowed off him while he looked at my face. He hadn't been drinking. Probably hadn't had a drink for days. "The cask didn't matter." He wasn't a drinker. That's not what mattered. He had got me to row slowly while he looked at the cliffs with clear eyes. His hands and his face were quiet and steady. His face was a mask, and, however much he told at whatever time, it would remain like that. Yet it wasn't a mask, it was a human face. Perhaps one can't see behind any face, and the unsearchable force in this man made me realise it.

But always, this night or that, it was the same face, the same man. Different aspects of the one persistent unity; though as I write that it seems too much like an "explanation", and even my stomach revolts at the word unity. Yet there is a containing outline in it, like the line that contained the face revealed in the twigs.

How one gets bogged! How much simpler it would have been if the first appearance had been the whole story, if I had come upon a man drinking himself to death in a melodramatic way, with a shocking final happening in the offing!

The air was darkening and there was a faint darkening in the sky, veiling the blue that had been high and serene so long; as if the sky had decided on a dark thought of its own. I saw heather stalks move in a wind eddy, and as I glanced along the path, that was no more than a sheep track, I remembered how Catherine had come towards me.

I looked at the ground between my legs and saw the earth, roots, moss, lichen, brilliant red beads of fungus, a green beetle; over the ridge a curlew called.

Then he had seen the light beyond the dark edges of

the cliffs, so that it seemed to run along the edges, and his face had reflected a memory within him as though it, too, were light, and his smile was held in his eyes.

That expression, when a woman saw that expression . . . and so at last I thought of Annabel as she had appeared.

Why had that experience drained the pith out of me, leaving behind so insuperable a reluctance even to think of it? I cannot tell. I didn't like it—even if that's too easy to say. Something within me didn't want to face it, would rather it hadn't happened. It produced a heaviness of spirit or malaise.

Yet if anyone had told me beforehand that I was going to have such an experience I would have imagined myself tremendously interested and excited, unable to think of anything else. The result was very different, so that I now wondered if we really did want such apparitions to appear, if we did want this kind of traffic across the border. I began to understand, as I never understood before, why the prehistoric hunter had his charms *against* the dead.

Yet it was Annabel . . . for whom, I had felt in my fashion, there was nothing I wouldn't have done here or anywhere.

Ah, not only that. It was so much more than that. The expression on her face, in her face. Of whatever illusion or delusion I could conceivably have been the victim, I certainly couldn't have been of that. Why? Because it was beyond any power of mine to invent or imagine, much less evoke. Explain anything else as one likes. That at least was something given to me; it came from outside.

Then a very strange thing happened as I sat there; much, indeed, as if I had been caught in my own puzzle picture of that old face in the tree. The eyes of the mind wander around as do the eyes of the face; then, in an instant, they *see*.

I suddenly saw, then, that the expression on Annabel's face was her farewell to Douglas Menzies on the night of the wreck. The intensity of her love for him was gathered into that moment and, holding it, her ineffable compassion. The smile in her eyes lived as no other light lives. Her hair was disordered and her throat bare. .

I was terribly moved, for I knew this was true. Never mind how it came about that I saw it: it was true. And with it came an extra truth, of which at that moment I was equally certain. It was this: within an experience of that kind there are no borders. Love destroys borders.

And long after the event, when the glow dies down and truth withdraws her face, one can still say: anyway, in that experience there is no *fear* of borders.

I looked up and saw Catherine coming.

The borders between us were down. Even the excitement, that romantic excitement of mine with its adolescent breathlessness, had grown out of itself. I saw her clearly and simply and what existed between Douglas Menzies and herself I was prepared to understand, even, if necessary, to ask about. There was something vivid and lovely, I realised, in her being herself, detached.

"Hallo," I said. "I was thinking about you."

Her eyes were on my.face and off.

I told her I should like to talk to her; I needed her advice; I didn't know what to do. "You're not in a hurry, are you?"

She took a moment, then said "No" doubtfully.

"Let's sit down over here. I think the midges are on the move. I hope the weather is not going to break. Do you think it is?"

"I hope not," she said.

We sat down where the wind was less fitful. "I have no one to talk to about Douglas Menzies. I never mention him in the hotel. I wish I knew if there was anything I could do."

She looked about the heather so I reached forward and plucked a solitary piece of cross-leaved heath, which was in full pale-and-pink bloom, and presented it to her.

As she took it her colour deepened and her lashes did not lift, then they lifted swiftly.

"Go on," I said. "Throw it at me and get it over."

She couldn't.

"Throw it away then," I said.

When she realised that she couldn't throw it away because it was a flower the dismay on her face was absurd.

"Did you think I was the worse of drink at the fire?" I asked.

"You were all well on," she said quite definitely.

"I hope I didn't say anything out of the way?"

"You said enough."

"I thought I hadn't said enough. You were so kind. An extraordinary business, wasn't it?"

"Awful," she said. "Dreadful."

"We might all have been burnt to cinders in our beds."

She glanced at me. "It was no laughing matter."

"Far from it," I agreed.

She dropped the flower in her lap. I looked at it lying there. "I am trying to say this," I said: "there's nothing I wouldn't do for Douglas Menzies and yourself."

I did not look at her. I gave her time.

"Only I would need to know more," I added quietly as I gazed over the near ridge. "I might then be able to do something to help. I don't know. But I think I might."

She never moved. She said nothing. I had to look at her.

Her face was like a summer storm that did not know where it was going to blow next. Her skin was flushed and her eyes stormy. The lashes looked wet.

So she was going to deny it. She was going to be angry. A pity, I thought.

"Look," I said sensibly. "I know I am interfering. But——"

"I don't know what you mean."

Oh, Lord! I thought. For whatever else she knew, she knew what I meant. Where did her stormy colour come from? It was the only thing we both knew at that moment. That she could have trotted out the old remark!

"I took him out in the boat with me yesterday afternoon," I said. "He looked at the cliffs. He was reminded of his music. We didn't say much, but I enjoyed it, and I think he did, too. I have got so far with him. Afterwards in his house we had a long talk. That's how I missed my dinner. He mentioned to me that you had told him about the rent—after hearing about it from me. So, you see, the three of us are in it somehow."

I used words to give her time, to make it easier for her. But also I realised clearly within myself that I was now prepared to take their relationship for granted and to help them both. I had at last arrived at this stage. At that moment there certainly wasn't much emotion left in me of any kind.

"I felt I had to tell him," she said out of her mood.

"Of course," I agreed. "But I am not quite sure of the effect. He passed it off; didn't say he would do anything. You can't press him—at least I can't—yet.

255

But I may. I would like to dot that factor one, too. Tell me, do you think he has any money?"

"I don't know."

"I wonder if he ever pays Mrs. Maclellan?"

After a moment she said, "She told me—some time ago—when she was going to wash out the milk pail one day she found three pounds in it."

I looked at her, but her expression was withdrawn, almost sombre. I had probed too deep and she couldn't readily get over it.

"Well, I am glad of that, if only for Mrs. Maclellan's sake. I love that woman. I had thought her sort of kindness had vanished from the world. It's old-fashioned a bit."

Suddenly I was bitter, heaven knows why. If she had got up and moved off at that moment I wouldn't have said a word.

I felt her looking at me. Let her look.

But we couldn't sit there in silence for ever. "Anyway, I'll do what I can," I said, "if I see him again. I can't stay more than two or three days."

She had a gift for silence, but I couldn't help her if she wouldn't be helped. Besides, I didn't want to help her much. The beautiful effect from thoughts of Annabel was wearing off.

"Two or three days," she repeated dully.

"Yes," I said. "I am going abroad—sailing in just over a week's time."

"What do you think should be done?" she asked with the same monotony.

"Frankly I think he should get out of there. The best thing might be to let the factor go ahead." I glanced at her and saw that her face had lost its flush. She had picked up the piece of *Erica tetralix* and was nibbling the end of the stalk with her finger nails, but she wasn't looking at what she was doing, she was staring in front of her, and suddenly I remembered that this was how she had appeared when she was sitting beside Douglas Menzies in the dell.

"You think so?" She looked blindly down at the bit of heath.

"Don't you think so?" I asked.

"I don't know," she said. Then she glanced up and away and a note of anguish came into her voice. "Oh, I just don't know!"

"What?" I asked shortly.

"He's in love with Annabel!"

Perhaps she spoke quietly enough but it sounded like a cry. It was certainly the kind of shattering statement that I couldn't take in all at once. Then its meaning *for her* came through.

Extraordinary how this sudden shift in "certainties" had been happening to me ever since I had come to Dalaskir. Always dead sure I knew what was what . . . then in a moment it wasn't that at all. An invisible hand shakes the kaleidoscope and the scene is startlingly new. The Major wasn't drowned even. I had been certain of the "intrigue" because the worse construction always seems the truer, and now even that gets kicked into a new pattern. Menzies might use Catherine as he used the rum, but she meant no more to him than that. Hence the poor girl's desolate cry. And what an appalling way of putting it: He's in love with Annabel! Good God, as if Annabel were alive.

This certainly was the last shake of the box and I didn't know what to say. That her love should be wasted on Menzies had the sense of loss in it that was bitter beyond enduring.

"I know he's in love with Annabel," I said. "He's looking for her." I tried to keep the bitterness out of

257

my voice but it was difficult. "He's also looking for the Wrecker. Do you know who the Wrecker is?" I tried to keep the hellish grin off my face.

The awful thing about a woman at such a moment is that she does not respond to what you say; I doubt if she actually hears it: she responds to what you feel. Her vivid distress was contained, but only just.

I went on about the Wrecker. I explained this particular element of the godhead; and I explained Menzies' quest. It was a hopeless quest, I said, because the Wrecker always had the last word first. But that would not stop Menzies searching, for he had the persistence, the remorseless sanity, of a remarkable man. It was not that he was expecting to find Annabel so much as that he was going to explore the road she had taken, and on that road he would have insights and each insight would be a milestone, and from one milestone he would set out for another, in that country which is the country beyond this, where Annabel was if she was anywhere. The Wrecker could not beat him but only knock him out, destroy him—so easy a kind of victory that it can be thrown back in the Wrecker's teeth. Not that Menzies, if he ever got the chance, would do the throwing. He was too big for that. He was bigger than the Wrecker. And what made him bigger was love, because love was the creative element, not the wrecking element, the creative element that made his music. And that's where Annabel came in. For she was part of the creative element that made him whole. Without that part, creation is non-human and a metaphysical delusion.

When at last my own words choked me I was ashamed to look at her. Yet I had got rid of something that at least left my head emptier. Then I looked at her.

The distress was gone. Not that she wasn't troubled;

yet she was stilled in some way beyond my comprehension. She could hardly have understood my words. She could not in this case even have got my mood, because a girl does not respond to an underlying bitterness with a troubled warm light that has positively a suggestion of shyness in it.

"I must go," she said.

As if our plans had come to a conclusion, as if we had decided exactly what to do about Menzies!

She got up and was moving away before I had pushed myself erect. She half turned and gave me a smile, a small, friendly, lovely smile. Then she was off on her light feet and I stood gaping after her.

When a man is lost he starts to think, for thinking is his only trusty weapon. It cleaves its way to the truth. A remarkable instrument, a reliable tool.

I tried to get hold of it and fumbled with cotton wool. I swore, probably because I knew what was coming. At times one gets a horrible premonition of what the thinking is going to arrive at before it starts. It's a beautifully intricate performance, a devastating phenomenon.

She could rely on me. I was committed to help Menzies, for I understood. I understood everything between them. For I understood about love. When a woman is shameless in her use of you her smile is beautiful. She probably thought me a wonderful fellow; the more wonderful the better. That I might love her a little, too, would help.

I stumbled between decks before I got back to Menzies. I was developing a habit of hanging on to him in black and engulfing seas. The fellow might have been a bollard. Though it was not the bollard that attracted at the moment, it was the fight against the Wrecker. I was all for it. That every sane person would think him mad made it perfect. Because every sane person, every dearly beloved critic, was stuffed with his common sense like a suet pudding. A bag of straw that you practised on with your bayonet. In the end, manure; good manure. Excellent stuff.

I rather felt like the stuff myself as I went round in circles, for when I approached the hotel I couldn't go in. They say that in a perfect State the delinquent will return to his prison like a gentleman conscious of the aberration which had made him a temporary *anti*. My aunt's left foot!

After I had whizzed through a few dim labyrinths, I came to myself, sitting on a grey rock which was as cold as my face. And in that moment, that still chill lucid moment, I saw Menzies in his place, a spare lean vision of him, his face, his eyes, in that lonely place that stretched out from him while he looked without looking and listened. I had the feeling that I knew him better than any other person on earth and yet I realised that I would never know him. But this did not offend, hardly disappointed even, for I realised, by a lifting further intuition, that what moves the spirit profoundly can never be fathomed. Like Annabel's compassion, it comes from the ultimate loneliness. Love is a mystery and the more you know of the beloved the less you know. And you have to go far before you know that. Great lovers meet always afresh, like strangers. I remembered the look on Menzies' face when he saw again the light on the rocks and on the sea tangled in chords of music; and I remembered his look also before I turned and saw Annabel in the doorway.

That brought me in on myself and when I looked deep I saw nothing.

So I got up and went back to the hotel. The Major was probably more on my level, I thought. A real good-going argument, no hits barred, on the road to hell with plenty of knockable things around, and eternity always in the offing like a punchball out of reach. British diplomacy had landed in tough places, but at least it had a wonderful tradition.

Lights were on so it couldn't be so late as I thought. I slipped in quietly, fearful of being trapped, and once in my room breathed with ease if not comfort as I put my candlestick on the chair and sat on my bed, which was turned down at the corner—by Catherine, of course. I looked at the white turn-over, the triangular fold, a theorem in geometry, smooth in all its dimensions and dead as Euclid. Presumably some woman had put even Euclid to bed and performed the last obsequies.

Such thoughts helped me for I knew that I had a bitter decision to make. I had to exorcise Catherine. That's what it came to. I had somehow to get rid of her and pull myself together and stop being a fool. I had the feeling of having grown so fast in so many dimensions since coming to this bewitched place, which presented spotted trout on its plates, not to mention an epochal halibut by the barrister, that I had got entangled like one of its wild briars with buds anywhere and thorns everywhere. I needed pruning back to the old familiar root which in its innocence had known such a lot about savages, and blood and sex rites, and religions. I had really been a simple fellow once.

By an odd sort of spite all my knowledge of savage rites of exorcism was worse than useless. I couldn't even properly think about them lest I stopped skating around like a water-beetle. Perhaps I was frightened. There was a sort of sickly choke in my gorge.

Catherine is stupid, I thought suddenly to myself. She's just damned stupid. And if I didn't know whether

I had hit something or been hit myself, still it was a good start. So I went on with what was sticking in my gorge.

For it was such an appalling thing to say: "He's in love with Annabel!" Good God, it was terrifying. Was she so preoccupied with herself that she had no idea at all what she was saying? And then when I had followed up and proved her right beyond what she could know, when I had introduced the Wrecker and the creative plane on which a great artist worked, when, in short, I had, with a sense of cruelty, blown her last hope sky high, what had she done? She had given me a smile and gone away, a smile that was like a wild rose opening before my eyes, shy and lovely.

Flabbergasting. That's what it was. Fatuous. Not just stupid. Anyone can be stupid. But it takes a woman in love to be fatuous. When a woman is deeply enough in love obstructions in her path are, in a queer sense, not there because she cannot believe that her love will not conquer all. It must, it is so great, it is so right, it is so eternally destined. And then with incredible cunning she will make use of a simpleton to help her round the obstructions which had in fact so preoccupied the very marrow of her manœuvre.

It made me tired. And Catherine, over and above, what was she after all but a simple country girl? There wasn't a move she could make that I couldn't foresee. And as for a gesture that would astonish me—my very neck was tired, stiff, and I slowly swivelled my head upon its creaking boredom. Heaven knows how long I sat staring at what I saw on top of the commode, which was on the other side of the bed's head. The drinking glass was of the small narrow kind which Sam Mor used to make a small whisky or nip visible. It was nearly full of water, and stuck in the water was the sprig of heath with its blossom, which I had earlier that evening presented to Catherine.

I went round the bed carefully, making no noise, ready to pounce. Then I sat down with slow care. I looked away and looked quickly back. When I put out my hand, the glass was hard and cold. But I didn't touch the heath. Not yet.

It took me a long time to summon my thinking powers, and when they had assembled they asked in one voice: Now why did she do that? It was a terrific, a shattering question. I confess it so frightened me that I kept the hounds of thought at heel for a bit. There was a tremor somewhere that made me gulp more than once.

Then I let the dogs loose.

(1) She had returned the only gift I had ever given her to show that there could be nothing between us. She had done it with grace, because she had that kind of nature. It was a sort of grave fun, a sweet gesture that only a boor would question.

(2) It was a scheming design to keep in with me, expressed in an amusing way. A deliberate act of a deeper dye than the fragile moony blossoms.

(3) If the tiny twig had meant anything to her at all she would have kept it.

(4) If it hadn't meant anything to her at all she wouldn't have had it to stick in a glass.

After thought (17) or thereby I kicked the dogs under the bed and went to the door. I felt in a bad way and knew I wouldn't sleep a wink. I didn't see why I should have to bear the whole brunt. If only I could see her for ten seconds, for two seconds, for one look. But the girl would be in bed, in her nightdress? I gravely replied, presumably to myself, that there would be nothing wrong with her in her nightdress. I had never been along the corridor past my own room. It was as crooked as the passage underneath, and I had not taken half a dozen exploratory steps when a door opened and Mrs. Brown appeared in her dressing-gown. We both stepped to the off side and back again at the same time and kept the game going to a deuce of beg pardons until her husband appeared and I stopped to say "Good evening", when she slipped by. He hadn't seen Sam Mor, had he? It didn't really matter, so I went back to my room.

Despite my wide and penetrating knowledge of women I had to admit in the end that I just hadn't the mistiest notion why she had committed this enigmatic act. So I went to bed. Three times during the night I struck a match. The tiny globes of pale and pink had a dreamy pearl-like haze.

15

I slept so deep in the end that the knock got me like a harpoon, or like the last summons for which no man may be late if he is going to save himself. Awake by the time I got to the door, I waited for her footsteps coming back so that she could not dodge me by going down the main staircase. There were back stairs. When I pulled my door open her face also flew open.

"I must see you," I began.

"Hsh!" Her look was frantic as she went on. I followed her.

In desperation she turned. I read her lips and so heard her wild, "Go back!"

"The same place," I said in a cracked voice for I was trying to whisper, "at lunch time."

Her face frowned like a witch's and shook at me. Her hand came out and gave me a fierce if imaginative shove. I caught it. She snatched it away and asked me in an intense whisper if I was mad.

"Promise," I said. ·

"Yes, yes." She was listening with all her cells and suddenly went quickly along the crooked passage. I don't know which door opened because by that time my own was closed and I was taking in some needed air in privacy.

My timing was so good because I had rehearsed the scene during the night, when it had seemed the only sensible way of making a definite appointment. Otherwise what guarantee had I that she would come along any path within a limited time?

Erica tetralix seemed to think my attitude restrained and reasonable. I counted her round bells again. Nine. We knew each other pretty well by this time. She was my treasure. "They're not going to make fools of us as easily as all that," I told her, and she all but rang a peal.

I began to laugh quietly as I thought of the door that sounded like Mrs. Sneddon's. If that lady had seen us, and me in my pyjamas, she might have come to a precipitate conclusion.

Though I was down bright and early the barrister was before me. The sky was hazed but in my opinion it would clear up by lunch time. He hoped so because Dan and himself were going to the Winter Isles, some dozen miles away. Apparently they were in the midst of a real lobster raid. Deep-sea stuff, I gathered, on a professional scale. This was his world of holiday and it suddenly fascinated me. I envied him.

"Like to come?"

"I would, very much. But—I'm fixed up for today."

"Some other time."

I thanked him and asked about the sea-birds. Johan came in with his breakfast as he was talking with a precision that was delightfully descriptive.

When they had all gathered it was an almost talkative morning meal, because a dull sky and a breeze made a good fishing day. The Major had come in last and, with Lachlan, was the last to depart. The Major hardly spoke to Lachlan, just grumphed and pointed to things. Lachlan was equally obdurate. Ian winked to Charlie in the driving seat. Perhaps there had been some bets on the outcome of the pantomime. It was good to see life coming back to its normal balance. If Lachlan and the Major each laboured under a point of view that had still to be expressed, they would express it. They went towards the gap in the mountains, far from Loch Dubh.

I avoided Sam Mor by going back into the hotel and then up to my room for my field glasses. My buoyancy was beginning to leak—though why should it? I turned to *Erica* . . . she wasn't there. She was gone, glass and all. She had vanished. My bed was unmade, the room untouched.

Somehow this knocked the pith clean out of me. The skin of water that the beetle skates on is very thin. But at least I had been doing my best.

I was surprised to find that I was not only nervous but physically weak; my muscles trembled. Deep in me I knew what the trouble was. This was the day of decision. The meeting with Catherine would have a termination fatally precise.

I tried to be annoyed over the removal of *Erica* but without effect. It was like a portent; a whisk of obscure magic. Of course it could only have been removed by Catherine. Not by Mrs. Sneddon anyway, I thought, searching for a precarious grip. I felt old and haggard.

I left the hotel without my binoculars and by noon I was in the appointed hollow. By two o'clock Catherine hadn't come. By three o'clock I had given up hope and fear and opened out my sandwiches but couldn't eat them because my mouth was as dry as the bed of the tiny burn that meandered by. But my brain was drier still and quite remorseless and as for those physical tremors they were gone like snow on the desert's dusty face. I was bitter, bitter and bleak. The Wrecker was my boon companion.

"Good afternoon!".

267

I looked up from my meditation over the sandwiches and there she was, bright and cheerful, like any young woman of the world. Her eyes flashed on me—and stayed the longest they had ever done. She didn't laugh outwardly, she wasn't so crude as that. When I began to get up she sat down.

"Haven't you eaten your lunch yet?" she inquired.

"I invited you for lunch."

"Did you?" Her politeness was surprised.

She was behaving in a civilised way. But it seemed needlessly heartless, even if it was the only way to get the whole thing over, as I knew only too well.

"Have a sandwich?"

"No, thank you. Johan had to run home so I stayed to help. I couldn't eat any more."

"Why did you remove *Erica*?"

"Erica?"

"The piece of heath."

"Is that the name? I know a girl named Erica. She's a very nice girl."

"Not so nice as my heath," I said.

She smiled.

I grudged her that smile.

"You haven't answered my question," I said doggedly.

"How do you know I took it away?"

"It was either you or Mrs. Sneddon."

As if I had said something incredibly fantastic she burst into laughter. She shook beauty from her eyes and her skin flushed like petals of the dog rose. Her teeth were milky and all there. She was all there herself in a fair way that would have made me ache if her delicious laughter hadn't helped me a little. She couldn't laugh like that and then be a death's head. Though **you** never knew with a woman.

268

"Why?" I insisted.

"It wasn't yours," she said.

I looked at her then and she put on an air of amusing defiance.

"But you gave *Erica* back the night before?" I challenged her.

"I gave you the loan of her—it," she corrected me.

My body settled down on its seat as if it had been hit on top of the head. "A loan!"

"If you had whispered like that Mrs. Sneddon wouldn't have heard you."

Where was I? Who was this? "A loan of her for the night?"

This time before her laugh she gave a yelp. Perhaps the name of Mrs. Sneddon brought that lady in person too close to my last remark. I don't know. A roe deer barks, but Catherine yelped like a puppy dog. My God, things began to gather inside me, like fingers, like hands about to catch a hurtling and invisible ball.

She saw them gathering. I saw her wariness getting ready.

"Catherine," I began.

"Please!" she said, the light in her eyes dancing away from mine like sparks.

"No fear!" I said. It was now or never.

"You're quite mad," she said.

"Am I?" I said.

But she had seated herself at a distance which permitted her to get to her feet before I could take matters in hand. Of all my intuitions, that one which concerned her capacity to run like a hind was uncommonly accurate. The hollow meandered with the dry burn, but when she rounded the first bend the wind struck her. She faltered and so, by the natural force in things, mine was a flying tackle. We rolled over twice.

I led her back by the hand to the sandwiches which she had remembered. She would remember anything, that girl, when it suited her, no matter what the moment. However, all this had taken longer than it takes to tell.

I asked her to sit beside me and she asked me if I would behave myself, so we got our voices back.

"You can do anything you like with me," I said, "and you know it."

"Eat your sandwiches then."

From the way I looked at the things, she got a little of her laughter back. Then she spied the piece of cake at two yards. It must have come in the way of my foot when I got up. It told its lopsided story with inanimate mirth. But then everything was arrested after its kind in this new light. The way she retrieved the piece of cake and put a black currant in her red-lipped mouth almost lifted me from where I sat. Her fair hair had issued from the sun and moon.

But can a man leave well alone? Can he thank God for the delight that splinters in kisses upon the dark side of his revolving planet when time and chance have combined in the rarest of all moments? He cannot. And he cannot because his revolting planet is composed of the sort of dough that would give indigestion to a moonbeam. Brutal stuff, full of violence and self-seeking and mastery and murder and duodenal ulcers.

"How the wind is getting up!" said Catherine.

I listened. "A storm," I said and I thought of Menzies. But I also thought that this was a cunning way of getting at my brutal intention.

We were silent for a little while, but I was far from thinking of anyone else, of men like Dan and the barrister at sea. The wind swished through the heather above our heads like a scythe.

"Do you mind if I tell you something?" I said. "It moved me a lot. It was when you said that Douglas Menzies is in love with Annabel."

Smiling, I glanced at her face and saw the last of the light going out of it. She looked around her knees and nipped off a piece of heather.

"He is," she said quietly, flatly.

I couldn't think of another word.

She looked at me sideways, with a curious detachment. "I thought you understood."

"I thought I did, and then I wondered." I couldn't look at her now.

She hadn't any more to say.

"Tell me," I said with the feelings of a criminal.

"I cannot."

"Please."

"You were asking about taking him away from the white house. But if Annabel is still there, for him . . . Oh, I don't know!"

I did not look at her. I took her hand and I kissed it.

"Do you think I'm mad?" she asked.

"I'm mad too."

"I know," she said. "That's why."

I was beginning to feel better.

"Go on," she said.

I looked up and saw the distress in her face. "Go on where?" I asked with some bewilderment.

"Say it," she said.

So she knew, my God, what was at the very core of the lump of dough. So I said it. For after all when I saw Douglas Menzies and herself in the dell, what was a fellow to think, what could he think?

"I knew it," she said.

"Did I show it as much as that?"

"Much more."

271

"What—how—what was much more?"

"It was awful."

When born dense a fellow had better wait. I waited.

"That was only the second time I saw him," she said, "since—since before Annabel died."

I had the odd sensation of falling down within myself like a shower of warm rain.

"The first time was at Easter when I came home then."

My brain was sodden, though with a powerful suggestion of growth in the rain, and rainbows.

"You couldn't do anything for him?" I managed to ask.

"No one could ever but Annabel."

"You loved Annabel?"

"Very much."

Then I got her to talk about Annabel.

Some of what Catherine told me I have already used in this narrative. She spoke simply now, and in speaking and listening we lost our self-conscious selves almost altogether but not quite, and what wasn't lost was warm and tender like the smile that sometimes came into Catherine's face. I asked her questions and she answered in pictures that I saw. But sometimes she would stop in the middle of a conversation between Annabel and herself, for there were things that she couldn't tell me. And Douglas Menzies moved around in the background, and in the foreground sometimes, like a brother, with that slight remoteness of the brother. "There's nothing I wouldn't do for him, for Annabel's sake, and for his own sake, too. So I thought I would tell him about the rent. I went to the house but I wouldn't go in, so he came back with me as far as where you saw us. I don't know what I expected to do. I almost felt sick. But I had to do something—Annabel would expect it of me. I don't know if you can understand."

"Yes. And I love you for it. What did he say?"

"About the rent? He asked me about it and I mentioned you and then I just saw that he was talking about it and it meant nothing. He didn't say if he would do anything or not. He can talk about something till you get that awful empty feeling that far in him it means nothing. I asked him if he was working and he said he was sometimes."

I waited and then asked her if he told what he was working at.

"I don't remember what he said but I got the feeling that it was music, far away—in the place where he is— I cannot explain, but—it was perhaps wonderful but it was terrible."

I gave her time.

"Then he asked me how I was getting on. So I tried to tell him. But it was no use. We had fallen away."

"Annabel wasn't there."

She gave me a quick flash and nodded, pleased that I understood.

Somehow she had made the relationship between the three of them extraordinarily vivid and as I sat there I wondered if I would tell her about my vision of Annabel. I decided I would.

I took my time: the row in the boat (but not the rum), the cliffs and the expression on his face, the music, Dan's invitation, the food we had picked up, the talk in the house, and then Annabel's appearance, which I described minutely in the same easy tones.

When she looked at me her eyes couldn't leave my face. Then she glanced away and her breathing came again shallow and fast. I took her hand but she was hardly conscious of this. I called her name and she gave me a curious strained smile.

"I have been thinking a lot about it," I said.

273

But she couldn't come back to words. Then I remembered that in the Highlands "second sight" or visions of the kind were or had been an almost common occurrence, so much so that it had got woven into the psychological background, part of the mind's texture, however subsequently the mind might be "enlightened". Like a folk tune. Then I remembered something else, namely, that the person who experienced "the sight" was affected afterwards by a feeling of exhaustion or revulsion, a malaise that could in extreme cases bring on physical sickness.

But I tried to speak reasonably. All that could have happened was that Menzies was capable of so intense a visualisation of Annabel at their parting that it could, at certain moments, get projected outside himself; not only that but also anyone with him, profoundly with him, might be able to see it too.

She seemed to be listening, but I fancy my words were just dry noises for when a gust of wind whined over us she cowered. I saw she was trembling.

"It's cold," she said.

I realised there was a shiver in my own skin. It was twenty minutes past six! She got up at once. She would have to run!

When we had parted, she turned and gave me her smile. "It was lovely talking to you." Then she was off.

Now that I was up I was shivering with cold. I danced around, and, having started dancing I kept at it with glorious abandon, warmed by the fire inside. Then I must get a glimpse of her, so I went cautiously up the slope.

First the sea came under the sky, then the sweep of land that culminated in the Head, and then I looked no farther because there were figures, small dark humans, along the cliff edge. A gust of wind choked me. I had the horrible sensation of being battered by the sea in the boat that these figures were looking down at.

My eyes roved and saw three men hurrying along the top of the braes from the direction of Balrunie. By the hotel, away below me to the left, a woman flapped in the wind until she got back into shelter; and away beyond that, the still white house. A man here and there, converging men. I saw Catherine below me, not far away, leaning against the wind. I answered the wild wave of her arm and started off at a run.

If it was Dan and the barrister, then they had waited too long at the Winter Isles and got caught in the storm. Which wasn't like Dan. A sudden fierce summer storm would be as familiar to him as a weather glass. My boyhood knowledge of these northern seas came back to me with so great an intimacy that it wiped out the years between. A terrific blow up and a blow over. He would have sheltered in the Isles. Unless he had broken down.

It was a sickening thought, and I tried not to think of the figures on the cliffs—waiting.

But they were waiting. The wreck.

I overhauled an old fisherman. Yes, it was Dan Maclellan and an hotel gentleman. The hotel had phoned to Balrunie to look out for the boat in Loch Runie. It was a westerly gale and God knows where she would hit the shore.

I left him and saw that the figures were stringing out to the south of the Head. So Dan wouldn't make Loch Runie. It was the welter of rocks now, the stack, and beyond that the wide raging channel that fetched up below the white house, and beyond that the spouting seaward cliffs of the long island. The death trap, with its merciless teeth everywhere.

I came among the men and I saw the heaving boat. She was small and the two figures on the oars were slowly bending toys. They were pulling her to sea, with her nose just off the wind and Dan on the inside heavy oar. When the gust hit her the oars stopped and when its vicious whine passed she was closer in. Dan was striving to gain seaway sidewise like a crab in order to open the channel. Perhaps he had thought he would open it wide enough to work across the channel and so come under the lea of the island. He would never do that now. A hellish gust drove us back and then I heard Sam Mor roar. Because of the treachery of the wind near the cliff-head Charlie had been all but sucked over. By the grace of chance he had got a handhold and crawled back. Sam Mor cursed him for a young fool.

When I got to my feet again she looked utterly help-less in the wallowing white-smitten seas. She had been losing seaway steadily but this had been offset in some measure by the fall back of the cliff from the Head towards the stack. Otherwise it would have been all over by this time.

When I realised that they were abreast of the narrow passage between the stack and the inner cliff I won-dered for a wild moment if Dan had been holding her up in order to fall down on it stern first, to fall down on that gateway which had so recently run with paradisal light. I got down on all fours and crawled forward. I heard Sam Mor's roar but I paid no attention. I flat-tened, and crept, and down below saw hell's own tumult, for the sea that burst on the stack's edge was met by a sea thrown back by the cliff in a spouting explosion of leaping water and fountained froth. I pushed myself back before I got to my knees. I did not look at Sam Mor.

But no one looked at anyone, only at the boat. Dan knew his rocks. Dan had to get round the stack on the weather side. That was the only fight, and he would fight the only fight to the end. He would do it coolly, and he would cry to the barrister when to hold and when to give way if that was necessary. And the barrister would obey him for this was their element.

A dreadful feeling of exhaustion came up from the slow movement of the oars. When I glanced back towards the Head I could see how far they had been driven in. They could never hold their own. They could only strive not to lose too much.

Slowly they fell down on the stack and, as they fell down on it, foot by foot they passed from view under it, close under it.

I looked at Sam Mor. His small eyes were slitted and green and the wind blew the water out of them. His head gave a slow shake on its own.

There was a general movement now round the bend, for the cliff that fell away from the Head ran straight inland from opposite the stack.

The stack was shaped like a loaf, perhaps fifty yards long on that weather side. If the boat was settling down under the water she had shipped, she would be heavy and not blown too easily, even if tougher to pull. There would be a throw of wind and sea off the stack on that seaward side. But however the mind juggled with chances it could not defeat the awful passage of time, let the minutes draw themselves out to however terrible a tension.

When reasonable hope was gone and no one looked at anyone there came a snorer of a gust that tossed us back. It was followed by a lull and in that lull which was surely an end we heard a cry. Charlie had gone back beyond the white house and as we looked he rose to his knees on a jutting pinnacle and waved to us and cried again.

We looked back towards the stack and in a few moments the boat came into the tumult at the point, with the gust's spume falling on her from the cliff above. Then her head swung back on Dan and she was all but broadside on. I saw him rise against his oar as though it were gripped by iron. The oar gave, and lifted and gripped again. On the edge of foundering they were still struggling, even if Dan was pulling now with his body's weight, the arms dead. Then a sea lifted them but did not throw them. They disappeared. But they came again, clear of the point. Dan was trying to get her bow round to the wind. I saw his head turn towards the barrister and their oars slowly worked against each other and slowly the boat's stem went round to the weather. All they could do now was hold her like that. Their heads drooped over the oars. We could see they were spent, utterly done.

But they were clear of the stack wall, in the landward swing of the water, and as they slowly dropped back towards us they looked flat, small, helpless, yet miraculously persistent. The swing and the heave, the snarl, the roar, the cavernous booming that trembled to our feet, the wind in our ears, our eyes half-blinded then terribly clear. As they came opposite the narrow passage inside the stack a swirl threw her stern round. Their oar blades were in the water and I saw Dan stir and slowly give way. The barrister put his weight against his blade. She was tossed and came on, but again she fell back, still on her keel. It was difficult to find thought in that chasm, so terrible was the fascination. Then near me I heard Sam Mor roar:

"God damn it, couldn't you go for it?"

I turned my head. "Davie has gone," cried the youth.

278

"Who the blazes," cried Sam Mor, "gave them permission to take the other rope?"

Men came round. Sam Mor towered solid and vengeful among them. Then Charlie said something about a rope at Dan's.

"Run, boy, as you never ran before," cried Sam Mor to Charlie.

And Charlie ran. As I followed him, my eye, leaping ahead, saw Mrs. Maclellan coming, bent and buffeted, like a stricken flapping bird. She fell back a step as Charlie stopped in front of her. I think everyone forgot the boat at that moment. Then Charlie was off again. There was a rope at Dan's.

She turned to follow Charlie, not trusting a man to find anything. I saw Charlie take the milk-pail ditch at a flying leap. He fell and picked himself up and was off like a deer.

I looked down at the boat. Charlie would be too late, even if ropes would be of help, which they couldn't be, not on those churning skerries and thrown from this height.

It was then I became aware of Menzies. I think he had been among us for a while. But somehow it had not been a time to look at him or think of him. I could not take my eyes off him as he went up to Sam Mor. I could not hear what he said for his voice did not rise. He was lean and knit and so composed that Sam Mor could only stare at him. "Let it down with a stone," Menzies said as he turned towards the cliff. The pallor on his face was a sort of light and he looked remorseless and pleasant.

Sam Mor got his voice back and cried out.

Menzies turned and smiled to him. "All right. Keep them back." He tied the bottom button of his jacket, got down on all fours, twisted round and put his legs over.

279

My heart sank in me then. I had the appalling sensation that all this had been arranged somewhere else. I was beset by a feeling that I cannot explain, that I can only call unreal. The fellow was doomed and here, before us, the action was being arranged. Words like "recurrence" and "the Wrecker" swung through me inaudible and blind.

I was flat on my stomach, watching him, each step and handhold. The way down was a zigzag. He went carefully flattening against the rock when the wind ripped at him. The bends were the danger spots and he negotiated them with a slow flawless motion. It was at the second bend that the gust got him and his feet swung away with the toes clawing for the crack that wasn't there. I heard Sam Mor's groan. The blood gathered and congested in Menzies' face as he drew himself up in a slow squirm, shifted a handhold swiftly, slid a few inches, got a purchase for his feet, put his forehead against the rock and lay.

When the gust passed, he turned his head over his shoulder to look for the boat.

The two men in the boat had seen the whole action for they were facing us as they still strove to keep her head to the seas. I could see the water rush and welter in her. It wouldn't take much to fill her now and she was only a few yards off. Dan would know of the cave, perhaps it had been behind his fight as a last dim hope. But his boat was beyond manœuvre and their strength was gone.

After Menzies had looked at them, he walked at a slant for several yards, then went down slowly feet first, slewed to one hand, to the other, and passed out of sight under a great bulge of rock. He was more than half way down.

Each wall of water raced and smashed along the

skerries then sucked down and out in a swirling motion. Nothing more deadly, more treacherous, could be conceived. As I watched Dan for a sign of what was happening to Menzies I began to see his craft getting out of control, turning into the piece of water-logged flotsam she was.

Then I saw Menzies again, well down, and I knew he would get down, and something moved in me very deeply towards the man. We could see his head and his shoulders. He was going steadily, easily, and when he stopped the water gushed up to his knees. He was down.

The boat now was being lifted, thrown, and sucked back, to lift again. When the barrister missed his stroke and fell away Dan moved past him to the bow and on his knees picked up the painter and coiled it. We saw the boat jerk as her forefoot touched bottom before she was sucked back. Then Dan straightened himself and when she rose next time and came on, he threw the rope from behind his hip so that it uncurled against the wind. Menzies moved to meet it and caught it as the seething wave got him. He went upright with the rush of water before he went under, then he rose behind it, streaming, and staggered back.

Next time the boat piled up on the skerry, and Menzies with a quick whip of the rope round a jut of rock held her against the recession. She slewed so violently that Dan and the barrister were emptied out, grabbing at the gunnel as they went. The gust came in a lashing spindrift; the wave seethed over, bumping the boat as it covered the men. The gust held to its top whine like a flight of demons caught by the teeth on a wire that wouldn't break.

Menzies had made the rope fast and as the water receded he followed it, using the rope for a rail. He ducked under the off side of the boat and hauled the barrister away by the neck. The barrister was hardly conscious but Menzies said something in his ear that stirred him to lay hold of the rope and stagger drunkenly before the next wave doubled him over. Meanwhile Menzies had clambered into the boat and gone aft. I saw him lean over the stern before he was all but covered. The boat crashed back on her seaward bilge as the water left her, but he had grabbed Dan before that old seaman had gone beyond reach.

The barrister was held by the rope and was retching so violently that he could not move, but he lifted his head clear of the next one. As he saw Menzies plunging back with Dan on his shoulders he turned to the cliff. In a little while all three were hard against the cliff where the rising tide swirled knee high. The few yards to the cave were too many, too deep and treacherous. In any case the cave would be a trap; they were better where they were if help came at once.

And help was at hand for many a look had been thrown behind by our crouching bodies. Charlie had had helpers and the right kind of stone was ready. A seaman's hands knotted the rope-end on the stone and Sam Mor lowered away as the seaman fed the coil to him. When the stone stuck Sam Mor pulled it back a yard or two and let it go to bounce clear before checking it once more. At last it slithered to Menzies' hand.

There was apparently a bit of an argument then between Menzies and the barrister, for Dan was plainly in a bad way. Though the barrister was still barking the sea froth from his lungs, his hands went mixing in with Menzies' to fasten the noose that wouldn't slip. Menzies finished the argument by lifting the noose over the barrister's head and passing it under his arms.

After pointing the way up under and round the overhang so that we could all see him, he raised his arm and Sam Mor said, "Take the strain" to the men on the rope behind.

I wanted to be on the rope but I lay where I was for I knew now that if the rope or the barrister got wedged I would start down before Sam Mor could stop me. But the big man was standing on the verge, for he had the rope to steady him, and he played the barrister like a heavy salmon in the back end, letting him cough away when he got his footing. When he fell over on a sheer face it was a straight pull if the rope ran clear. Up he came, scrambling and pushing off with what pith was left in him, until we hauled him clean in over the edge and well back.

It was only then I saw how many were there, including Brown and Sneddon and the Major. Lachlan had been on the rope and over towards the house I saw Mrs. Maclellan and Catherine. I gave them a wave and Catherine lifted her hand.

Ian had another stone and down the rope went once more.

Menzies had got Dan laid out on a narrow ledge and was working on him. When the stone reached him he acknowledged it, but went on with his task until we saw Dan's hands stir. When Dan sat up he doubled over but slowly straightened again. Menzies seemed to be in no hurry now at all, so I knew he was anxious about Dan.

Presently it was clear that he intended they should come up on the rope together. Dan instructed him how to make the double noose and when they were ready Menzies signalled the route to Sam Mor. "Take the strain," said Sam Mor over his shoulder, "and for God's sake, easy!"

If Menzies thought they could have come up the way he went down, with him behind giving Dan a lift, it did not turn out like that. But at the first slither he got his knees against the rock, and as Sam Mor gave him time he got his feet and so he was able to ease Dan's face clear and walk up, leaning back over the space below. But it was not easy, for Dan's feet were in his way, but when he came round with a whack Sam Mor gave him time.

When the gust screamed Sam Mor cursed those who had come too near the edge. As if he hadn't enough on his hands as it was! His cheeks were red as a winter fire and the water whipped from his eyes ran down them. He was solid as a stack and as steady. When the defeated fury raced to the hills he blinked and waited for the two bodies, huddled on the ledge. Menzies had an arm under Dan's neck and was talking to him as though they were on a journey together. I saw the aftermath of the smile on his face as he looked up at Sam Mor and raised his hand.

The nearer they came the more Menzies took control, for he wasn't going to have any choking strain on Dan now. And when at last they came to the edge, he leant away, pulling on Dan's noose and easing him over, before he slipped, and held, and came in over under Sam Mor's fist.

As they went back from the cliff Menzies removed his noose.

They stopped and Sam Mor stood to his full height and looked at him. "Great work!" he said and he put out his hand. Menzies took it and smiled. We all looked and no one could speak.

There was a greyness under the weather on Menzies' face and his feet were light. From a star of blood on the back of his right hand a small trickle ran down.

Dan was sitting up and blinking the shadows from his eyes. He had nothing to vomit and that weakened him, and exasperated him a little, too, for he told his wife to be quiet. Not that she was asking him much though she was on her knees.

Ian said, "You have drunk too much of the Atlantic: it's another drink you need now."

Dan smiled back. "Ay," he said.

"Did you bring a drop, Charlie?" Sam Mor asked.

"No," said Charlie, who had just driven the hotel car to the sheepfank.

Menzies stood looking at Dan's face but said nothing. And I tried not to think of the rum in his house.

The barrister came up to Dan. His face was blue and his teeth chattering. "All right, Dan?"

"Fine," said Dan. There was a strange air of sadness about him.

"Out of this at once," yelled Sam Mor going into action, "or it will be pneumonia next!"

Mrs. Maclellan went up to Menzies and took his hand. She did not shake it; she pressed it between her own. The tears were running down her face and she did not know what to say. Then suddenly she kissed his hand.

As she made to turn away he raised her hand and saluted it, smiling to her with an understanding that was rare and light, and somehow I knew at that moment that Annabel was the invisible one with them.

I saw Catherine's face. Ian and Lachlan got hold of Dan and I was only too glad to give them and others a hand to carry him to the car.

The car went off and the rest of us followed to the main road. I saw the Major stumping on ahead, with a stagger now and then. It was as near Menzies as he would ever come, I thought, and for a moment all of us were fateful figures and separate.

From the road I looked back and saw Mrs. Maclellan, accompanied by Catherine, hurrying home doubtless to prepare hot bottles and drinks for Dan.

But around the white house there was no life of any kind now and from its chimneys came no smoke.

16

The deserted appearance of the white house went with me. Now and then a man looked over his shoulder in its direction. Then I saw that Lachlan was walking just in front of me, alone, so I made up on him. As he turned his face I saw a curious pallor in its tan and I recognised at once the expression that is left on a musician's face when he has played something that moved him deeply. Even the light in his blue eyes was strangely withdrawn. And I was aware that, perhaps more than any of us, this man had been stirred by what Douglas Menzies had done. It was like an old heroic story of the Highlands about which pipe tunes are made. He was quiet in manner and we did not say much, but somehow I felt completely at ease. This unexpected companionableness was like the opening of a door to places which we would yet visit together. When we parted at the hotel he gave me a glance and in it was understanding of why we could not speak readily of what Menzies had done.

There was much commotion in and about the hotel, for dinner was late and Sam Mor's stock of drink on the run. The barrister was in bed and Dan had been sent home in dry clothes, with a hot strong drink inside him. After dinner Sam Mor caught me and took me into his small office.

"It's been a time!" he said, blowing.

"How is Dan?"

"Nothing internal, I think. He's got a mauling. But, man, he's sad."

"He had a sort of farewell look."

The old twinkle came into the small eyes. "You've hit it. A farewell it was and it got Dan pretty bad, though he wouldn't say as much. Apparently it was the magneto. But he's covered, thanks to the barrister. I told him he would get a better boat from the insurance, but he wasn't strong enough to lose his love of the old one. They had been in a few dirty seas together."

I sat down abruptly on two cases of whisky, for I had thought Dan's sadness was the approaching shadow of death. Sam Mor poured me a dram without measuring it. "I have never been so moved by any one man's action and I have seen a few. I take my hat off to him," and he took off the cap that wasn't on his head until his sweeping hand hit the bottle and upset it. Some spirit was lost but all he said was "Ach!" His tribute to Menzies could hardly have flown higher.

And so it started. Up to this point it had never occurred to me to call on Menzies that night. But Sam Mor was fresh from serving drinks to men who as they warmed up would have said what they had to say about Menzies on the cliff, and he had had a drink or two himself. The picture of Menzies all alone in that cold house was too much for their old social instincts. "It isn't right," said Sam Mor. "It isn't natural. Not after what he did." He was ashamed of the thought of it.

I realised I did not want to go; the reluctance rose into my gorge, and there was a thin excitement below it.

"Do you think he would take the wet clothes off himself?" asked Sam Mor.

I met his eyes which were regarding me critically, then I looked away. I didn't know what to say.

"He may be lying there ill, in a high fever. If a man doesn't get right food, how can he have the resistance?"

I began to see the force of his remarks.

"Who else," said Sam Mor, "could call on him to see how he is, if nothing more?"

There was no one else, as he knew, and everyone knew.

"Take half a bottle with you—as a medicine," said Sam Mor and he reached for a flat half bottle wrapped in tissue paper.

Still I could not say I would go, but I took out my pocket book.

"Never mind," said Sam Mor, "just now."

"Let me see—that's thirty shillings."

"Make it a pound, if you must, but not a penny more." And not a penny more would he take.

With the bottle in my pocket, I went up to my bedroom feeling I must think this out. At my door I looked along the dimly lit crooked corridor and Catherine, leaning back, saw me. She hesitated for a listening moment then came lightly.

"Sam Mor thinks I should go and see him," I said.

"You should," she whispered and before I quite got my bearings she kissed me sweetly and was gone.

I went into my room. I had made such resolutions about never intruding on Catherine in the hotel that her own swift act was incredibly surprising. It turned the basic excitement into an upper tumult. I would go certainly. I sat down and the candle flame flickered. The wind rose to a hollow moan round some chimney stacks.

As I knew I was going, there was no point in being reluctant, yet I couldn't get up. I am not trying to suggest here that I had any premonition of what was to happen. I hadn't—not consciously, anyhow, if I must be exact. I just felt I didn't want to intrude on him. It was too soon; like taking a friendship for granted when our relationship was something infinitely more tentative than that. They didn't know that, but I did.

Yet what could be more human, more natural, as Sam Mor had said, than to call on him, at least, and ask how he was? He had been grey enough after his sea plungings. Not to do it would be inhuman *on any level.* This struck me with clarity and force.

I took a turn about the room and then, without any conscious prompting, fished his typescript out of my bag and sat down again beside the candle. I could not concentrate on the writing and turned the pages over, looking at a sentence here and there. I was reluctant to read it as though I could not bring myself to meet something that was in and behind it, apart from the words. At the same time the quality of what I did read confirmed the need for going. The typescript might help if ever our talk got round to the future, to discussing what he should do, how he might exist, while his real work was being considered by someone who mattered. Anything rather than, at a critical moment, being left without a direction, even a suggestion. I had the notion that Catherine was behind me in thinking like this. I decided to take it with me.

Going downstairs I expected the Major to appear, as though there was a lot of fate about. As I was putting on my rainproof coat, the sitting-room door opened on voices and the Major closed it behind him. He looked at me in his jowled assessing way. The man's eyes would be the last part of him to die.

"Have a drink." It was neither a question nor an order, merely his way of taking something for granted.

I followed him into the dining-room, saying I had just had one and would not have any more.

He paid no attention and produced his bottle. He was obviously fed up with his friends at the moment. I said I was going out.

"Where?"

"I was thinking of calling on Menzies, see how he is." I looked at him.

"Hm," he said.

I waited.

"Like my opinion?"

"I should."

This touched him in some way. He poured out a drink. "Sure you won't have one?"

I thanked him. No.

"What's bothering you?"

"I suppose I don't want to interfere."

"Hmf. Handing it back to me?"

I realised that I was. I realised that I was wanting to be told by everyone to go, even the Major. So I smiled and waited.

"No harm in going, I suppose," conceded the Major. "You can always make another night of it." He drank.

"Sam Mor thinks someone should go."

"Hell!" said the Major. "These old women!"

"You didn't speak to Menzies today?"

He looked at me with a glitter in his eye. "No. Why should I speak to him?"

"He did pretty well."

"What are you trying to say?"

"Well," I said, "you seem to understand him better than anyone else, know the road he's on."

In slow motion he set down his glass on the table and his features gathered their congested look. "What road?"

He had spoken often enough of the road to hell, so I did not answer. But as I saw the pressure increase in his face and knew an explosion was not far off, I said, "Why don't you come with me?"

The suddenness of the invitation staggered him a bit. It rather staggered myself; as though I had been living in two worlds and all in a moment wanted them to meet beyond me.

But the Major as usual was searching for motive. He could never get beyond that. The personal was always being invaded, the ego touched. His actual presence could be felt like a dark electric field. There had probably been a lot of talk in the sitting-room about "that man". Probably more than enough for the Major.

"To do what?" he asked.

"Well, to talk to him. He would interest you, I'm sure. He has penetrated some odd regions."

"Oh? What regions?"

"Of the human mind. He's not just drinking."

"Really? Not just drinking?"

He could take any kind of remark to himself, but I answered innocently enough, "No. His music . . . his thought . . . the tragedy . . ." I stopped, then added, "He's making an effort to see what it's all about."

"Good God! Gone that way definitely, has he? I more than suspected it." His lips met and pursed with a sort of vindictive pleasure that was yet belied by something at a deeper level. I had noticed that whenever Menzies was mentioned the worm of bitter inwit got crawling around and exciting his nether regions. I suppose I knew that they could never meet; it was fantastic to expect it; I would have been horribly embarrassed, no doubt, if he had offered to accompany me. But something kept me there.

"I don't think it's a bad way. He seems to me to be making an effort, at least, to come to grips with the enigma." I hoped I was speaking with a fanciful air, out of deference to the Major's age and experience, but I realised that whatever I said, and however I said it, the result would appear to be a probe at the Major. The fanciful in some mysterious way became fatal.

Yet by seeming to invite the Major's help, I kept by an ever narrower margin on his right side, and as the talk went on I got a quite vivid impression of what was troubling him at the deep level: he was jealous of Menzies. He knew that Menzies was the only one who could stand beside him at his utmost reach—and then go beyond. This particularly exasperated the Major because he had assured himself that there was no beyond. That any man should think there was, that any "musical fellow" in particular could hope to poke his head through that black wall . . . Clearly madness lay that way, if the fellow wasn't mad already.

"You wouldn't get that impression if you talked to him," I said. "He doesn't jib at anything; he takes all his fences."

"He'll break his bloody neck," said the Major.

"He's not likely to die in his bed," I agreed.

We were looking at each other now and I realised that the unspoken conversation which had been going on all the time had reached a point where things were pretty stark. So I turned away, disengaging as lightly as I could, but with my heart uncomfortably beating and a quiver all over. He didn't actually directly order me to get out, for he was more darkly involved than ever Lachlan had managed to leave him, but he muttered something that was harsh enough.

Outside the wind got me and then after I had passed the sitting-room window and before I could find my torch I bumped into someone. It was Lachlan.

"I wouldn't advise you to see the Major now," I said.

"I wasn't going," said Lachlan in a voice that sounded quiet and remote as he held himself away against the wind.

"Looking for someone?" I thought I might help him.

"No," he said. " It's a dark, stormy night."

The way he spoke made me wonder. "I am going along to the white house," I said.

"It's not too easy on a night like this."

"I have my torch." I switched it on and off.

"In that case you may be all right. But I could come part of the way with you if you like."

"Not at all," I said, suddenly realising that he must have been waiting to guide me but didn't like to say so, didn't want it even to appear that he had. I was aware of a warm human intimacy in the night while the wind whistled in our ears.

"Are you sure you'll be all right now?" he asked.

"Yes, fine. Thank you very much."

"There's just that broken bit of bridge below the sheepfank."

"I know it."

"The only danger, maybe, is in walking past the house."

To the precipice. He had thought it all out. I switched on my torch and saw his hand, took it and shook it and thanked him again.

As I went on I laughed into the wind. For somehow that short meeting had been extraordinarily uplifting. Revealing, too, as though in the absurd thicket of his relations with the Major I suddenly saw Lachlan's real face.

Stories in everyone; and when I asked the Major to come with me I had probably been moved by the weird notion that all stories should meet in one story. No wonder the Major was never quite sure if I was a simpleton. In each one all the stories met. If I hadn't met the Major that first night, would my first conversation with Menzies have been different, would I have shied away from it too soon? Would I be here now?

But that brought Menzies so near all in a moment that absurd questions of the kind got torn away by the wind and my original reluctance to go to the white house came back. In a blind surge of feeling I wished I had taken Lachlan with me. But I would have had to take him into the house. Why not? Why not, indeed, why not take a full deputation, including the Major? I switched the torch off for a beam of light shuts a man and his thoughts too closely within its circle. In a moment the wild night had me, and presently I was able to discern the dim greyness of the road's surface.

Below the sheepfank the small flat bridge which spanned the burn from the dell had got disrupted. But I knew the spot well, for we had carried Dan here to the waiting car. I put my hand in my pocket for my torch and it landed on the flat bottle of whisky. Perhaps I had better put this in the pocket of my rainproof so that it needn't be seen until the right moment. As I drew it out it slipped from the tissue paper and smashed at my feet. I hadn't even stumbled. My dismay was intense. I stood in the howling night like a cheated fool.

When I had removed the pieces of glass off the track and dropped them in a hole, I followed the electric beam for some distance then switched it off and stood, trying to see the house. The cliffs had all their stops out. The boom, the thunder and the depth. A primordial performance with the wind tossing the overtones into space. Black humps that seemed to move made me think of the dog. It was a night for the brute. I didn't want to use the torch.

I went on carefully until I felt the looming bulk of the house and presently I saw the light from the window in front. So he was there.

As I gathered myself and my wits I became the prey of a delusion that hit my back like a cold sheet. The cliffs in the freedom of their night had gone a stage beyond their wild uproar and were now producing a fantastic but coherent symphony of sound. I heard it, lost the theme and heard it again. I stalked the unblinded window —and saw Douglas Menzies at the piano.

His back was towards me in the off left corner of the room. The lamp was on the folding card table beside him. He was playing with an assurance that matched the storm. I thought I heard his voice now and then punch out notes, lifting the piano's effort to a higher definition, a more triumphant assertion. The playing was muffled by the room and by the storm, but as I stood there, staring and lost, what ranged and raged through space was here at the heart of it, one with its creation.

I have tried to write more about this but have struck it out, for at the best now I can get but dimly what I experienced then. Upon some of the notions of these few extraordinary days, I can be as critical as the next; indeed, where the abnormal manifestation is concerned, I find I cannot normally be quite objective because of a latent urge to be sceptical. There are things we may not want to believe. But of one thing I remain quite sure: we do experience in certain reaches of the spirit what we cannot communicate. And there may be a stage beyond mine, where those who could find the words must perforce remain silent before those who could not understand them. When Pilate asked his famous question about truth, he was met by this silence.

Perhaps I should strike that out, too, for there seems

little point in fumbling now. But perhaps less in being ashamed of it. I don't know. I remember leaning against the wall by the window, pinned there by the wind, and staring away towards the stack which I heard but could not see. Grandeur, devastation, unbounded force . . . they were the shiver on the skin, blind from achieving nothing, dark without knowing. . . . In there at the piano was something other . . . I turned my head and looked in. He was playing more slowly, with a curious concentration, as though watching what his hands were doing. I watched, too, and listened, and was beset by that wonder to which there is no end and no key. His head lifted a little. He was not watching his hands, he was listening. And I was caught up in a way I cannot now even remember, though I remember, as it were, its country, its climate. My eyes came back to the door where I had seen Annabel. It was closed. Nearer to me was the table with its confusion of papers. White papers were on the floor. A confusion like a bed from which the spirit had risen. I brought my face farther along the window pane and saw the dog standing in front of the fireplace, head outthrust, glowering at me. There was a gleam of teeth.

As I straightened up against the wall, I hardly knew what to do, for there was a strong urge in me to go away. Then before I could decide anything I was moving noiselessly back along the wall, one hand against it, until I was round the corner. Now I all but fell in my haste, but as I rounded the next corner I came into shelter and stood, hearkening. What was I doing? I didn't mind running away if that's what I should do. Misery has an abject taste. I stood there for a few moments, lost. Then I went on round the house, stumbled and got up as if the dog were on top of me. Not that I minded the dog. The brute would have been a diversion. I kept going with a breathless caution until I came into the wind again and stole along the other gable wall in order to look back along the front of the house. If the dog had not disturbed him, I would go away now.

I saw the dark loom of his body against the light that streamed out from the window beyond him and at once I went forward, calling "Good evening" cheerfully from a few paces.

He did not answer.

"I had to come," I said; "everyone is so anxious to know how you are."

"It's you."

"Yes. A bit late to call, I know."

He opened the door and I stood until he said, "Come in," then he shoved the door shut. His body brushed mine in the dark but in no time the door to his sitting-room was open and as I entered, blinking, I heard the dog growl.

I spoke of the general concern for his welfare with a light-heartedness that grew on me. I made quite a tale of the half bottle of whisky which Sam Mor had insisted I should bring for the pneumonia.

"Sit down," he said.

I thanked him. I wasn't going to stay a minute but the boys were really anxious, I explained again. As I sat down the left side of my rainproof slid off my knee from the weight of the typescript in its pocket. But I wasn't taking off my coat, for I was leaving in no time. Indeed I wondered what had caused all my reluctance to come.

"How is Dan?" he asked.

"Feeling very sorry for himself. He loved that boat of his, and the insurance isn't everything apparently."

"He got a nasty one," he said. "The sudden check

298

on the boat when he went over. He'll be on his back for a time."

"There can't be any real internal injury because they had him on his two feet, I understand."

"Good."

"And you are really none the worse yourself?"

"Not a bit."

He was sitting in the same chair and I saw the milk-pail on the floor. I knew he wasn't going to offer me a drink. He hadn't been drinking. He was quiet and anonymous. Anonymous to me. That's the only word I can think of. But I did not mind, because the elation in me was a sudden gift. And after his storm of music there would be a lull in the man. So I spoke with unusual ease, a positive social glow, because I was going in a minute.

I can remember giving a bright description of the tumult I saw in the narrow channel between the stack and the land and then sheering off it lest it might seem an indirect reference to "the slow movement" of that same spot.

But he wasn't interested in description. What was going to be my last remark was a half-veiled compliment to his rescue work against all the chances, and when I had made it I gave my coat a hitch and the envelope containing his typescript fell on the floor. I felt my face sting as I stooped, picked it up, gave it a roll and stuck it back in its pocket.

"Chances," he repeated.

When I glanced at him I could not be certain that he had recognised the packet.

"Well, they were rather against you, weren't they?"

"The statistical account."

I wouldn't say he was amused but a certain light of interest was in his eyes. I couldn't quite get what thought or faint irony had stirred in him, so I said, "Yes, it's a statistical age."

"The next move. You can see it coming."

"It's come, by gum," I said. "We're rationed by it. Statistics all the time."

"Even getting philosophically conditioned by them."

Who knows what thread of recent thought in him had now got a twist, but I guessed at once that he was referring to the scientist's statistical way of dealing with those radioactive atoms which so spontaneously and unaccountably give up the ghost. There had been a few controversial articles on the subject in *Serpent* about a year ago. Perhaps he had read some of them, and it certainly would never require much in the way of reading for him to pick out what mattered. In this case, of course, what mattered was that no one could tell when any particular atom in the radioactive material was going to disintegrate or decay, and nothing that the physicist could do with heat, pressure, or anything else, would make it, so to speak, die before its time. When the individual atom, the basis of all, was governed by so uncertain a principle in the matter of life and death, how could anything be foretold or predicted about the behaviour of the material as a whole? And the physicist's answer was quite explicit: a certain proportion of the atoms in the given material did in fact bust or decay in a given time. That always happened. Thus statistics could settle the affair of prediction with absolute certainty, and, accordingly, for all practical purposes, the individual atom could be ignored.

It was the kind of topic that had enough implications to be going on with, particularly for an individualist like Menzies. As we sparred away—I was going in just another minute—he came alive and I got that sensation again, as always in his presence, of space about to

300

open up, and whether the space was outward or inward the expansive effect was the same.

"That the individual atom has significance only in relation to the group shouldn't today be so difficult to grasp as all that," he suggested.

"The individual atom has no significance in itself? Oh, come!" I said, and sat down but in an upright way, for in no time we would be off if I didn't watch out.

"According to the new look in physics it only has significance statistically. Or so I gather."

"Perhaps it has. But I am not sure that it is the business of physics to go into significance anyhow."

"Of what, then?"

"Philosophy."

"But individual philosophies bust as incalculably as individual atoms. The dressmaker of the new look has it all taped."

"But the dressmaker, the individual, is there?"

"You haven't made the revolution in yourself. The dressmaker is the statistical account."

"You might as well say God is the statistical account."

"Or more precisely: God is statistics. Given the statistics the answer is assured. You need nothing more. To bother about anything more is a waste of time."

"But, look, when the blessed atom busts, there must have been a reason for its busting, even if we don't or can't know it."

"Cause and effect. The old classical determinism. Difficult to get away from, isn't it?"

"That may be. But it does matter."

"Only to an old mental habit. No scientist worries about any individual atom in a gas chamber. So long as he knows quantity, pressure, temperature—statistics of that kind—he knows what's going to happen, knows when the explosion is going to take place, the pistons work, the wheels go round, not to mention the wider merry-go-round. To attempt to trace what happens to each individual atom might take him to infinity and then it wouldn't matter."

"I had heard of humans as ants and bees, but not as atoms in a gas chamber."

"Not as atoms in a gas chamber? Oh, come!" he said.

So he worked the smile off my face, and for me that extraordinary night began.

Our knowledge of atomic physics was probably equally elementary, but that an atom should explode, decay, for no conceivable reason and yet fulfil a statistical function with mathematical certitude was a tail-end of research that could be grasped by the layman and even wagged. When science hits the right note it sets the overtones going. And for a musician overtones ascend into regions that are more, or other, than three-dimensional.

Somewhere hereabouts, anyhow, the initial sparring lost its simple cut-and-thrust and began to wander, meander, curve back and loop on. Sometimes I can feel lost in the impatient certainty of knowing where I am. Talk of this kind has more than the excitement of a drug. In a sense it is man's supreme debauch. But with luck it has its still moments, when the overtones are heard: the strange, the intoxicated, silence. Then the deep breath—and in the corner of thought's eye whisks the disappearing tail of a new and still more elusive implication, and in no time the harsh throat lifts its tally-ho and the hunt is on; that most mysterious hunt after the invisible fox that with equal ease can slip through a thicket of statistics of the infinitesimal or dodge behind stars in an island universe. We hadn't reached the stars yet. But we would.

I can hardly use a word now that for me isn't over-charged. Mere mention of a thicket of statistics and I am waiting for the face to appear. I did wait for it in the sense that I began to feel it coming, that he could explain as it were from *inside* the atom why it gave up the ghost or why its ghost was given up. I know this must sound quite fantastic. It irritated me even then. For I find that though in the ordinary way I may be tolerant of supernatural or other similar manifestations, like this one of understanding the involuntary "death" of the atom, I become sceptical to the point of intoler-ance when brought slap up against even its direct argumentation, much less what purports to be the thing itself.

Anyway, when I felt it coming and when his words were looping about it and about in a way that seemed to me more than indecisive, I challenged him directly to tell me if he did really know what happened inside the blessed atom.

He looked at me. And he was silent.

There was a smile in his eyes and the outer corner of his left eyelid quivered very slightly in a critical, understanding humour. The absence of the superior or complacent was complete. He was detached and human and friendly, though friendly is too warm a word for what I felt was strangely anonymous, yet the humour was there and the compelling latent force or reality of the man; it was waiting there, but communication could not be made, and this for some reason affected me in an uncomfortably naked way. I have said that I could never know the man. It went deeper than that; deep as the realisation that none of us can ever, at this point, meet; the awful realisation of the stranger.

But that cannot be borne for more than a moment, except by those who have learned to bear it. And I wasn't in the mood to bear much in the way of mystery, however affected. Either he knew and could not put his knowledge in words (an arguable proposition in itself) or he could find words which would not convey meaning to me.

I am aware that this is the Pilate situation again, and, with the least encouragement, it becomes the Pilate complex. But I can to some extent understand that Christ had a conception of truth which Pilate had not and which therefore, however expressed, Pilate could not understand. One man cannot convey to another even the taste of a strawberry if that other hasn't already tasted the berry. And to suggest that Christ should have used words even though Pilate could not understand them was to make of that face-to-face profound situation an occasion for propaganda. And even the propaganda would have been futile to the unending, the universal, company of Pilates. Truth does not ask itself the truth. Truth was in the silence.

Something of this I can get, and if it may seem naive to say so, still there are times when naivety can make one sweat. Anyhow, in my own limited or argumentative way I could be as persistent as Menzies in his weird realm and I was troubled by the possibility that his silence meant nothing much, that it might even be a trick which I was expected to understand.

But when something began to come out of the thicket that had to do with the radioactivity of the atom and whether this activity included a *psychic* activity, a drift set in towards the question: *where* did the psychic activity inhere and *how?* If added from the outside then it was a miraculous creation—and I certainly didn't want that. At such a moment the miracle makes nonsense of everything, shuts the mind up. And mind now was the bother. To call it a function of matter seemed abstract, woolly. I preferred the concrete word excretion. The atom or the atomic thicket excreted mind. Accordingly, if it is an excretion then it is part of the atomic function to excrete it. But even an atom cannot excrete an excretion that isn't there to be excreted. Remarkable how much at home one feels with the notion of excretion, but comfort alas! is not all. Somewhere mind inhered, but where and how? And the face in the statistical thicket was suddenly seen, and it was the face of Psyche, and her silent look was as forbearing as Menzies'.

So we borrowed Psyche's wings and took flight to the universes of stars and planets where there was enough matter to do a fair amount of psychic excretion. I had to admit it, almost straight off. I may have toyed with the notion of life on another planet before, but now I saw that to deny it would be such a presumption of our solitary importance in the scheme of things entire that it bordered on a less reputable mental condition than that of simple idiocy; a "provincialism" beyond the slickest cosmopolitan use of that word. Statistics began to blush at the possibility of the entertainment of such a notion. It takes a lot to make statistics blush.

But if on one extra planet, then on millions, in all the uncountable universes that waltz around even in such space as we have turned a telescopic eye upon. Millions of Pilates ask their question and millions of Christs are silent. Though that, too, was a presumption, another piece of our one-planetary importance. For at least I knew from my anthropological work that among primitive tribes each selected from the psychic keyboard its own particular chord and developed that. And if they differed thus one from another on one small wandering planet, how about the differences elsewhere through all space and time? If in a few years we have

305

got to know so much about the basic atom, how much shall we know a million years hence when our earth should still be spinning comfortably? Would it be unknown then why the radioactive atom so spontaneously gives up the ghost? Was it known on another planet already?

It was a debauch of a thicket, I admit. I could wish now that I had argued less, asked fewer questions and listened more. But that's now. Then even the congestion of talk seemed to thicken the psychic atmosphere. The beautiful austere realm of mathematical physics became interpenetrated by the very mentalism which so marvellously created it. There was an immanence of mind or spirit greater than I had ever previously experienced, and by being far reaching it was very near. Words, as I have said, became overcharged. They were like notes that when struck produce overtones. The realm of mathematical physics, the realm of music. The planes tilt.

But there was something more, and that was, in a word, the sudden insight. It always came suddenly. The mist, the verbiage, cleared and lo! there was what had not been seen. The true work of art produces the sense of surprise, delight, but the great work also produces something more. What had been unthinkable is in a moment apprehended.

So remarks dropped earlier by Menzies, like the one: "God has a different system", begin to take on as much meaning as extra insights can give them. There have been insights, therefore there will be more—unless the end of understanding has been reached, which is probably absurd.

I began to see that Menzies could not turn back. The insights cannot be revoked. Even in the physical inquiry the physicist must go on.

But I need not pursue our looping arabesques through new concepts of phenomena like matter and force, hitherto regarded in the light of a fundamental dualism but now seen to be complementary aspects of a new "unity", just like old space and time. Heaven alone knew what insights for a clear apprehension of this new or "other system" were awaiting us here!

Yet all this hardly hints at what was between us in that paper-strewn lamp-lit room, with the sea booming from the cliffs and the wind whirling round the gable-ends. Menzies' love for Annabel was taken for granted, like the memory of a profound understanding, a warmth, a light. In the loneliness, the bleakness, it was there. It evoked the dark enigma of the Wrecker. It was never mentioned.

Once when I glimpsed his face which in the ordinary sense showed no personal emotion at all yet was alive with interest, that refinement of the mask, I had an intuition of the bleakness, the loneliness, of the human condition that strips nakedness to the grey bone and is terrifying beyond all further insights of terror. What horror, what tragic meaningless horrors, the Wrecker works on man, from without—and from within.

Against that darkness man has the light, the warmth, the other insight which love has fashioned for him as his sole weapon on the eternal quest. I saw rather than thought this. I thought of Annabel.

Shortly after that the grey morning stood in the window.

The time had come.

As I got up the typescript slipped again from the pocket that was too shallow for it. As I lifted it I glanced at him. He knew. There was that smile between us.

"I thought perhaps we might have got round to it."

"I know," he said.

"Perhaps—some other time?"

He nodded as he turned away and I laid it on the table. Then as I faced him to say good night I saw him stick the empty black bottle in an outside pocket.

He was going down the cliff.

I could not speak.

"Shall we go?" he said and made a gesture against the dog.

"You're not going down?"

"Yes."

"But—I don't want a drink——" The words would hardly come.

"It's not for you—unless you wait until I come up. I'll open the door."

He went ahead.

I must have felt stupefied because when I saw the lamp still burning on the card table all I could think was that it should be put out. Then I saw the dog between the card table and the piano and I turned after Menzies, who was waiting for me to close the room door before he opened the outside one.

It still was blowing hard but the sting was gone.

In that outside world he saw I had to say something.

"I want a drop for Dan," he explained. "The tide is out."

It explained so much that my mind lost focus and I began to go with him. At last I knew why he hadn't offered Dan that badly needed drink on the cliff-top. He had had none in the house.

Suddenly I got a scent, a fragrance, as if some woman had passed at a little distance, and in a corner of the garden I saw a bunch of tall stocks. They had an incredible freshness of colour as though magically trans-

308

ported into their sheltered corner from somewhere clean outside the world of storm. Nevermore will these flowers, seen, be separated from Annabel.

He approached the verge carefully over the last few paces and looked down. I did not wish to go so near, upright, but I was suddenly aware of his concentrated gaze and edged forward. Part of the stern of Dan's boat was visible and quite whole. Clearly as the tide rose she had been swept into the cave—the rock conformation must thrust the water that way—and then as it ebbed she had got stuck. Neither of us spoke, but —what if Dan's boat could be salvaged? He got down on his hands and knees and put his legs over.

Flat on my chest I watched each step he took with so utter a concentration that nothing existed beyond his movements. I did not think he was going too confidently: I felt he was going too lightly. But I was no more than a silent cry telling him for God's sake to be careful. He negotiated the second bend, where so recently he had lost his foothold, with a slow ease, and was off again, on the slant, but too lightly, surely too lightly. Then it was straight down and, after a yard, I saw him pause, saw his forehead touch, lean against, the rock and I knew within me the moment of dizziness that can come from too sudden an effort, from the body that has endured too much on too little, the dark attack on the unslept body whose muscles suddenly quiver and tremble and on the mind that knows a place must be found at once to lie down on or all will fall away. I saw him move and fumble uncertainly; then he dropped a foot or so and was checked; his hands scrambled as his body slewed sideways; for two or three seconds he seemed to hold, but inch by inch he was slipping; then he slid and rolled over. The last bound was into space before his body met the jagged skerries.

My face was in the turf when I heard the whine beside me. It was the dog. He had come too quickly and though his hind legs ploughed under him they just failed to stop him and he went over. His yelp was a hellish scream as he hurtled down, leaving the smell of hell's brimstone in the wind.

But already the feeling of sickness was ebbing and, shedding my coat, I put my feet over.

Normally I am rather uncomfortable with heights and more than once have sworn never to tackle a rock face again. On this occasion that feeling of unease (which can so quickly develop a horrible kind of panic) was completely absent. And the sheer astonishment of this, with the utterly unaccustomed feeling of mastery in it, helped me. I was confident, and after I had negotiated the second bend I slanted down what was a narrow rocky fold or path with such certainty that I began to feel the tremors coming. Too much effort too quickly. I lay over at full stretch on my side; waited for that treacherous trembling to pass and for that "second wind" which the flesh needs before it can go on until exhaustion alone can drop it. I had to reach Menzies.

I reached him and he was dead. He had indeed never moved.

The tide must have been about full out for when the wave smashed the water sucked back among vivid brown tangle-weed, yet rising up through them or me was a cry, like the wild seabird's cry, in that destroying and desolate place.

I squatted beside him for some time, then hauled his body away and staggered with it until I got it on the narrow ledge where so recently he had revived Dan. His back was broken and his right arm, but there was no blood visible except in his right hand and on the end of the jaw bone under the right ear. His face was drained and expressionless and his eyes were staring sightless at the sky. I looked at his face, for I stood very close to this man and there were few places to which I wouldn't have gone with him. I closed his eyes and his mouth and sat beside him with my hands on his face.

I must have been there a long time before I became aware of movement and saw that the dog was not quite dead. The body was badly smashed. I caught a hind pad and dragged it to a spot where I could drop the brute over into the sea.

How the dog came to be there, how that odd illusion of a brimstone smell had affected me on the cliff top, I did not try to work out. It's not that I was too utterly spent, body and soul, to bother, it just did not matter.

As I turned back I got a full view of Dan's boat, so I began to examine her. What we had seen was the port quarter. She was canted over on the smashed planking of the starboard side. Her stem had been stove in. She was a wreck.

Beyond her was the cave and as I stared into its recess I remembered the cask of rum. I was not interested. I could not think and wanted to rest. Hours would pass before the hotel would come awake and Catherine knock on my door.

Catherine was the first warmth of life that came to me, and her face and hair were round, like a sun, a sunniness, far away. It vanished as it came nearer and was with me. I rested on the wood of Dan's boat where I could see Menzies on his ledge.

Gradually the world came back and I began to think; at least I realised that I would have to explain how it all happened. I would have to tell Sam Mor and the others. There might be an inquiry. I might have to tell the

Procurator Fiscal. About the rum. About going for a bottle of rum. The cask.

My gorge rose. Blast them, it was too much. They would never see that it didn't matter. It would be a sensational story. Not that that would matter either, but still I couldn't stomach it. Christ, they wouldn't understand. I couldn't tell them. In all that transcended the dodges and the law, I would have to be silent.

I was bitter and somehow deeply hurt, pierced.

My eyes roved over Dan's boat. The planking had sprung from the stem. Naked rivets, broken ribs, gashed edges. Then out of that detached vision of the wreck a thought half formed. In no time it was complete. My story would be that we had seen just enough of Dan's boat from the top of the cliff to think her worth salvaging and with this aim in view had started down the cliff. We had sat talking all night in our full sober senses. I could even show Sam Mor the broken bits of the half bottle of whisky—and what irony was here! For at the moment of the breakage it had seemed almost like a futile senseless interference from outside, an illustration of how the Wrecker worked. It was still an illustration, but I could use it.

The cask of rum, however, would remain—and might easily be found when the wind went down and the small boat came with those who must inspect the scene of the accident and the wreck. Man's curiosity in front of a strange cave in ordinary times went so deep that the investigation of this cave would be inevitable. I must destroy the cask.

At once I got up and went into the cave, slithering over the wet sea wrack, and round the inner bend. The funnelled wind whirled about me but I groped forward until my hands met the cask and withdrew the spile on top. Then, stooping, I ran my left hand down the head of the cask, withdrew the second spile, and waited for the gush against my palm. There was no gush. I kicked the cask. It gave an empty boom.

When even several matches struck at once would flare only for a moment or two before getting blown out it took me a little time to discover what had happened. The two inner bilge hoops, one on either side, had snapped but they still adhered to the cask because the hoops themselves were almost eaten through with the rust which remained caked on the wood.

I attacked that cask with heavy stones until the staves fell asunder, then I threw the two heads and the staves into the sea. I did the job thoroughly, taking my time, and even, as I came out each time to the cave mouth, glancing up the cliffs to make sure that I was not being overlooked.

While I was doing this I had one very strong memory of Menzies. It was when I had, on my first visit to the cave, turned away from the cask and seen his still figure against the outer light.

Now in my comings and goings I tried as it were not to look for him.

Why I should still be haunted by this particular vision I cannot explain even to myself. But he remains, standing there, looking at me, not with any menace but with something else which is strangely more than understanding. For I could not see his face then; though there are times when I fancy I see it now.

However, with the task done my story of an attempted salvage of the boat was complete. And in view of what Menzies had accomplished on the cliff face before the people of that place, it was never doubted. And in any case he would in fact have tried to do for Dan's boat what he had done for Dan himself.

As I went back towards him my mind was cleansed of its bitterness. All I could do now was wait until Sam Mor became uneasy and sent someone, hours hence, to find out why I hadn't returned.

I got a curious shock when I looked on his face. The eyes were not completely closed and the lips were just apart. Once I had seen a smile on a dead man's face which had contained not only the fine essence of his character but also the extraordinary suggestion of a further knowledge, as if a last strange insight had broken upon him. I believe this is not an uncommon occurrence. I had no doubt helped to compose Menzies' face. Anyway, the expression was hardly a smile but rather a characteristic or veiled intensity arrested in quietude . . . from having heard the struck note and knowing what the note meant.

I went out a pace or two and squatted where I could be more readily seen. The exercise in the cave had warmed me up. When I found myself staring at the spot beside me where his body had landed I remembered that passage in his story where he described how the woman on the cliff top (who was Annabel) had seen the body on the skerries, the body that had his face. I remembered his word "recurrence". But I did not speculate much, and I could not think of Annabel. In this place of cliff and cave and smashing sea even enigma seemed pointless. How could one believe that this merciless machinery was the prelude to anything further in the way of knowledge or quest? As a finishing piece of mockery it could only be stared at.

Then I heard what I thought was a far human shout. I looked up the cliff and saw Sam Mor's head. I arose and walked to Menzies' body and signalled that he was dead. Sam Mor did not move, and now near him appeared Catherine's face, the fair hair blown from her brows. Sam Mor thrust her back and came again and signalled to me. I understood. Men would come with the rope.

They came and I hitched up Menzies' body and my own and slowly they drew us to the top.

They had come quickly because Catherine from her bedroom window had seen the white house on fire. I suppose at the back of my mind I must have understood that the only way the dog could have got out of that room was through the window. What had disturbed the brute so violently I don't know, even if I do know that it wouldn't have required more than a glancing whack from that tough body to have upset the rickety card table and thrown the burning lamp on the floor. And once the papers were on fire the only outlet for the dog was through the window. The relationship between man and dog is no doubt the oldest of all relationships between man and beast. I leave it at that.

Sam Mor and Ian and Charlie and two other local men were there. When we had talked and I had seen the smoke torn by the wind from the smouldering house I looked along the track to the sheepfank and saw Catherine standing alone. "I'll tell Catherine what happened," I said and I walked towards her.

17

Shortly after she had graduated the following summer
Catherine and I got married. Before then I had spells
of writing down what appears in the foregoing pages.
We have now been married about two years and things
have gone so well with us that I can sit here above the
hollow, where we had so often met, and look down the
flow of the land towards the ruins of the white house
with a quiet wonder. Perhaps I let my manuscript lie
untouched because of some odd notions in it like that of
"recurrence". I hardly know. We are on holiday, staying with Catherine's people, and a couple of hours ago,
just before lunch, she came into the house with a bunch
of stocks. If I smiled, knowing where she had gathered
them, I said nothing and Catherine ignored me. In
the realm of Highland superstition she is a whole golden
bough in herself and I think I have now done everything
except bow to the new moon. She bows three times and
then looks enchanted, but what she wishes for I don't
know, though I suspect it is not for anything new so
much as for the continuance of what she thinks we have
in health and happiness. Enchanting the gods may be
a way of keeping them reasonable in the matter of
mortal possessions. Over difficulties of this kind, which
I encounter in remote times before legal documents
regarding possessions were invented, she can in a
moment be extremely illuminating and helpful. I am

afraid she does not judge an anthropologist's capacity by his theories let them be never so subtle, at least not in the first place.

After we arrived yesterday I had a long talk with Sam Mor. This is the second season the Major has not turned up and what has happened to him no one knows. "He may have found a better hole," said Sam Mor, "but I hope not his last one." His humour stirred up an affection for the Major and I promised to look up a London address which he gave me, even while I wondered if Menzies' death was the real cause of his not coming back. The Sneddons have also fallen away. But the barrister and Dan are busy as ever in a new boat and the barrister has been helpful with suggestions for installing a temporary electric system in the hotel over against the coming of "the hydro-electric scheme". "Perhaps we had enough of the candles," said Sam Mor.

"You think a new day is dawning for the Highlands?"

"More light," said Sam Mor, and we shook with laughter for no particular reason.

Today the sun is shining and far beyond the quiet cliffs the sea glitters. What light is there, and space, and infinite quietude!

I was recalled by a shout and looking up the slope towards the house I saw Catherine and Catherine's mother holding her small grandson by the hand. This business of waving he hasn't quite mastered but when Catherine left them he howled without any prompting.

"What on earth kept you?" I asked.

"Your belongings," she said. "But I'll make a real man of him yet." She paused to wave the bunch of stocks at them and then she was off.

She was at once full of business and a little beyond herself, eager and bright.

When we came to the crest of the slope she stopped involuntarily before the view of Loch Runie, sweeping in from the sea. The prospect was a fair one, near and far, and the sea water, from the sun behind us, was a living blue; varied and austere the wide scene was, asleep and yet awake in its sleep. And, like something forgotten, came back to me "the other landscape".

When I glanced at Catherine I saw her eyes travelling down that far prospect until they rested on the small cemetery. When she looked at me there was more than the light of that world in her eyes. Then she went on.

I was again haunted for a little way by the picture that Douglas Menzies had evoked of Annabel on the cliff top, of her eyes travelling down the sea.

Scraps of the talk came back which we had had in the white house, but in a moment they were like some ogham script, scrawled on stones, about something beyond what could be said, something other. And though nothing of this other might be known, or nothing that could be conveyed, yet equal to it and indeed in some mysterious way going beyond it was the sheer wonder of man's being on its quest. For of that now I had no doubt.

In the cemetery Catherine stopped before the headstone, a low rounded piece of local rock which we had had dressed on one side to take the simple incised inscription: DOUGLAS AND ANNABEL MENZIES.

I was standing a little behind her, for when she has her own business to do I have learned to leave her alone. Her head was bowed slightly. Then she gave them the flowers.

If you have enjoyed this book and would like to receive details of other Walker Adventure titles, please write to:

Adventure Editor
Walker and Company
720 Fifth Avenue
New York, NY 10019